D1711038

ONE RIDE

Hellions Motorcycle Club

CHELSEA CAMARON

One Ride

A Hellions Ride

Hell Raisers Demanding Extreme Chaos

USA Today Bestselling Author

Chelsea Camaron

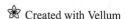 Created with Vellum

CONTENT WARNING

This book contains strong language, strong sexual situations, and violence. Please do not buy if any of this if any of this offends you.

This is not meant to be a true or exact depiction of a motorcycle club rather a work of fiction meant to entertain.

STAY UP TO DATE

Do you want to get bonus scenes, sale updates, new release information and more?
Click here to sign up for my newsletter!

Want to get an email direct to you with every new release or sale?
Follow me on Bookbub!

Connect directly with me anytime at:
www.authorchelseacamaron.com
Facebook
Twitter
Instagram

HELLIONS MC

In Memory of

Haywood Dail

You were my Dad's best friend, close as a brother.
Thank you for being the light hearted man you were.
You are missed by everyone who knew you. My first
bike ride with someone other than my dad was with you,
and one I will never forget. An angel now, watching
over all the S.O.B.'s. Gone but never forgotten.

Ride or Die, your Harley was part of who you were.
Missing the laughs we all shared with you. We will
carry you with us always.

> *The whispers in the wind...*
> *The rumbles of the exhaust...*
> *The pavement passing by...*
> *Still with us with every ride.*
> *Always.*

ALSO IN THIS SERIES:

Hellions Ride Series:

HELLIONS RIDE ON SERIES:

Hellions Motorcycle Club Second Generation

ONE RIDE

Their forbidden attraction couldn't be denied.

Can one ride turn lust into love?

Delilah "Doll" Reklinger has never been in danger before. As the only child of Roundman, Haywood's Hellions motorcycle club president, she has always been protected.

When a threat to Roundman's club gets too close to his precious doll, he does the only thing he can think of —sends her away until his enemy is in the ground.

Talon "Tripp" Crews lives his life from one ride to the next. As the Catawba Hellions motorcycle club chapter president, he doesn't hesitate to answer Roundman's call for help.

One ride across the country sounds simple enough.

One ride tempted by a forbidden desire is far from easy.

One ride changes everything for everyone.

*** This is a motorcycle club romance. This book contains strong language, strong sexual situations, violence, and is not suitable for readers under the age of eighteen. This is a work of fiction and is not meant to be a true or exact depiction of a motorcycle club but rather a book meant to entertain. ***

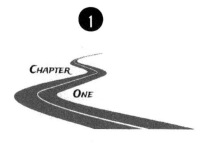

ONE ENCOUNTER

S hit! *This one is going to be a mess to clean up,* I think to myself.

Pulling up to the clubhouse, I realize today's barbecue is not just for the local Haywood's Landing Hellions, but also for our affiliate charter and chapter clubs. Rather than the usual fifty or so bikers with their families, it's more like two hundred of them here today.

It's a sight that most would be intimidated by. For me, it's comfort. It's the safety found in my family. Most of all, it's my home.

Once a year, sometimes twice, my dad invites all of the partnering motorcycle clubs out for a huge barbecue. The Hellion's control all of Coastal North and South Carolina, as well as a few areas in the Piedmont and Appalachian areas of North Carolina. They provide protection, shelter, food, and fun for all affiliate clubs traveling through. The Hellions are respected and run Carolina Country. Some of the clubs we protect passing through our territories are into the more illegal side of motorcycle club life, while others are more of a band of brothers traveling together. Our club walks a fine line in what they do and do not participate in. As a female, I'm sure there is much more that goes on in the club than I will ever be made aware of. Having such a large area to cover, Dad makes sure to show his appreciation for the smaller charters and chapters whenever possible. Times like this are about family and relaxing; business is off the table.

Our thirty-acre compound area is now littered with bikes, trikes, and cars. Burly bikers abound. Ol' ladies and kids are squealing and smiling at every turn. The kids are enjoying the food, games, bounce houses, and pony rides. It's like a mini-freaking-carnival. With all the ol' ladies present, the barflies and hang around whores are at a minimum. Some aren't so bad, but most annoy the shit out of me. They all respect the ol' ladies and wives, though. It's a good thing they know their place, too. My dad doesn't tolerate any disrespect of a claimed woman in his club by anyone, but especially not from a bar-bitch just looking for a night with a Hellion.

Getting out of my car, I smile. My girls are here today, standing on the other side of the lot, waving to me. Savannah Mae and Caroline are my two very best friends, my survival sisters in this crazy lifestyle. Savannah 'Sass' Perchton and I have been best friends from childhood.

Her dad, 'Danza', is a Hellion original, along with my dad, Roundman, their friend, 'Frisco', and the late 'Rocky' Fowler. The four men created the MC as a way to ride together and stay safe thirty-two years ago when they were in their twenties. Rocky and his wife passed away in a car accident a few years back. Their only daughter, Dina, was in college at the time, with no other family. The Lawson family and the Hellions MC have made sure to be a support system for her as much as she will possibly allow. She's the reason Sass and I went to college in Charlotte. Our dads felt it was a good way to keep an eye on us, Dina and Maggie Lawson, another

Hellion princess all at the same time. Dina is a couple of years older than us. She's settled in life. She has a great husband and two beautiful daughters. Maggie and Dina both took care of Sass and I while we were in college. Especially the first two years, we were young and had been sheltered so much by growing up in our small town run by the Hellions that college was a wild experience. Dina and Maggie are like older sisters for both of us.

Freshman year, we decided to attempt dorm life. That's where we met Caroline Milton. We lasted one semester in the dorm, before my dad put us in an apartment and we brought Caroline with us. She's the complete opposite of Sass and me. Caroline majored in business, specifically accounting, where Sass and I took an easier path, one not involving so much math, choosing arts and communications.

I stifle a giggle as I realize this is Caroline's first time at a large club event. Of course, she knows that Sass and I have biker Dads, but her schedule has never allowed her to be with us for a party. She's clearly overdressed in her cocktail length, spaghetti strapped dress, and wedge-heeled sandals. The dress isn't overly formal, but its fitted and not the casual feel that these barbecues are meant for. Sass and I are both in jean shorts and tank tops. Denim and leather are safe bets for anything at the clubhouse. A sundress would've been a bit more suitable for her to wear. Although, I don't think Caroline is one to ever dress casually except when cleaning her house or something, and that's a serious maybe. I doubt she even owns a pair of yoga pants.

After college graduation, Caroline stayed in Charlotte. She works with Kenna, one of Dina and Maggie's friends. Sass and I, on the other hand, came back to the coast to work for the Hellions storage business and motorcycle garage. I run the storage office, while Sass is like a "girl Friday", answering phones, doing parts runs and stuff for the bike shop. We share a condo on the beach because at twenty-five, neither of us wanted to live back at home, even though we both know we are never out of the reach of our parents or any of the Hellions. This has been our world for two and half years, living at the beach, while working beside our dads.

Weaving my way through the hordes of bikes towards my friends, I feel at peace, even amongst the chaos. Gazing around me, I admire the many motorcycles in our courtyard, each decked out in chrome and leather. I hug my girls for our typical greeting, as I reach them.

Together, we make our way inside the clubhouse where I nod and wave greetings at my extended family. Taking in the many unfamiliar faces, I smile knowing I'm safe even with these "strangers" around. It's an unspoken code women are protected and cherished in the Hellions. I'm no one's target for trouble here, and it's not because this is our territory; it's because I'm a lady of the Hellions for life, ride until I die.

The affiliates seem to understand who I am, even without introduction. I'm not an ol' lady. There is no cut on my back. I'm not claimed with a property patch. That doesn't mean I'm available either. No, I'm not one to be found riding bitch on anyone's bike. There is only one motorcycle I'm permitted to place my derriere on and those opportunities are few and far between. My dad refuses to let me ride with anyone but him.

I'm not available to guys outside the club either, which suits me just fine. I was born into this life. My heart beats to the same steady tick of a Harley Davidson V-twin engine. I'm Delilah 'Doll' Reklinger. Princess to the Haywood's Hellions MC. Daughter of 'Roundman', Hellion original and Prez for the last thirty two years. I'm the kid sister that each of these badass bikers looks out for. They will gladly kick your ass all because you simply looked at me. I'm a daughter to each and every ol' lady to nurture, love, and treat like one of their own. This is my world, my home, and my happiness.

aywood's Hellions' annual barbecue is one of the best parties of the year. Due to business needs, last year we were unable to attend, though. Roundman scheduled the run so our absence was no sign of disrespect for our parent chapter.

This year, we're expected and happy to oblige. When Roundman or any patched Hellion calls, we answer. Each charter may have their own Prez, but we all answer to the Haywood's Hellions and Roundman.

All the charters are represented today, complete with families in tow. The turnout is outstanding for the small town of Haywood's Landing, North Carolina. The compound is located in the boondocks, making functions like these a non-issue for the neighbors.

Taking it all in around us, my crew and I are relaxing, leaning up against the bar when Rex smacks my chest as he tips his beer bottle in the direction of three females. One of them clearly didn't get the message, this is an MC event. She is dressed more for a day of shopping, or a night out at a club than a barbecue at the clubhouse.

"Those are definitely not hang around hoes," Rex states.

"That's for damn sure. They're walking with class and a whole lot of confidence. None of them are hangin' on a man and no property patches in sight. Aw shit, Rex, fresh pussy for you." I reply, laughing.

Drexel 'Rex' Crews, is my cousin, Vice Prez of my Catawba Hellions chapter, and my lifelong best friend. We are the Piedmont chapter to the Haywood's Hellions, located in Catawba, North Carolina, about an hour outside of Charlotte.

Our moms are sisters who both had us out of wedlock and at a young age. We were taken in by our grandparents and raised more like brothers, and we proudly carry our Grandpa's last name. Only eighteen months apart in age, we are still, and have always been, inseparable. Rex's mom tries, whereas my mom bailed early on. Our grandmother passed when we were eight or nine and our grandfather followed in our teens. Having no one to really care for us, we roamed the streets.

Aunt Jolene, Rex's mom, tried; but she worked so much to provide a house and food for us that there wasn't enough time in the days for her to keep up. Drugs, alcohol, petty theft, and girls were our day to day until a chance meeting with Roundman and his boys at a gas station one day. He set us straight and set us up. We owe everything we have to him.

Rex is a ladies man with little to no standards. His only real boundary is that of an ol' lady. If you don't want Rex to hit on your woman, then you damn sure better claim her. Hang around hoes, sisters, friends, exes, and complete strangers are all fair game in his mind; married or not. As long as it's new pussy, he's happy. There are no encore performances.

'Hit it, get it, and go. No repeats' is the motto Rex lives by.

"That dress is screaming to be plucked off. She needs to be devoured by D-Rex, my brother. She just doesn't know it yet," he says with a snicker as he steps away in the direction of his new conquest.

The brunette in the dress may be what has caught Rex's attention, but my eyes are glued to the long, blonde and straight-haired beauty next to the dress. Her face is round and flawless, her skin smooth like that of a glass doll. She's in a black Harley Davidson tank top and short as sin jean shorts. Damn, this broad is stacked; nice rack, skinny with a plump ass that's screaming to be smacked. I watch as she laughs, carefree, with her friends as Rex joins them.

I begin to approach when I see Roundman walk to her. She hugs him innocently and it dawns on me exactly who she is. That's Roundman's Doll she's off limits. All lust filled thoughts I have are momentarily gone. She isn't just any Hellions princess, she's *the* Hellion princess. We had to keep an eye on her from afar when she lived in Charlotte.

Rex waves me over after he finishes greeting Roundman with a hand shake, pull into a half-hug, back slap that we men do. I follow suit after my approach.

"Glad to see you and Rex could make it, Tripp." Roundman greets.

"There's no place we'd rather be." I reply, while thinking, '*Well other than balls deep in your daughter.*' That's one place I certainly would rather be. Damn, I can't be thinking like this. Roundman would cut my dick off if he knew.

"Tripp, Rex, this is my daughter, Doll, and her friends, Sass and Caroline," Roundman introduces.

That is a quick way to squash my lust filled thoughts, actually hearing the words *my daughter*. Blondie is a doll alright, Roundman's Doll. She's one of a kind, that's for sure. You shelter and protect a beauty like her. She's the kind of doll you treat like fragile china; wrap it up and store it on a shelf for safe keeping. I don't know why we haven't officially met before. Although these events are crowded, one would think we would have met. I've always come here focused on business, so maybe that's why.

These broads are far from fresh pussy, and far

beyond off limits. I hope Rex realizes this isn't territory he wants to dip his dick in.

Doll extends her hand to me, bringing me back into the moment. "Doll is what the boys call me. My name is Delilah. This is Savannah, otherwise known as 'Sass', and Caroline, our friend. It's nice to meet you," She greets. As I shake her hand, she stands up on her tiptoes, while tugging on my shoulder to pull me down then she kisses my cheek.

The touch of her soft lips to my skin ignites a fire burning inside of me just under the surface. Her touch sends adrenaline coursing through my body. Before I can respond, there is a harsh voice, snapping me out of it.

"Doll, Sass, Caroline! Asses in the kitchen!"

Looking in the direction of the noise, I see Danza in the kitchen doorway, bellowing for the girls. They giggle as they sashay away. My eyes roam up and down her back side as she goes. Damn, what an ass she's got. It's one of those moments, *I hate to see you go, but I love to watch you leave.* Fuck me, what a strut! That girl is a heartbreaker with one swish of those luscious hips. *Tame it, Tripp.*

"Sass is Danza's daughter. Every time someone gets near our girls, he calls them to the kitchen. Won't see 'em again." Roundman laughs, "Our Hellion princesses are tucked safely away for the rest of the evenin'."

After the girls leave, Rex and I shoot the shit with Roundman for a bit. Outside of sermon times, no business is ever discussed between clubs. Those are Roundman's rules and we are chartered clubs to him. We are Hellions always. Brothers without hesitation. Allies and friends, yes. Business partners, of course. And although, my territory is mine to run Roundman respects his chapter leaders and doesn't impose, but ultimately, I answer to him.

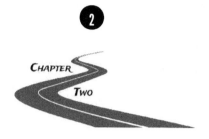

CHAPTER
TWO

ONE DAY AFTER

C lean up after the barbecue is always a chore. Well, actually, cleaning up after anything with these guys is never a pleasurable experience, regardless of the size of the event. This barbecue is on a much larger scale, though. Danza quickly called us to go in the kitchen yesterday, therefore our drinking and socializing was kept to a minimum. Looking around me, I'm kind of thankful for his overprotective ass. Cleaning this with a hangover would have sucked.

At the time, however, I was slightly irritated. I was introducing myself to this guy named Tripp. Or is he Rex? I don't know, but either way, he is hot as hell.

He's at least six feet two inches tall because he is slightly taller than my dad, who is right at six feet. His dark brown hair was pulled back in a knot on the back of his head, the top grown out and the underneath shaved. His face is one of pure masculinity; a strong jaw line, pronounced nose, and hazel eyes with golden flecks.

It's been way too long since I've been laid because watching his jaw muscle twitch while he was standing there was turning me on. I pulled him down just so I could brush my lips above that spot. His broad shoulders were tight under my delicate hand. Splaying my fingers across them to pull him to me, sent an electric shock through my body. The ink adorning his forearms was detailed and in our brief encounter, I couldn't take it all in, making me wonder what's under his clothing.

Too bad he has shown zero interest in me. His blatant disregard of me has made it clear that my lust filled thoughts are not reciprocated. I'm off limits to him even if he does want me, though. All the Hellions respect my dad too much to ever date me, fuck me, or do more than protect me. Don't get me wrong, I'm close with almost all the boys, they are my older brothers or uncles, but no matter how hard I flirt, they never cross the line. Never am I given a second glance from any of them. I've dated pretty boys, but it quickly fizzles. I need the adrenaline, the chaos, the protection, and the lifestyle.

At least one of us was getting some sort of attention. With the way his friend was looking at Caroline, his attraction and intentions were clear. Caroline was not impressed, however. It takes a lot to get her attention. She has aspirations, a career, and goals far beyond that of a motorcycle club.

My mystery man was more concerned with my father. His patches let me know he's a Catawba Hellion and the Prez at that. Well, that explains why he carries such a serious demeanor. The level of his responsibility is a tough burden to carry. His crew depends on, and trusts, his instincts and instructions. I wish I knew his name, not his road-name "Tripp" or "Rex" but his real name. At least then, in my fantasies, I would know what to call him. My B.O.B (battery operated boyfriend) will just have to settle for being Tripp, or Rex, for now. I like the name Rex better, so Rex it will be.

Looking around me, I shake off my thoughts of the encounter with what's his name to start gathering the trash off the floor and tables of the clubhouse. It's a simple warehouse-style building with an open floor plan. There is a kitchen in the back with four restrooms just off to the side of that. In the vast space of the common area, there is a fully stocked bar, pool tables and darts in one corner, dining tables off in another, and a DJ area with a dance floor in the middle.

There used to be a stage, but it was taken down a few years back. Bikers and rockers together, yeah, this building isn't big enough for the egos. A lead singer decided to openly flirt with an ol' lady, which was a clear sign of disrespect to Frisco, her man. In a moment of jealousy and rage, Frisco jumped on stage and began punching the singer in the head with his own fucking mic. When his band mates tried to pull Frisco off, the brothers stepped in and shit got ugly. My dad finally had to move in and control the situation. The damage was already done, though. The singer ended up with a broken jaw and nose, while the other band members were roughed up but nothing serious. The next day the stage was taken down and no more outsiders have been allowed since.

Making my way outdoors, I take a moment to enjoy my surroundings. The clubhouse is the first of many buildings on the compound. My dad owns fifty acres out in the country of Haywood's Landing; a small coastal

North Carolina town. Thirty of it is compound land which is surrounded by a privacy fence that is eight feet tall with barbwire running across the top and security cameras mounted along the way. The front gates open to the space of the lot for parking where, in the center, there are three flag poles, our American flag, our POW/KIA memorial flag, and our Hellions flag are all proudly on display. The clubhouse is the first building due to the fact it's where most club events occur.

Finished with my small break, I continue cleaning up. Once I've gathered all the trash from the clubhouse, I head out to the pit to dump my trash bag. The pit is a concrete slab with a few posts holding up an A-frame tin roof. Under the shelter are pig cookers, gas grills, charcoal grills, and the oyster tables for oyster roasts. The tables are six feet long, wooden with a stainless steel top, and in the middle, there is a square hole cut out that a bucket goes under. When the oysters are ready, they are dumped on the open table to be shelled and eaten. When finished, you drop the shells in the hole to the bucket to be tossed. This is nice because anytime we cook for large crowd's cleanup is easy. Later today, a prospect will be out here, cleaning the grills and pig cooker and hosing off the concrete.

The open grass area beside the pit is used for horse-shoes, badminton, volleyball, and the kids' toys for barbecues and parties. Beyond that are the boys' shops, the duplexes, and the cave.

Dad does not allow drinking and driving, and some of the brothers don't have homes. To give everyone a place, he's had a bunch of duplex-type buildings put in. Each home has four separate bedrooms with their own full bathrooms. They share a common area with a couch, love seat, TV, and small kitchenette. Each bedroom is assigned to a patched member, even the ones who don't live here full time have their own room. They hold the key in order to keep their private space just that, private. The married guys even have a room in case they need a place to crash for any reason. There are two buildings reserved for guest clubs passing through under our protection. After last night, every room is full, some even shared, and tents and campers fill the lot.

The shops in the back are basically sheds for the boys to store their bikes and belongings in. They're roomy but not huge. There is enough for toolboxes, some workout space, and motorcycles, of course.

The cave is the other building on the compound. It's a large, one room building with a table inside, that's all I know. I've never seen the interior. That building is for sermon; only patched Hellions are allowed, no women ever. That is where business is discussed, members are voted on, and decisions are made. Prospects don't even go in to clean it. That is the one building that the

Hellions clean for themselves. Not a prospect, not an o'l lady, a princess, or even a hired maid have permission to enter the cave. Only two people hold keys to that building, my dad and Danza, the VP.

Out of the corner of my eye, I catch movement over by the duplexes. Looking up, I see Sass making her way over to me. The walk of shame is evident in her stature. Her hair is a mess, clothes wrinkled, her shirt is on inside-out, and her face is flushed in what looks to be a mix of satisfaction and anger.

Damn it, I can't believe she's done it. We have a rule: don't sleep with Haywood's Hellions. Sure, we flirt, but as the saying goes, *'don't shit where you sleep'*. Fuck, this can't be good. Although, maybe it was a member from a different charter. Since we don't have to see them all the time, the situation would be more tolerable than one of the local brothers. We flirt with all the boys, but neither of us has hooked up with a Hellion before.

"Doll, don't ask. I see the look on your face. If my dad asks, I was with you last night."

"Sass, you know I've always got you, but exactly who were you with last night? And why do you look like you are holding back tears?" I ask, full of concern for my friend.

"Tank. And I should've known better," she says with her voice trembling as she fights to push back the tears.

Shit, of all the Haywood's Hellions, Tank is the worst she could've hooked up with. He's a man-whore. Bigger than that, they have a genuine friendship, or so I thought.

"What the hell happened?"

She takes a minute and pulls herself together. "What happened? What happened! Oh Doll, that man just gave me the absolute best night of my life. Everything the girls say about him is true and then some. I wake up this morning thinking there will be more of last night, when he kicks me out. *Me*, that fucker kicks *me* out like I'm a *bar-bitch*."

"Oh, Sass. Did you think for one second Tank, of all people, would treat you special?"

"I'm not club pussy. I'm not a bar-fly. I'm Savannah Mae Mother-Fucking Perchton. We've danced around each other for two years. Two damn years, Doll! We have laughed, flirted, and talked. I've shared my real dreams with him, told him shit I haven't told anyone but you. Yes, I thought I was someone special to him. At least I thought I was until this morning," she replies with anger now replacing the sadness she began with.

"You are someone special. He's too blind to see anything beyond his brothers and where to put his dick next. You know this! They're all like this for the most part."

Shrugging her shoulders, she huffs before the anger

sets back into her voice. "Well, lesson fucking learned. Doll, I want more than being Danza's daughter, working for the club, and knowing my dad is never going to let anyone near me. No more bikers for me. I'm ready for a relationship, not a quick fuck. I thought Tank was, too. Just the other day, he was saying, 'I'm thirty five years old. I need to stop acting fucking twenty.' It was my mistake for thinking he was hinting at something. I got his message today, loud and clear."

She's now filled with determination and vigor. Uh-oh, this is her sassy side coming out in full force. It's going to suck to be Tank.

"Well, babe, I don't know what to tell you. Anything less than a biker just won't do. You crave the vibration of a bike, your arms around your man, and the wind in your hair as the miles of pavement move below you."

"Not anymore, you'll see Doll. I'm moving on. Now, let's get this place cleaned up before they have sermon. There is a big meeting today, that's why everyone stayed overnight. Dad said the cave will be full for a while, and that's all I know." Looking at me with curiosity and concern, she asks, "Your dad isn't passing the gavel, is he? Why else would they need everyone here?"

"I don't know, girl. It's not my place. Let's get this done and go shopping. You need some retail therapy."

Shopping, how every girl fixes things. Sass and I

may not be the girly girls, but who doesn't love a new pair of shoes when dealing with life's woes? My heart hurts for my best friend, yet this is a decision she has to make for herself. In time, she may see things differently, though when the hurt cuts that deep, time, distance, good friends, and booze are the ultimate healers. I'll stick by her through the time, give her the distance from the club, and I'll share as many drinks as it takes for my girl.

Waking up, I rub the sleep out of my eyes. The throb radiating through my head reminds me of the very good time I had last night. Looking over at the clock, I realize it's time to dismiss my guest and get ready for sermon.

She's lying on her stomach, hand up under the pillow. Her golden brown hair is covering her face and the pillow. Watching her breathing pattern, it's evident she's still asleep. Sliding the covers off her, I expose the round curve of her ass, which is calling to be slapped.

The sound radiates through the quiet of the room as

I do just that. Lifting her head in surprise, she smiles up at me. Damn, she's a hot mess in the morning; make up smeared, hair everywhere, and she has the *'I've been worked over look'* in her eyes.

"Good morning, handsome," she coos at me. I really hate that fucking endearment.

"Ain't nothing handsome about me, it's time for you to go," I reply, already over the idea of having any form of conversation with her.

There weren't many single females around last night. When the ol' ladies and kids are around, the club whores are kept to a minimum. This chick is a friend of an ol' lady, or at least, I think that's what she said last night. I do vaguely recall her saying something about she's never been with a biker before. She's cute enough, but the reality is, I had a certain blonde in my head and needed a release. She was willing and available, so yeah, I took advantage of it.

She reaches her hand under the covers and begins to stroke my dick. As it comes to life, I lay there while images of one special blonde invade my brain. When my bedmate then leans over to kiss my chest, I gently push her head down to guide her where I want her mouth. She moves in an attempt to climb on to me, though.

"Oh, no, baby. You woke it up, you're gonna finish it. With. Your. Mouth."

She makes a pouty face for a moment to show her displeasure at my wish. Fuck that, I'm done with her pussy, but she's going to finish what she started. I gesture with my hands, *what are you waiting for?* When she still doesn't act accordingly, I sigh.

"Suck. My. Dick. Or get the fuck out, the choice is yours. I got shit to do, so make your decision quick."

She starts at the task, her gag reflex not allowing her to take me all the way. For being as wild as she was last night, she's a timid prude this morning. This is the worst blowjob I've ever been given. She's not even playing with my piercing. I didn't get that part of my anatomy pierced for my pleasure alone. I know my dick is large and it's a lot to take in, but damn, she could use her hand or flick her tongue on my jewelry. Nope. Fucking nothing, she's just sucking with a slight bob of her head. Fuck this! I'm over it. My hand can finish the job better. When I reach down and grab her hair and tug her off me, her mouth comes off my dick with a pop, as she looks up at me with her lips still forming an 'O'. Confusion is written all over her expression, as my irritation with her lack of oral skills visible in mine.

"It's been real, but it's time to go."

"I'm not finished yet," she replies, meekly.

"Yes, you are. I'm never gonna finish with the way you suck dick, and I've got shit to do, so it's time for you to go."

"You're kicking me out? Do you know who I am?"

"Nope, sure don't. Don't really give a flying fuck, either. Time to go."

She huffs and puffs as she climbs off the bed and collects her clothing. She keeps looking over at me. I'm not going to stop her if that's what she's thinking. She is cute, but she's nothing remarkable or memorable. She's going to get the hell out of this room, then I'm going into the bathroom to shower. We have an important sermon today and afterward my crew is heading back to Catawba.

After the bitch finally gets the point and leaves, I saunter to the bathroom to start the shower. Letting the warm water cascade over my body, I wash away the grime of last night, and my thoughts automatically drift to Doll. Picturing her smile, her skin, her body, takes my dick from hard to rock hard.

Release, I need release to get this broad out of my head. Imagining running my rough, calloused hands, over her soft, smooth, perfect skin, I begin to stroke. Each pull of my shaft is bringing the sensations of being inside her more vividly to life in my imagination. Her voice is that of an angel, I can imagine her screaming out my name as I get her off, my large hands cupping her full, luscious breasts, while moving down to squeeze her plump, full ass, with her secure up against me. The face of a doll, the body of a pin up model, and the personality to fit my lifestyle; Doll is everything any man would want.

Tightening my grip as if her pussy were milking me, I increase my pace. The muscles throughout my body are becoming rigid under the pressure, the tension in my balls building, as I finally find my release. In that instant, I think of that simple kiss on my cheek and imagining the feel of her lips wrapped around my dick. My cum is now floating down the drain, and my body and mind are relaxed.

I finish washing, knowing I've got to get Doll out of my head. Fuck, I can't be getting off to Roundman's daughter. I have to get this shit under control.

With my hair still wet from my shower, I leave it down to dry. I dress in the usual jeans and black t-shirt, finished with my black boots. Hearing the sounds coming from Rex's room, I know he's busy, but at least, awake. Grabbing my cut to throw on, I step out of the duplex into the compound lot.

"Tripp, hey brother, how's it going?" Tank greets as he approaches me.

Tank is exactly that, a tank. He's not as tall as me; around five foot ten or so, I would say. Broad shoulders and arms show the man is familiar with a gym. I'm built, but he's stacked. His arms are covered in full sleeve tattoos that go from his neck all the way down, a skull even covering his left hand on one side and his sleeve stopping at his right wrist on the other. The intricate designs are eye catching. The metal in his face adds to his persona as well. His ears are gaged with a lip ring in place, probably for the ladies. His presence is intimidating to most people. Underneath it all, though, he's hilarious and a big kid, once you get to know him. He's come to Charlotte a handful of times and stayed at our compound. He's fun to drink with and the women flock to him. He loves to mess with the pretty boys in collared shirts when we go out and has been known to fuck their bitches right in front of them. He's fierce, he's loyal, and he's everything that represents a Hellion.

"Tank, brother." I reply while we greet in the man half hug, back slap.

Hearing a noise behind us, we both turn around to catch the sight of Doll and Sass bending over to pick up trash. Tank whistles and I laugh just before Doll and Sass abruptly stand and glare over at us.

"Fuck you, Tank." Sass yells over to us.

"Oh, baby, you know you want to."

The girls are making their way over in an aggressive march. Shit, they're not happy with the flirtatious behavior of my brother.

"Let me tell you something, Frank Thomas Oleander. I've fucked you once. I won't fuck you twice. Take all those thoughts from your pea-sized brain and tell them to your pea-sized penis."

I watch as Doll flinches at Sass's words. Damn. Now I see why they call her Sass. Doll reaches out to grab Sass and pull her back. Instead, Sass steps closer, toe-to-toe with Tank, she stands strong against him. He takes the opportunity to grab her ass and pull her closer, rubbing up against her. I can't tell if he's going to fuck her right here on the spot, or cuss her out.

"Oh, baby, that sassy mouth," he croons, "I know just how to shut you the fuck up. And last night, my dick sure as shit wasn't pea-sized as you were begging for more. Talk your shit, but you know you want more. You know there's gonna be more. That sassy ass is mine, Savannah. I know it, you know it; you just don't wanna admit it. It's all good, baby. No one else will ever match up to what I gave you."

"Keep dreaming, Tank. Badass biker... Fucking shit-head... Controlling ass pricks. You, my dad, and every other fucking Hellion here can kiss my ass. I'm done with this shit. Never. Again."

With that, she backs away then turns and storms off. Doll is standing there, stunned.

"Tank, how could you? You fucked her, fine, you're both grown ass adults, but you didn't have to treat her like a bar-bitch. You know better. Even I fucking expected more from you," Doll chastises.

He starts shaking his head as her words begin to sink in. "I'm sorry, Doll. It's not like that. She isn't a bar-bitch. I'm not looking to settle down, though. The white picket fence and shit isn't for me."

"She doesn't want a white picket fence, dumbass. Neither, Sass or I, feel ready for the complications of a serious relationship. Sometimes chicks are out to have a good time and see where it goes, not get married right off the bat. Why do men make such quick assumptions?" Doll's frustrations are rolling off her with each word.

"I fucked up, Doll. My bad. You know I can't give her what she needs or wants, not long term. It's a good time, that's all. I didn't mean to be harsh this morning. It was just habit, that's all," he says running his hand through his hair.

"'My bad.' That's all you're gonna say?" Doll lowers her voice, mocking Tank to his face. "'My bad. It's a habit.' Man, fuck you, Tank!"

And before either of us can respond, Doll is off at a slow jog to catch up with her friend. Meanwhile, Tank is still shaking his head, running his hand through his short, dark hair, sighing.

I sigh as well. "Do I even want to know, brother?"

"Nah, man. I fucked up, it's what I do. Danza is gonna fucking kill me when he finds out," Tank replies as the relaxed tone of his voice is replaced with tension and something else that might even be sadness.

"She's an adult. Danza won't be happy, but I'm sure

he'll understand. She's the one who's pissed enough she seems ready to cut your balls off." I say, thinking, *'Damn, he really messed this one up.'*

"It is what it is. Fuck her, man. Come on, let's get to sermon."

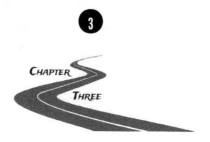

CHAPTER THREE

3

ONE ORDINARY DAY

Doll

It's another day at the office. For a little over two years now, Sass and I have been out of college and playing secretary for the Hellion's owned businesses. Sass works in the garage next door to my office. She handles customers, phones, ordering parts, and billing. The boys have a three bay motorcycle garage for comprehensive work and two additional lifts in the back to provide maintenance services to the bikes. My dad believes in higher education. The boys that work there all went to school and are ASE (Automotive Service Excellence) certified mechanics, for the boys that work on the few cars that come in. Ruben, known as 'Ruby' to everyone, is also certified by MMI, Motorcycle Mechanics Institute. He oversees everything for the garage.

My dad regrets giving me this job. I'm around too much and therefore, I figure out more than he would like for me to know. He didn't want me off the property, though, so he has to deal. You can't have it both ways, Roundman.

Looking at my board, there are thirteen available units. Ugh, that number. Superstitions don't usually get to me, but Friday the thirteenth and anything with that number, always seem to be a bad omen for me.

Running a mini storage facility is a tedious task. Keeping up the accounts, billing the late ones, tracking the people moving in and out, looking for the available units, the repossessions, the auctions, it's a lot of paper-work. We have one hundred and thirty five regular units broken into seven buildings inside this lot. There are also two additional storage unit buildings available outside of the regular space, adjoined to the Hellions compound area. The Hellions don't sell drugs. They don't actively sell guns; the occasional trade or sale, maybe, but not anything on a consistent basis.

Those additional forty units are for special business deals with Hellion connections and range in size from the closet-space-size of a five by ten, to the one-car-garage-size of the ten by twenty units. For these special buildings, the shipments come in on a schedule, and they're stored appropriately in however many units are needed until the product is ready to be moved again. I don't know for sure what is stored, though I have my suspicions, we all do. The Hellions provide transportation, storage, and protection after our clients have already sealed and filled the containers. This means we're responsible for the crates while they're in our territory, and the contents of the crates don't matter.

Being the overprotective type, my dad tries not to involve me in that side of the business often. It's not abnormal for club members to be kept away from it, either. We have a few upstanding, law-abiding members of the Hellions, people that don't want to get their hands dirty, like the Lawson's.

Harold "Roscoe" Lawson and his ol' lady, Marguerite, along with their daughter Maggie, her husband, and her older brother, Harrison, are all patched members that don't get involved in business. Dina and her husband, Ryder, are the same way. They all live in Charlotte, except Roscoe and Marguerite. That doesn't make them less of a member; it just means they don't get a cut out of that portion of the Hellion funds. We're all still a family.

Looking over my paperwork, I update the available board. Calling the people who are late with their rent drives me insane. There's always some excuse. Those who don't pay, lose their stuff to auctions, which are a nightmare. These people get certified letters, yet they always call after the auction asking for their stuff. It's gone, sweetheart. Gone. Next time, pay your bill. Business is business, nothing personal.

My dad gave me this job to keep me close and to avoid doing the paperwork himself. My dad has kept me close ever since my mother died when I was eleven from breast cancer. It was hard to watch her deteriorate and pass away. I don't remember much else about her. My four years away at the University of North Carolina, Charlotte were the most out of sight he's let me be. And even if I was technically out of sight, I was never out of mind; I had to check in with Dina or one of the Lawson family members. Somebody always knew where I was or what was going on with me. I'm a grown ass woman, but at the heart of it all, I'll always be my daddy's little girl.

Thirteen transports this week. Damn, it's going to be busy.

Shaking my head, I laugh off the weird feeling I get at the number thirteen. I know, it's stupid as fuck, but something about that particular number has always been unsettling. It's almost as bad as six-six-six. Oh, hell, just thinking of it gives me a moment of dread, which seems twisted since I'm not a man that unnerves easily. I've got the Hellions insignia tattooed on my back. A V-twin motorcycle engine with wrenches crossing over it, a skull is centered between the motor, and flames swirling around. Needles, skulls, spiders, and snakes, don't shake me, but stupid number superstitions cause me that moment of pause. Every man has a quirk or two.

Thankfully, the phone ringing on my desk shakes me out of my stupid thoughts.

"Crews Transports."

"Yo, got a nine-one-oh. Take it from the South Carolina border stop, on the Georgia side. Keep it close, Tripp, and it comes to the storage lot. Off-load isn't necessary. There'll be three Mack trucks needed for this one, you'll be locking and rolling in Georgia."

"Three trucks? And we aren't providing the trailers? Roundman, this is different," I reply. This is not our usual protocol.

"Delatorre scheduled this run. I know we usually do smaller, but we've got over ten years transporting with him; he'll have the trailers done right."

"We'll have no choice but to pass through at least two weigh stations crossing the state lines. Pass the message, the trailers need to make weight precisely, leave no room for error. I'll start to map the routes and send those stopping points to you. With that mileage, we'll need to double up drivers because of the hours behind the wheel. I'm gonna need Tank up here to fill one of the spots driving a Mack. I'll assign five ride along cars; one for each truck, one to scout ahead for road checks, and one to follow behind for any tails or trouble," I answer as I start planning out my job.

This is what I do, I maintain a trucking company. Rex and I own Crews Transports together. We do the usual scout for jobs online, bid on the runs, and travel with anything from transport, passenger vans, all the way up to full on eighteen-wheeler tractor-trailer loads. The company is completely legit, other than the nine-one-oh runs we take for the Hellions. The numbers nine-one-oh, the area code for the Haywood's Hellions, is the way we mark our transports for the club versus our regular business.

Typically, when old man Delatorre needs a transport, it's one trailer or two box trucks. He packs the trailers or box trucks. We either pick up the box truck as it is, or we pull up our Mack truck to his trailer, lock it in, and roll. What's in the trailers is not my concern, the weight of the contents is. Delatorre is good business, he's honorable and wouldn't do anything to put any of us at risk. Knowing this is his run, I'm confident that every-thing will go smoothly. Delatorre isn't a man you say no to anyways, so we are taking the job regardless. It's just nice to not have to look over your shoulder like you would with a new client.

"Alright, Tripp. Get the shit ready. Tank will be there in three days and the shipment is to be picked up in five."

"Got it, Roundman, over and out."

Looks like the transport number has just moved to sixteen now instead of thirteen. Business is good. Life is good.

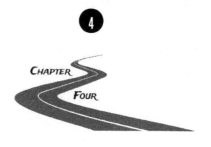

CHAPTER

FOUR

One Regret

S trolling over to the garage to pick up Sass from our work day, I can hear her shouting outside the building.

"What is it, Tank? Are you afraid of commitment? Or afraid of rejection? You may be one badass biker, but the way I see it, when it comes to relationships, you're full of fear. What are you sooo afraid of?"

As I enter her office, I see her standing there, poking her finger at Tank's chest. She's red in the face, full of fury, anger, and blatant defiance. Tank's face is distorted with his own anger and, perhaps, regret.

"Shut the fuck up, Sass. Why are you making this into something it's not? We fucked. You wanted it, fucking begged for it. If I knew you were going to turn into a stage-five clinger, then drunk or not, I would've sent your ass packing," Tank roars back at her.

"Whoa, you two! Calm the hell down. I can hear you outside. Y'all were friends before, cut this shit out. Enough with the hateful remarks," I say, trying to defuse the situation.

"That's what I fucking came here for, to fix shit. Then, fucking Sass, turns into a psycho bitch. I never promised happily ever after. A fucking orgasm, Savannah Mae, that's what I promised. And that's what the fuck I delivered. All this other shit you're spewing, fuck off."

With that, Tank storms out, leaving Sass standing in front of me utterly speechless. Walking up to Sass, I wrap my arms around her. She drops her head on my shoulder and begins to cry.

"I fucked up, Doll. I keep pushing, and I need to shut up. He's been up front. I knew damn well what I was doing. I thought one night, just one night, would be enough. But he's like a drug and one hit is never gonna be enough," she sobs into me, her body trembling with emotions.

"Shhh, Sass. It'll work out. Y'all need space, and you can't push him," I console, holding her close.

"You're right. He's more than another guy I've fucked, Doll. He's Tank. He's my Frank. We talk, we hang out, and I've fucked it all up. I never should've let this happen," she states, drying her eyes.

"Are you saying you regret sleeping with Tank?" I ask, stunned at her last remark.

He is older than us and has always been wild. They've become really close in the last two years, hanging out, talking, and becoming genuine friends, however, Sass has wanted to hook up with Tank since we were teenagers.

"Hell, no, I have no regrets there. Being with him for even one night was so much more than I ever could've imagined it to be. My one regret is my reaction to sleeping with him. This life isn't for me, Doll. I thought it was, but it's not. Tank is the first and last Hellion I'm sleeping with. I want something more. It's time for me to get serious about my life. To find someone who will commit to me, not to a club. I want to get married, have two-point-five kids and a white picket fence, not go to rallies and chase tailpipes in the wind."

"Come on, Sass, you love this club. It's family. And a white fucking fence? You have never wanted that," I say shocked, stepping back from my friend.

"The club will always be family, but this isn't my future. Doll, come on, be understanding. Let things be like they were in Charlotte where we freely picked up regular guys and dated. Neither of us have had a relationship since coming back to Haywood's Landing. How do we know that we aren't meant to be with someone that isn't a Hellion? Maybe I'm ready for a relationship now." Her eyes are pleading with me to agree and I've never been able to resist Sass.

Whether I agree with what she's saying or attempting to do, doesn't matter. If she wants to go out and try something new, as her best friend I'm along for the ride, that's a given.

"Alright, we'll go out. I love you, Savannah. I want you to be happy whether it's with a suit, a biker, or hell, even a rock star. Promise me though, no white picket fence…at least paint that shit black." We both break out into giggles at that and head home.

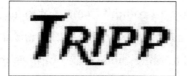

E verything is set up for the transport. Tank and I will be riding in a rig together, Rex will be riding with Frisco, and the third Mack truck will have Coach and Alfie paired for driving. John-boy, Conductor, Perry, Slice, and Dukes will be driving the cargo vans for our look out vehicles and added man power should something go wrong. All elements are arranged.

"We heading out on the town tonight, man?" Tank asks.

"You know it, brother." I smile and fist pound him.

"Good. I need this time away to get my mind off shit," he responds, shaking his head.

"You need to fuck that feisty one out of your system," Rex states, as he looks over at Tank with laughter in his eyes.

"Damn straight, I do. No regrets, that's the way I've lived my life. Then I have to go and fuck everything up by giving into something I knew I shouldn't have. Time and time again, I wanted to fuck her, but knew it would mess everything up. Damn it, I did it anyway and now I need to get her outta my system, that's all."

"A change in scenery, some new pussy, and a lot of alcohol will help man," I say as I lead the way outside.

The whole crew comes out with us to a local bar. The place is one we frequent regularly. The beer is cold,

the locals support us, and the barflies love us. Within a
few minutes, Rex is off in the back stock room with
some random hookup. This is definitely what Tank and I
both need. He can't shake Sass, and I can't get Doll
outta my head. Damn, at least Tank got laid before the
broad took up residence in his every thought.

After entering the bar, we pass by the booths that
line the right side wall. Sauntering through the open
middle space, we make our way to the long bar on the
left. Tessie, our usual bartender, already has our first
beers out and waiting. She's a cute, petite, dark haired
girl. She's nice enough. Rex tapped her once a few years
back; she took it in stride. She's a single mom trying to
get by, and gave into one night of lust. She's never
asked him for anything more than the one night in the
very stock room he's off banging someone else in right
now. I'm pretty sure she may be the one repeat Rex has
had, but neither of them shows it. Once, twice, whatever, they don't act like it's a regular hook up. Towards
the back of the bar, there are two open rooms with two
pool tables each. There is an area to throw darts in the
back of each of these corner rooms. They usually fill up,
but as a Hellion, once we enter, our room empties.

A few beers later, Tank and I are playing pool in the
back corner room. Three women come over to our
game. For a bit they watch and giggle to each other. One

is a bottle blonde, short only five foot, one or two. She's wearing a black mini skirt that barely covers her ass, a navy blue halter top that her boobs are screaming to be let loose from, topped off with those fuck me heels that women love to wear and men love to feel digging into their backsides. The other two have dark hair, one is taller, maybe five eight or nine, the shorter one closer to the blonde's height. The taller broad, is in a little black strapless number that she clearly doesn't realize one ass cheek is already hanging out of. The shorter one, obviously more reserved than the other two, is in jeans and a fitted shirt. She walks away, returning to wherever they came from.

The blonde approaches me, with a smile that says seduction. She licks her lips as she trails her finger over my cut. Stopping, she breathes into my ear.

"I have a pocket you can sink into, biker." She whispers.

"Is that so?" I reply, looking over at Tank. Her taller friend has now approached him and is mauling his face in what I believe to be extremely drunk kisses. I watch as Tank wraps his hand in her hair. Tightly, he pulls back on her, to slow her pace. He's taking control, and soon going to take what he wants. Returning my attention back to the barfly beside me, I move so she's pinned between me and the pool table.

Taking the hint, she pulls me up against her. I lean down, she thinks I'm going to kiss her, but instead I whisper, as I breathe heavily on her neck.

"Baby, are you sure? Be ready, I'm going to fuck you hard, fast, and rough. Right here, in front of your friend, my brother, and whoever decides to walk in. Once I start, I'm not gonna stop. Say no now, and walk the fuck away. Otherwise, take your panties off and stick them in my pocket. Then turn around and bend your ass over the pool table bitch."

Without hesitating, her panties are now in my pocket. Pulling her skirt over her waist, her bare ass is now shaking in front of me. Getting a condom out, I unbutton my jeans and stroke my dick. As I'm getting hard, I look over to see Tank is already working his girl over. Her legs are wrapped around his waist, arms around his neck, and her head back as she's moaning in ecstasy. Damn, they were quick to get to it.

Reaching around her front with my right hand, I slide up her thigh. At her juncture, I slowly tease her pussy lips with my fingers. Spreading them apart, I circle her clit as she rocks back on to me, seeking more. I increase the pressure and the pace on her clit. My dick is hard pressing against her ass. She looks over her shoulder, down at my dick. Seeing the silver jewelry at the tip, she smiles.

"Fuck me, biker. Take that big, pierced cock and fuck my ass."

If that's what the hell the slut wants, who the hell am I to say no? The bitch wants it rough, fine. She'll feel this shit for days. I push her head down onto the pool table. Removing my hand from her clit, I roll the condom on. I kick her legs further apart. Taking a few moments to finger her pussy, I use her own juices to start inserting my finger in her ass. Once she adjusts to the first finger, I add a second. With my other hand, I'm rubbing the head of my penis against her clit, letting the piercing apply that added sensation. She's now rocking back rhythmically on three fingers. I remove my fingers and slowly insert the tip of my cock. I give her body a moment to adjust to my girth, as I inch in further. She's tiny and there is no way I'll be balls deep without hurting her. Her ass is tight and the lube from the condom isn't enough. Once I'm inside her a good bit, I reach around with my left hand and massage her breast at the same time I begin rubbing circles on her clit. I tease the entrance to her pussy with my fingers. As I do, she rocks back engulfing my dick in her ass. It's warm, soft, and so tight. I insert two fingers inside her pussy as I pinch her nipple. She rocks against me as I begin pumping both my dick and my fingers in and out of her. She's clinching around me as her orgasm is building.

"Oh, oh, oh…yes…I'm coming." She screams out

so loud Tank and his play thing stop fucking to turn and watch us.

As she's going through the aftershocks of her orgasm, she starts to raise her head up. I push it back down, as I remove my hand from her pussy and my dick from her ass.

"I'm not finished yet. Bitch, stay put." I say as I hold her down onto the pool table.

Fast and hard, I thrust my dick in her pussy now. I set a quick, intense pace, ready to get off and move on. Within a few hard thrusts, I allow my mind a moment of wondering, imagining the face of a doll, I come in the condom. Finishing, I pull out. Removing the condom, I tie off the top, and toss it in the trashcan in the room. Adjusting myself, I zip up my pants. Looking over, I see Tank is finished as well. His girl is already sporting a pouty face while mine is still bent over the pool table like she doesn't know what just happened.

Deciding I am done for the night, I grab my beer, and nod to Tank that it's time to go. He follows me out of the room, leaving the two barflies behind. They both call out to us. Rather than turn around and acknowledge them, I flip my middle finger over my head at them as we make our way by the bar towards the exit door.

Even after my release, Doll's face is still circling my mind. Damn, I can't shake her. Fuck me. I throw an extra hundred on the bar for Tessie, like I do every week. She's a devoted mom and dealing with my boy's when we're here ain't easy. Nodding to Rex and raising my hand up, all the boys start making their way outside. We climb on our bikes and head home to rest for the upcoming job.

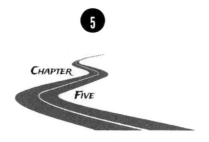

5

CHAPTER

FIVE

ONE OPPORTUNITY

Today is a slow day at the office. Sass is serious about letting go of this lifestyle. She loves her dad and the family we have, but she really wants more. Full of mixed emotions, I begin to question what I want in the future. When my mom was alive, I didn't spend as much time at the clubhouse or around the guys. After she died, my dad took me everywhere with him, so this is all I know.

Settling down with a man sounds appealing, but playing domestic goddess does not. Kids are cute, but I don't know about being tied down. I like the freedom to go off whenever I want, wherever I want, nothing holding me back. At twenty-five, I feel like I'm settling into myself. I don't need the baggage of a serious commitment. I do need to get laid though. Damn, it's been awhile and BOB is nice, but battery operated toys aren't the same as a man's warm breath on your neck as he's thrusting in and out of you.

The chiming bell on the front door shakes me back to reality. Looking up, I see a tall Latino man and a seemingly scared small woman.

"Hi, welcome to Landing's Storage. I'm Delilah. How can I help you?" I reach to shake his hand.

"Lookin' for Roundman." He says, shaking my hand quickly while subtly squeezing the back of his companion's neck.

"Just a moment, may I tell him your name," feeling apprehensive at his presence.

"Delatorre."

Turning to my desk, I dial my dad over in the cave. "Hey Daddy. A Mr. Delatorre is here to see you." I say into the phone. Dad makes a growl, which is his way of saying he will be right over.

Smiling at my guests, I ask, "He's on his way. May I get you some water, Mr. Delatorre and … I'm sorry, what was your name?"

"Amy, my name is Amy Mitchell." She stammers.

Delatorre's grip must have gotten tighter around her neck at her response, because she hunches her shoulders in a defensive manner. He's obviously in control of her and this situation. It's making me uncomfortable, but I'm here alone at the moment.

"Some water would be fine, Doll." Delatorre responds.

Getting the water, the hair on the back of my neck stands up. How does he know to call me Doll? I told him my name is Delilah. Instincts are screaming at me that this is not a nice guy. Trouble is brewing and his name is in the thick of it.

My dad stomps in. "Who the fuck are you?" He barks with agitation evident in his stance.

"Daddy, this is Mr. Delatorre." I interject watching my dad's reaction intently. My dad is a master at reading people.

"You may be a Delatorre, but you're not Oscar Delatorre. He's the only Delatorre I'll meet with. I'll ask you one more time, as my patience is non-existent. Who. The. Fuck. Are. You?"

"Felix Delatorre, I'm Oscar Delatorre's son. He's become ill and I've taken over the business dealings."

"In my office, Delatorre." My dad replies, pointing in the direction of his private door.

He begins to guide Amy in front of him. My dad raises his hand in a stopping gesture.

"She stays out here. No women in my office. This business does not relate to them, Delatorre."

He seems to want to argue for a moment, but stops himself. The cold stare he leaves Amy with is a harsh reminder to keep her mouth shut, act a certain way, of what exactly I'm not so sure. The look on my dad's face lets me know this isn't a welcomed guest. Amy sits down in the chair that faces my desk. Head bowed, she looks defeated, broken, and lost.

"Can I get you anything, Amy?"

For a long moment, she sits there, unmoving and not speaking. Then with a raspy, trembling voice, she speaks up.

"Help me." That's all she says.

Hearing a noise behind me, I look up. Before I can respond, the office door opens and the men walk out. Studying Amy, her body becomes rigid at Felix's presence. Looking more closely, her face seems to have some underlying bruising that is still healing but clearly covered up by makeup. Why did I not notice this before?

Grabbing a business card, I scribble my cell phone number down while trying not to be seen. Walking over to Amy, I extend my hand to her.

"It was a pleasure to meet you, Amy." She shakes my hand and I feel her trembling as I pass her the business card. I don't know what exactly I can do for her, but I can't miss this one opportunity I have to help her.

Felix and Amy leave. My dad seems more annoyed than usual. I sense something big is going on. My instincts are confirmed when my dad calls a sermon in the cave for the Hellions. My heart is heavy with worry for our boys.

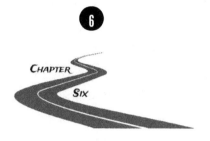

ONE MISTAKE

Women's intuition. That sixth sense. We often ignore it, and make excuses for the nagging feeling of dread, danger, or doom. Sass and I are out at Booties, a nightclub here on Emerald Isle, not far from our condo. She's determined to meet a regular guy. I want to cut loose, have fun, and not have a Hellion taga-long. Bad idea this was.

There aren't many nightclubs on the island, as it's called, or even in town if we were to venture back over the bridge. Now having a few drinks in us, we're both feeling comfortable and ready to mingle. We hit the dance floor. After a song or two, we are joined by two pretty boys. Sass seems to really enjoy dancing and chatting with her new friend, Nick, leaving me stuck entertaining Alton, Nick's friend.

The guys are nice enough and cute in that preppy, country club way. Both are dressed in khaki's and pastel polo shirts. Real men wear pink and all that bullshit. Give me a break. I want a man in jeans, a t-shirt, boots, and sporting some ink. If you're too much of a pussy to go under the needle for the opportunity to be completely creative with the canvas known as your body, then you're definitely too pussy to be with me. The collared shirts and sports coats, they just don't do it for me.

When we left the condo tonight, I couldn't shake the feeling that someone was around. Here at the club, hours later, I still feel like something isn't right. Looking around me, everyone and everything appears to be like any other night out, business as usual. I'm probably overreacting because we went out without a prospect or a member. Rarely do Sass and I go anywhere without a man with us. Not that I need a man, I'm perfectly capable of changing a tire and all that, but my dad insists the Hellions look out for us at all times.

Suddenly feeling claustrophobic, I decide to leave the dance floor and head to the bar. The club isn't very big. Entering, you find a doorman table for keeping the

ID's of the under twenty-one people. Once past the doorman, it's open dance floor space. To the right is the bar with a few of those gambling machines, to the left are a few table and chairs. Off in the corner is the DJ set up on a platform. Straight back leads to the restrooms and stock room.

Alton follows me like a trained puppy, as I reach the bar. Rolling my eyes, I can't help but think, '*man up son. If you want me, make a move because right now, you're boring the shit out of me*'. I order a beer in a bottle, not on tap. This late in the evening, the kegs have been changed out, and the newer keg hasn't been on ice as long. Warm beer is piss beer. Beer on tap that is crispy, ice cold is refreshing, but if it ain't cold I don't want it. Alton orders a Razzle Dazzle. Really? Ugh, there was a brief moment, and I do mean brief, where I considered sleeping with him tonight. Scratch an itch so to speak. Ordering a mixed drink and making a face at my beer; damn, you might as well have ordered a martini pretty boy.

"What is a Razzle Dazzle exactly?" I ask because curious minds want to know and all that.

"Vodka, cranberry juice, lime juice, mint leaf, and blueberries." Alton answers with a proud smile.

"Trying to hide the liquor taste?" I ask as a statement as much as a question. I'm so dumbfounded that a man would order a chick drink.

"It's very good and you don't taste the alcohol."

"What about a simple beer? Like a Bud? Or hell, have a Corona with lime? You don't drink Crown and Coke, or Jack and Coke do ya?"

"No. Beer never has been a taste I could become accustomed to. And liquors, whiskeys, bourbons, are all good, but not for me if you can taste them."

What the hell? If he can't choke down a real man's drink, he sure as shit doesn't have any ink hiding under those clothes. We finish our drinks with little more said. Sass comes over to whisper that she's going home with Nick. Lovely, now asshat Alton is going to expect to go home with me. I'm over this night. Everything has felt off today, and it's not getting any better.

Alton, being the gentlemen that he is, wants to escort me home. Having taken a cab here, I wasn't left with many options, other than to offend pretty boy and call another cab or let him drive me home. Not feeling threatened by Alton, I choose to allow him to drive me home.

Something is still nagging and pulling at me in the back of my mind. This all feels wrong, going out was a mistake. Letting Savannah go home with Nick was an even bigger mistake. He may be sweet, but he's not her type, even if she doesn't know what her type is at the moment.

We arrive at my condo. Alton walks me to the front

door like any well-mannered, southern boy would do. He leans in for a kiss. I'm not sure why exactly, but I allow it. Waiting for a spark or something, I continue to kiss him. Nothing. No spark, no flame, no fireworks; hell, I don't even get the tiniest amount of friction. I'm so dead to Alton, a boy scout couldn't start a fire. He tries to advance the kiss. I pull back. Looking at him, the façade slips, and his irritation with me shows.

"Delilah, you know you want me. Why be a prude now?"

"Prude? Want you? What the fuck have you been smoking? I danced with you a few times, we talked, had a few drinks. That does not entitle you to have something more, douchebag."

He grabs me a little too firmly, pushing me into my front door.

"Alton, no, I don't want this from you. Go home, you need to leave." I state firmly as a warning before things get out of hand.

He makes no move to loosen his grip on me. My adrenaline kicks in. Fight or flight mode begins as my mind races for what to do next. Suddenly, his lips crash down on mine, hard. He's trying to pry my mouth open. When I don't yield to him, he bites my lip, drawing blood. I begin trying to push him off me, when I hear a voice.

"I believe she said for you to leave."

In shock at the interruption, Alton pulls away. "Who the hell are you?" He asks. My veins run cold at the man standing in the breezeway. He should not be here. He's not someone who should know where I live.

"The person who is going to make sure you leave Miss Reklinger alone."

"You're a damn tease and not worth the hassle." Alton says, stomping off.

Waiting for Alton to get around the corner, I'm in a stare down with my unwelcomed guest, who is now only a few inches away.

"This is none of your concern. I had everything under control, Mr. Delatorre. Why the fuck are you here?" I ask, wiping the little bit of blood off my lips.

"I came to return this." He says handing me back the business card I gave Amy. "And to inform you that Amy is none of your concern. You need to be aware, I can find you easily."

Not knowing what to say, I stand there with an uneasy expression on my face. Felix Delatorre is walking away. The man carries himself with such confidence you know he means every word he says. He's tall, over six feet, and he clearly works out. His cockiness is what's most alarming. He comes across as the man who owns the world. This can be a dangerous attitude to have. And raises the question, can he back it up?

Separating the trucks doesn't make me comfortable. We've had two cars following us from the beginning. Since they are making no serious attempt to hide themselves, my instinct screams to deviate from the original plan. Sending the code to split the group early is not a decision I'm a hundred percent comfortable with, but it's the best one to make. The trucks are spaced out in half hour intervals to keep distance between the loads and not draw attention. Now we are switching our directions. The routes were planned to be different, but the break off was not intended to occur this soon.

Checking in, I let Roundman know we will be delayed. Something in this doesn't feel right. This is not at all how any of our previous dealings with Delatorre have gone down. I rub my hand on the back of my neck, trying to work away the tension radiating throughout my body.

"You straight, Tripp?" Tank asks as he's changing gears.

"Yeah, I'm alright. Shit feels off though. Not our typical run." My phone rings before we can talk more.

"Crews," I answer.

"The caddy followed you on the break off. Stay aware. He's closing in on your six. Do you want me to send extra wheels?" Conductor states with his normal firm tone.

The tail watched who has the double up on back up, damn it. Tank and I decided to stick with only one of the additional cars and let the others have two each. We have Slice, Tank, and me. Slice being our additional car, while the other two trucks have two cars with them. They're clearly following the truck with the least man power. Conductor calls in informing me that the Cadillac SVT has four men inside, the other small car has three men, leaving the three of us against seven. The odds aren't bad, but shit isn't good either. We're armed, but it's drama we don't need following us home.

"No, call Slice. Tell him to back off us, and circle around. We'll be at the truck stop in Lumbee. If they follow us in there, we'll chat. Slice is to make no moves, just wait and watch. Understood?"

Finishing up my phone call, Tank is already making the appropriate turns to get us to the location. He pulls the truck up to the diesel pumps and stops. I ready my Glock. Tucking the pistol in the waist of my jeans against my back, I exit the truck as Tank is prepping his weapon and logging the miles and hours. Sure enough, as planned, the caddy pulls in behind us. What's surprising is the boldness of the car, as it parks directly behind our rig. Glancing over my shoulder, I'm aware of Slice arriving. He's parked out of sight from the caddy's location. If things go wrong, he's close enough to step in and help while Tank leaves.

I nod to Tank making him aware, the shipment comes first. He's not to exit the truck. If these boys want to fuck around, he's to pull off and leave Slice to back me up. The other boys will catch up and cover him. Knowing there is a risk, but also knowing this is my job, I approach the vehicle. Aware of my weapon, but not showing any signs of being armed I tap the window.

The car has four tattooed Hispanic men inside. The guy in the passenger seat rolls down his window with a smirk of arrogance on his face.

"Can I help you boys with anything?"

The fucker actually chuckles at me. My anger boils immediately.

"I'm Pablo. We work for Mr. Delatorre. Consider us quality assurance."

"Well, Pablo." I stretch out his name, my annoyance evident in my tone. "I don't know who the hell Mr. Delatorre is, or you, for that matter. We are a corporate transport company. Nothing we ship is for private individuals. So, mister quality ASS....urance, you're already fucking up your job. If you would back your car up and pull away, you might have enough time to catch up to whatever truck it is you are supposed to be on its

ASS for insurance. This ASS has a delivery and dead-line to make." I step back off the window and cross my arms over my chest.

"That's your story.....mister....I didn't catch your name. What is it?"

"You didn't catch my name because you have no need for my name, Amigo. Now turn your fucking car around and be on your way." I start to walk away, but I'm halted momentarily as his last words are said out of the window.

"Mr. Crews, I know who you are. We will leave you, as you have assured me our shipment is safe. Your other boys better be as quick witted and quiet with details as you are. See you around, Talon."

I don't look back as I hear the car start and then pull away. I fill the truck up with fuel as I run my fingers through my long hair. He called me by my given name, not Tripp. My business lists everything as Tripp Crews. The trucks are all unmarked, no business names, only our licensing numbers for the state Department of Transportation checks. Who the hell is Pablo? What is he to Delatorre? How much does he know? Having someone we're in Hellions business with know my real first name isn't an issue. Being confronted on a trans-port, however, that screams trouble. Taking this job has become one huge mistake for the Hellions. Shit just got real deep. Fuck me.

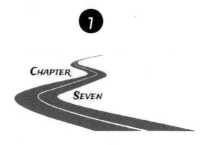

ONE THREAT

The weekends always pass much too quickly. Savannah spent the entire weekend with Nick. Glad that hookup is working out so well for her. We're getting ready for work. My bestie has a glow and a smile on her face that I haven't seen in a very long time. Maybe Nick will be good for her.

I've been on edge since the encounter with Mr. Felix Delatorre. Part of me wants to tell my dad what happened, but the other part knows that would cause

problems. My dad is extremely over protective. Delatorre is right; I shouldn't have stuck my nose in his business with Amy. She obviously didn't use the card.
Maybe I misread her plea for help.

All the way to work, I've been thinking of the situation with Felix. The domino effect this would have on
the Hellions business would not be good. I don't know
how much money he spends for our transport and storage. What I do know is my dad and his boys. The
minute I tell him Delatorre showed up at my doorstep,
business ties will be severed. That's the least of what
concerns me. My dad going off the deep end, feeling
that I am in some way threatened, that concerns me. He
and the other Hellions walk a fine line. One wrong
move, people are going to federal prison, not just an
over nighter at the county jail. Having a client dispute
would run the risk of blowing the whole transport business wide open.

Gathering my resolve, I make the only decision
there is to make. Keep my mouth shut. From now on,
I'll keep close to Hellion grounds, try not to be alone,
and keep focused on everything surrounding me. As
much as my dad would make this problem go away for
me, it's not good for the Hellions as a whole.

Even as a female, I know the club comes first.
That's the first rule of being an ol' lady: understanding
the club is always priority one. I'm no one's ol' lady, but

I keep the club focus as my first priority. There are more things to consider than my own insecurity here. In time, I'm sure Felix Delatorre will tire of whatever cat and mouse game he's attempting to play and move on. People depend on the Hellions for a lot. I won't risk the security of the club, as a whole, for my own dumb decision to help a stranger. Who knows, Amy might've been high that day. It could've been a test against the Hellions and how much we'll be involved in Felix's business and personal life. Either way, it was my mistake to reach out to her and it's my mistake to face alone.

Settling in at work, I'm busy catching up on messages from the weekend. The door chimes, alerting me that someone has entered. Once again, Amy is almost pushed ahead of Felix Delatorre. The one person I want to not exist in my little bubble of the world is back in my very office. Damn it. The fresh bruises across Amy's face are clearly evident now. I no longer question what I saw on her before. Her lip is swollen and cut like its healing from a recent altercation. She's in a mess, but what, if anything, can I possibly do? What kind of man is Felix Delatorre to prance her around in public looking like this? The abuse is obvious. Is he not concerned with the ramifications of such behaviors? Is he big enough that he truly feels above the law?

"Hello, Delilah." He snarls. Clearly, he's not happy

about something. The foreboding feeling that shit is about to hit the fan engulfs me.

"Mr. Delatorre, what can I do for you?" I ask making sure to steady my voice to cold indifference. Never let anyone see you are affected or vulnerable. Weakness is like love, hold it close to your heart and only show it to those who will protect and cherish it.

"Where is your father?"

Before I can answer, my dad emerges from his office. He must have been watching the camera monitors in his office.

"Delatorre, what do you want?"

Felix leaves Amy standing off to the side as he approaches me. He's now standing to my right, inside my bubble. He's too close for comfort. His arrogance and irritability is coming off him in waves.

"My shipment seems to have taken a detour, Mr. Reklinger. I'm here to ensure that everything is on schedule."

"And what exactly does your presence in my office do for your transport? Riddle me that, Delatorre?"

"I have men following each vehicle. My presence here is only brief to make sure my message is clear." He steps closer to me, bringing the back of his hand up to stroke my cheek. I back away. "Tsk, Tsk, Delilah, remember I know how to get to you day or night. Do not shy away from me."

Before I can reply, my dad has Delatorre against a wall, by his throat. I watch in shock as Delatorre squirms against my dad, gasping for air.

"Let me make my message clear, mother fucker. You ever lay one fucking finger on my daughter again I'll cut them all off and feed them to you for dinner. Business is business. You stay the fuck away from my family. Your shipment's on its way and I'll say when the fuck you'll get it now." My dad drops his hand from Delatorre's throat, and shoves him roughly one last time.

Felix, the sick fucker, laughs. That's right, laughs in my dad's face. "Oh Roundman, your code of honor to protect your women is such a joke. I've already been to your precious Doll's home. Fuck with my transport, I will get to her again." Looking at me, he continues. "Fuck with my personal life again and you won't see another day."

My dad pulls the .357 Magnum from my desk drawer. Shit is seriously about to hit the fan. Amy screams in fear. Delatorre quickly backhands her. She falls to the floor, holding her already battered face. Blood trickles from her now reopened lip wound.

"You're a dead fucker, Delatorre. Let me make this clear. Get the fuck out of my office. You won't know when or where, but I promise you if it's the last mother fucking thing I do, you'll pay for threatening my daughter."

"I will leave for now. Be warned, yourself. Don't fuck with my transport, Reklinger. If I don't have my shipment in Virginia on time, and complete, your daughter isn't going to be the only one I'll fuck with. I will take every single one of those bitches you Hellions keep so close. Each time they cry out for one of you Hellions, I will make them choke on my dick, while I carve my name across their breasts. Then while they bleed out, my boys will fuck them in every way imaginable. Their torture and deaths will be on your shoulders, and I will make it slow and painful. And your precious Doll here, will watch each and every single one of them all the way until their last breath."

He yanks Amy up from the floor by her hair, half dragging her out of the door. My dad lowers the gun and glares at me. He's more than ready to kill Delatorre, but won't because of my presence.

"Did you know he knew where you lived?" I don't answer. I don't know how to answer. My dad is red with rage. I'm scared to move. This man, burly, big, and scary has always been my teddy bear, until this very moment. My body is trembling as the adrenaline is slowing down.

"Answer me Doll. Fucking answer me!" My dad roars, slamming the drawer shut.

"Yes." I whisper.

"And you didn't fucking tell me? Shit, Doll, do you know what he could've already done to you? Damn it to hell! He knows more about all of us than I realized."

"I'm sorry, Daddy. I didn't want you to flip out and get into trouble." I say weakly.

"Flip out and get into trouble? Fuck me, Doll. You never put yourself in danger for me or any fucker! Damn it. Stay put. You go nowhere alone, and you stay here on the compound. Are we clear?"

"Yes, sir." I answer. Tears flowing down my face as the fear sets in. After giving my dad the rundown on exactly what happened with Delatorre at my front door, including my evening with Alton, I'm overwhelmed with thoughts of what will happen next.

His last words before walking into his office are on repeat in my head. "What's done is done, what's been said, can't be unsaid. This fucker found my daughter. This fucker came to my territory and threatened the people I love. This fucker is going to the ground."

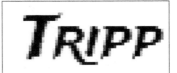

Hanging up the phone, I run my fingers across my jaw. Damn it, I don't know what went down, but shit got serious. Roundman is calling for a meeting in the cave. An off-schedule sermon with zero notice means trouble. Considering our encounter with Don Juan Pablo and his troop, I would say we're in some shit. And they would be my target numero uno.

"What's going on Tripp?" Tank asks. "I just got a text from my crew that sermon has been called immediately. That means as soon as we pull in, everyone is waiting in the cave for us. We've been followed. And now you've got the look like someone killed your damn dog."

"I don't have a clue man. Roundman said hold the shipments tight. Call the crew to catch up and every patched member is required at sermon."

"Hammer down son, let's get home." Tank replies as he pushes the gas pedal. Due to our lack of knowledge of what is contained in the trailer, we can only exceed the speed limit in places we know we won't get pulled over. Although we have most of the police stations in our back pockets and on our payroll, there are always those one or two cops that want to do everything by the books.

———

P ulling into the lot, we quickly unhook, and secure our trailer. My crew arrives, as well as the other two transport trucks. We make our way inside the cave. The room is bland, void of real decoration outside of the black and red of our colors. The flags on the walls are Hellions insignias, and the few pictures in frames are our Hellions history living on through captured memories of previous events. In the middle is a long rectangular table that seats sixteen. Chairs along the walls fill the remaining space, with a large standing safe in the far back corner.

Tank is a Haywood's Landing Hellion; he's the Road Chief to be exact. He takes his place at the long rectangular table. Officers only at the table, patched members take the side seats along the walls of the room. I take my seat beside Rex, four places down from Tank and six places down from Roundman. As Prez and VP of our chapter, we get table seats.

Roundman calls the sermon to order. He sits there quietly, his age suddenly apparent to me. Roundman is tall, built, and covered in ink, full sleeves that go up his neck. His long graying hair pulled back and his goatee does nothing to hide the serious look crossing his face. He's fifty-eight, but most days he carries himself with the agility and attitude of a much younger man, with a lifetime ahead of him. The look he has in this moment is one of worry and one of age. He's obviously bothered by something.

"Fellas, Oscar Delatorre has fallen ill. He has passed his business dealings down to his son Felix Delatorre. We've completed the first half of the transport under Felix's command. He does his business much differently than his father."

I shake my head; this can't be good. Sharing the specifics of business dealings with all the active members is definitely out of our normal procedures, big shit is going down. Roundman takes this time to catch everyone up on the side business we have.

"Bottom line, Felix is a control freak with some bigger issues. He threatened not only Doll, but every Hellion woman. He plays dirty boys, and needs to be taught a lesson. He's clever. I underestimated him. He came on board under a guise of being Oscar and the job was agreed upon long before I knew it wasn't a job for Oscar, but one for Felix. Therefore, we're goin' on lock down for families. Pack your wives, girlfriends, moms and children. Get them settled into the duplexes. As for each of you, go to work, and be normal. Set up a schedule so the compound is double or triple guarded now. We're going to complete the transport, as that is the business transaction. Then we're going to teach the fucker that Hellion women are off limits, even in conversation. Danza, Tank, Tripp, Frisco, and Rex stay behind. The rest of you are dismissed to pack your shit. I want every single one of you and your families accounted for on the compound TONIGHT! No fucking around! Dismissed." He slams the gavel down.

Once everyone exits the cave, Roundman continues. "Danza, the girls aren't safe. He knows where the condo is. He confronted Doll on the front porch when she returned from a date."

A date? Doll was on a date, hmmm. I wonder who with. Is he a Hellion? A suit? I'm quickly brought back out of my thoughts.

"He's made it clear. He can get to them if he wants to. Until he's eliminated the girls aren't safe. Typically, I would put them on lock down with everyone else. This time, I'm not comfortable with that. I don't want them anywhere near what I'm going to do to that son of a bitch. Let's send the girls off on a ride while we take care of the issue. After we bury the fucker, we can bring them home. There are club affiliations nationwide that we can send them to that will keep them protected and safe."

Danza replies, "Damn it. I don't like the idea of them being so far away. He's already gotten too close, though. If that piece of shit knows where Savannah and

Delilah live, it's serious trouble for the girls. Neither of them seem to know how to shut their mouths to stay safe. I'm in."

"Alright, let's head over to the office and let the girls know." Roundman states and we leave the cave.

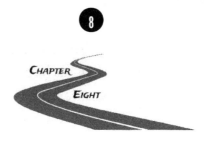

ONE REQUEST

M y dad is on his way over to my office. Savannah is here, all of a sudden, at the request of her dad. Given the threat of Felix Delatorre, I have a feeling a lock down is coming. The door chimes and I look up to see Tank walk in first. He approaches Sass and I. Standing, I greet him with a hug. I move out of the way as he pulls Sass into him. Reluctantly, she hugs him back. I can hear him talking to her.

"Sass, be mad at me all you fucking want. Please, right now, keep that sexy as sin mouth of yours shut.

Don't fight this okay? For me, please. I need to know you're safe so I can do my job."

Before either of us can further question what he's referring to, the door chimes. In walks the familiar face from my recent fantasies. His shoulder length dark brown hair is hanging down now, rather than pulled back as it was on our first encounter. His face set in a stone like frame of seriousness. The golden hazel of his eyes is sparkling with lust and passion as he stares straight at me. He's in jeans, a navy blue t-shirt, black boots, and his cut. His friend from the barbecue is with him, as well as my dad, Danza, and Frisco.

Frisco reaches me first. He's short compared to the others, about five feet, eight inches. He's trim and hand-some. For a biker, he's clean cut. His tattoos aren't visible unless he removes his shirt. He has salt and pepper hair and eyes so dark, I could almost swear they were black. For a man in his late fifties, he's still handsome. He's one of the few Hellions that could play the part of a suit easily. Although, if you tell him that, he will laugh in your face and say, *"Not even in my casket will I wear a damn suit."* Frisco smiles down at me, his dimples lighting up his face as he hugs me. He hugs Sass, as she's still staring at Tank.

Frisco moves to the back wall of my office, beside the door to my dad's private office. When you walk in the front door, it leads to an open space with four chairs, two on each side of the door and my desk lined to the right wall, but facing the door. I have file cabinets on the wall behind my desk and then, an office door that leads to a bathroom and my dad's private office. Tank moves to sit in a front chair.

Danza hugs me quickly before reaching over to Sass. He hugs her as he growls, "Stop with your attitude toward Tank. Shit's real serious Sass. You've been killin' him with your eyes since we walked in the door. I've had enough." With that, my best friend's face softens and she moves to sit against my desk.

For once, my dad didn't enter and greet me, rather, he stares. An awkward silence encompasses the room. Tripp and Rex are standing in the doorway by the chair Tank is occupying.

"Doll, you remember Tripp?" My dad asks, pointing to the man of my recent dreams. Damn, I've had his name wrong this whole time. Definitely should've paid better attention at the barbecue introductions. Being the flirt that I am, I step forward and once again extend my hand to Tripp, as he shakes my hand, I step closer so I can pull him to me.

"He's one that's hard to forget." I say as I pull his shoulder down to kiss him on the cheek. The charge zings through my body at the touch of my lips to his cheek. I step back and move to shake hands with Rex.

All the greetings now complete, my dad is still eerily silent.

"Is someone going to tell me why the hell y'all are taking up my office space?" My annoyance is now over-taking my patience.

The more time I stand in close proximity of Tripp the more I want to inspect every detail of his naked body. I don't want to get to know him. Hell, I've had a couple of battery operated initiated orgasms with his face in my mind, while calling out the wrong name. None of the details matter, what he can do for my body is what I want to know. If he's not into me for sex, then, quite frankly, I want him to leave. He's a distraction of the lust filled kind.

"Sit down, Delilah." My dad commands. He never uses my given name; I've been his doll my entire life. Shit.

Doing as I am told, I back up and slide my butt up to be sitting on my desk. Bracing myself for serious news, I grip the edge of the desk and look down.

"Big things are going on. You and Savannah are going to go on a ride for a few weeks."

"Huh?" I mutter.

"Pack a small bag for the bikes, you and Sass are going on a ride with Tripp and Rex." My dad states firmly.

"Tripp and Rex? You're sending us away? With

them? Why exactly? We've never been sent away before. What the hell, Dad?" I ask as I hop off my desk and stand with my hands on my hips.

"Roundman, why are they coming with us? Wouldn't you rather Danza or Tank take them out of the area?" Tripp asks with that serious demeanor he always has.

"No, I need Danza and Tank here. You two will take the girls."

"And what if we don't want to go, Dad? What will you do then?" I ask with a firmness I've never had when addressing my dad before.

Any other time a trip wouldn't bother me. I know my dad is going to take this time to handle Delatorre, that's not my issue with going away. This trip means days and nights with merely inches between Tripp and me on his bike.

"Delilah, I don't ask any fucking thing of you. This is my one request. Go away with Tripp on this ride. Have fun while you travel if that makes it better, but stay safe. Put your attitude away and listen to me and to Tripp. This is for you, my Doll. To keep you safe."

"I don't want to go. Delatorre is an ass, but he won't come to my house again, he's bluffing." I say, not really believing myself.

"Damn it, Delilah! You. Will. Fucking. Go!" with that my dad stomps to his office.

"Not negotiable, Sass, so shut your fucking trap before you even start." Danza says, as his way of backing up what we already know. He follows my dad into the back office.

Tank, Tripp, Frisco, and Rex follow Danza. Sass and I stand by my desk in disbelief of what just occurred.

"Roundman, you're sure 'bout this?" I ask once we are in the privacy of his office. Of all the things he could ask of me, this is what I end up with. No fucking way. How do I say no? The office is small; only a desk, a chair, a safe, and two file cabinets are contained in the room. Having six grown men in the small space is cramped. Tension coursing through each of us is filling the room and sending everyone's adrenaline into overdrive.

"Are you fucking questioning me, Tripp? Because I know you're not stupid enough to question me." Roundman states, the tension is rolling off him in waves. The room is suddenly feeling even smaller.

"I'm not questioning sending the girls on a ride. I thought you'd want me and Rex to work on Delatorre."

"No, I need our daughters kept safe. They've both got a knack for not only running their mouths, but also sticking their noses where they don't belong. The last thing I need to worry about right now is Doll and Sass. I trust you and Rex to keep them safe. Tank here, would be too busy fucking Savannah to stay on task. As for the rest of us, those girls have us all wrapped around their little fingers, and won't listen like they need to. They've gotta keep their mouths shut and stay out of trouble. You two are my best options." Roundman says firmly, while Danza is giving Tank the death glare.

Tank coughs at the mention of fucking Sass. Roundman is perceptive. Does he see the way his daughter winds me up? Every minute that ticks by I feel the walls closing in. Danza has yet to remove his eyes from Tank.

Pulling an envelope out of the drawer, Roundman walks over to me. Toe to toe, I stand taller than him, but he's no less intimidating.

"Keep them safe. Don't fuck around, Tripp. She's a beautiful girl. Hellion or not, you fuck over my kid, I will feed you your balls for breakfast. She's off limits. Sass is off limits. Got it?"

"Got it." Taking the envelope, that I know is full of money, I hand it to Rex for safe keeping.

Roundman is in his safe. He comes out with a sealed, letter sized envelope.

"This stays on you Tripp, and only you. Map out your travels, head to Broadus, Montana. When you get to the Shifter's compound, go see Dyson. You know the Shifter's Pack. Keep yourself and those two broads in check. We're fuckin' good with 'em, and we're gonna stay fuckin' good with 'em. They're a strong affiliate, and I don't want any disrespect whatsoever between our clubs, understood? This envelope is important for the Blackout transport, and they're expecting it."

"Got it." I reply, what else is there to say?

There's a lot to this ride and it's going to require every bit of my focus and attention to the details around us. Roundman sits behind his desk as we work with Tank on the details of our route. After two hours, every-thing is ready. We exit the small office to the front lobby. Leaving Tank to deal with a very pissed off Danza, a stressed out Roundman, and Frisco, who I have a feeling, may find Tank's situation funny.

"Alright, let's go darlin'," I say to Doll as I stride out the door of the building.

One ride together. Go across the country and back. One ride to get her out of my system for good. One ride to keep her safe. Our one ride begins now.

ONE RIDE BEGINS

M y dad insists my car stay at the office. Hell, getting him to let me pack my own bag is about as much compromise as Roundman is willing to give. He wants me to let a prospect go pack my bag. Really? How could he want a fucking prospect all up in my panty drawer? That is so not happening. Now, I'm in the front of my office getting ready to ride bitch on Tripp's bike. Butterflies are taking over my stomach. I've only ever ridden with my dad or driven myself.

"Wait just a fucking minute." I hear Tank roar, as he's storming outside.

My nervous energy is now full blown anxiety. Shit is going down. I'm in danger from a women beating criminal. My dad is going to kill Delatorre, I know it. To add to that, Tank is storming around. And fucking great, Danza and my dad are close behind him, yelling.

"Get your ass back in the office. I'm not done with you, Tank. You fuck her over, I'm gonna have your balls, mother fucker. That's my daughter!" Danza yells, charging at Tank.

Tank halts and turns to face Danza. "Let me say goodbye, then you can have my fucking balls, Danza."

Sass is standing there, helmet in hand, and a blank stare on her face. Tank pulls her into him. He tucks her into his chest with his chin resting on her head. I can hear him as he's talking to her.

"Savannah, don't be sassy. This is serious. Stay safe, don't run your mouth. This is all so you can come home." And with that he releases her and walks quickly back into the office.

Tears in her eyes, she looks over to her dad. His hard stance and face, letting his feelings on the situation be known.

"It's not like that, Daddy. Leave him alone. He's my friend, that's all. I promise you on everything I am, I'm not with one of the brothers, and especially not Tank."

Her voice is void of emotion, making it clear, she is done.

Tank slumps slightly at her words. Does he have unspoken feelings? Or is it because Danza knows and will have his balls regardless?

Her tone affirms her recent decision. My Savannah Mae "Sass" Perchton no longer wants the life we grew up in. I don't know what that means for this ride. Hell, I don't know what it means for the future. What I do know, is when my best friend looks her dad in the eyes and says Tank is just her friend, that's the truth. Whatever feelings she may have had are gone. Whatever possibilities could have been, no longer exist. Tank is and always has been important to her. The opportunity of a future for them to build something together is gone. I have no doubts she cares for him, as he does for her. They both realize they can't be together for different reasons and, on different terms, they have come to know and accept this.

Danza shakes his head and runs his fingers through his long brown hair. In this moment, his age shows, the worry lines crease his brow, and the twinkle in his eye now full of distress.

"Okay, Sass. I'll let him be, on your word that there's nothing there. Baby girl, listen to Tripp and Rex, stay outta trouble and keep your fucking mouth shut." With that he turns around and goes back inside.

My dad is leaning inside the doorframe watching me. I mouth the words, 'I love you, Daddy'. He nods his head in acknowledgement. I put the half shell helmet on my head. Looking over, Savannah has dropped in behind Rex. Tripp is on his bike, engine started, the unique tick of the Harley Davidson engine rumbling all around me. He has no sissy bar. This is going to make for an even closer ride than I'm used to. I place my hand on his shoulder. He watches me intently as I swing my leg over and settle in behind him.

My jean clad legs leave little wiggle room as I try to find my place. Typically, I could use the sissy bar to push back against and give myself some space. Having nothing but Tripp, I lean into him as I push my weight into my butt and downwards onto the foot pegs. I settle my hands gently on his hips. Apparently, he can sense my unease, or my weight differential is not comfortable to him because he grabs my hands one at a time and pulls me up against him. My chest now firmly against his back. My head is resting on his shoulder. My thighs wrapped tightly to him as the vibration of the bike radiates up my core. He's brought my hands up to cradle his chest. I couldn't get any closer if I wanted to. This is by far the most erotic moment I've had on a bike ever, and we haven't moved yet.

He releases the brake slowly and gently turns the throttle. With a calm and controlled thrust we take off out of the parking lot. The movement of his foot as he changes gears gives a slight shift of his leg. Each subtle change draws me into him more. As we accelerate, the bike comes to life beneath me. The wind against my face feels like wild abandonment. Even through my clothes, the bikes vibrations radiate to my core tingling through my body, making me aware of the freedom in this moment. The quiet around us as the miles go by. The steady rhythm of the bike is calming to my soul.

I've ridden with my dad more times than I can count. I have my own Harley Davidson Sportster. Driving itself is liberating. It's a feeling of fierce independence. Never in my life did I imagine anything feeling better than that. Until now. This is home, this is peace, and this is how it's supposed to be.

I've never had ol' lady aspirations. I'm a Hellion, with or without being tied to a brother. In this moment, it's not about being an ol' lady; it's about being one with your man, being one with the road, and being one with your bike. It's about being one with the ride. This is a moment of clarity for me, as I realize why women want to be ol' ladies. They have this one moment, where they have a connection, and later make a commitment. All to live for that one moment, one connection, one commitment, and one ride.

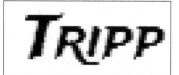

U sually bitches are crawling all over me when they climb on my bike. Not Doll, she looks for a way to support herself. The bike we're on is not mine; rather, it's a club bike. Had I known Doll would be riding with me, I would've taken the time to install a sissy bar. We would still be close but at least she would have somewhere to rest her back.

As she leans into the curves with me, it's easy to get lost in the ride. Her arms wrapped around me, one of her hands tight against my heart. Her chest up against my back as the steady rise and fall of her breathing lets me know she's relaxed and comfortable. The loud rumble of the engine, the power of the bike under me, and the softness of a woman behind me is all consuming. Life is not about the breaths you take, but the moments that take your breath away. This is one of those moments. For this one moment, everything feels right in a way that it never has before.

Without thinking, I reach my left hand down and gently squeeze her thigh. Never before, have I felt the desire to connect with anyone. She relaxes further into me. Her left hand begins tracing circles over my heart.

Every minute ticking by feels intimate in a way I've never experienced before. My chest constricts at the thought of being close to someone. I don't live the lifestyle for that. Protect Doll, yes, I will. Beyond that, she's off limits. Putting those thoughts back into perspective, I quickly remove my hand from her thigh and back to my handlebar.

Feeling me tense and pull on the throttle to accelerate us further, Doll stills her hand and tightens behind me. She feels the sting of the rejection I just dished out. Perceptive, just like her father; I'll be quick to remember that as well. I've got a job to do, and a very serious one at that. My boys rely on me to keep them safe and out of jail, given the nature of our business. For me, this task feels so much more, I can't explain it, but on a deeper level, this ride feels like it's everything.

ON OUR WAY

At the condo, I stuff a backpack quickly. Knowing Tripp and I shared a moment on the bike, entices me to pack my pretty panties, just in case. Even if Tripp remains honorable to the fact that I'm Roundman's daughter, I still deserve to feel sexy.

Does the man have to be so honorable though? Seriously, I get it. I'm Roundman's Doll. I'm so far off limits, I'm on another planet. It doesn't mean I plan to make it easy for him. He's hot. Any red blooded woman would want a sample of him. Daddy doesn't need to know about one hookup.

Knowing that Delatorre could already be watching me causes a moment of insecurity. I'm not naïve enough to ever think the club was perfectly legitimate and safe. Never have I had someone follow me home though. Then again, I was raised to keep my nose out of other people's business. My dumbass broke the cardinal rule of 'turn your head and look the other way'. See no evil, hear no evil, and speak no evil. I saw it, spoke to it and watched it backhand a defenseless woman who looked like a stiff wind could blow her over.

Some broad comes in all broken, I feel bad, and get involved. If it was another MC, I never would've given her a second thought. That would be their club business. But no, this Amy bitch comes along and I fall for her victim game. The Hellions are now in danger, a long term business deal long gone, and a shit load of people on lock down because I had a moment of kindness for a stranger. This is why good people don't get involved. They get burned.

My frustration is at its boiling point. Packing is relatively easy when you know you will be wearing jeans and a t-shirt every day. Heels aren't made for a bike ride; therefore, they will remain in my closet. I did squeeze in one little black dress and one pair of flats in the event we get to go out. It's springtime so I only need to pack basics. Fitting toiletries and clothes for an unknown amount of time into a backpack is not an easy task. Given the bike has no sissy bar, I have to fit what I need in a back pack to stay on me and in the two small saddlebags the bike has.

Stepping outside, I look over at Sass, who is already settled behind Rex. Tripp is on his bike, his tattered jeans, black boots, t-shirt, and Hellions cut all add to the sex appeal that is undeniably him. His hands resting on the gas tank on top of his half shell helmet, his long hair is knotted low on the back of his neck, and a black bandana covers his head. Following his gaze, I see him focused on the ocean view that can be seen through the breezeway of our condo. From our balcony, the view is breathtaking. His face is tight showing he's deep in thought; about what, I don't know. While watching him, something deep inside of me yearns to know more about this man.

T he smell of salt in the air, the crashing of the waves in the distance, and the sounds of seagulls surround me. The tranquility of the beach, the calm, the peace, and the serenity one can find here shows why so many decide to vacation, retire, or choose to live here. It's the great escape.

Turning my head as I come out of my musings, I see her standing in front of me. Her stare pulls at something deep inside that I've never felt before. Running my hand across my chest absently, our eyes lock. Her gaze does nothing to tame the unknown yearning building inside of me.

She's a job. She's a Hellion. She's off limits. I remind myself over and over again as she walks over to me. When she reaches the bike, she pulls her backpack over her arms, settling it into place on her shoulders. She's braiding her hair to keep it from tangling in the wind.

"Do I need to switch the bikes or stop and add a sissy bar before we leave the area? Charlotte is a long ride." I ask not sure if she's up for the discomfort of the five-hour ride.

If need be, we can go back to the compound, add a sissy bar or trade the bike to something more comfort-able for her, like an Ultra Classic or Screaming Eagle. I'm sure one of the guys would have a full dresser, weekender ride.

"I've been farther than Charlotte with nothing to lean on, Tripp. I got this, no worries, let's go. The quicker we leave, the more my dad can focus and get this over with." She replies in a somewhat somber tone.

She's going to miss home. This is the first sign of sadness she's shown. Anger, surprise, and defiance have all been ever present, but this is the first sign of discomfort and sadness.

I crank the bike as she puts on her helmet. Revving the throttle for the hell of it, she climbs on. She settles in behind me. Her hands are lower this time as she pulls tight against me. She is wrapped around my waist, her hands are roaming my abdomen, causing my muscles to twitch involuntarily through my clothing.

The weather is nice, the company is quiet, and the scenery much better on the back roads as we head out. Avoiding the interstate, we stick with the country roads, nothing but pavement and pine trees as we make our way back to my home. The more Doll settles herself in behind me, the more I find myself relaxing into the ride.

Arriving in town, we pull up to my house. Something inside me twists as I think, having Doll on this ride, I could get used to having someone on the back of my bike. I pull the bike through my back gate. The garage is full with my truck and two motorcycles. Rex and I live together. He has a shop in the back for his car and bike; there is enough room back here for these two bikes to be stored safely. Our house is small, two bedrooms, two bathrooms, a living room, and a kitchen.

We pull the bikes in, and turn them off as the girls both climb off. Grabbing the contents of the saddlebags, Rex and I lead the way in through the back door. This leads in through the kitchen. It's painted in an ugly ass blue color. The realtor called the kitchen décor French country, whatever the fuck that means. It's a house, a place to eat, sleep, shit, shower, and fuck. No more, no less.

"Sass, you can take Rex's room tonight. He'll show you where to put your things. Doll, follow me and you can crash in my room."

"Where will you two sleep?" Doll asks with genuine interest.

"On the couch and in the chair," I answer blankly.

What a dumb question. I can't leave them here alone, but I'm sure as shit not sharing a room with her if I can help it. There will be enough of that on this trip, why start my test in self-control early?

"Sass and I can share a room so you both don't have to give up your space." She says somewhat timidly.

Grabbing her hand, I guide her to my bedroom. "We're only here two days tops. Once Delatorre has his shipment, we go on the move. For now, Roundman wants things to look normal. It's one, maybe two nights,

Rex and I have slept on far worse than a couch and a chair. Make yourself at home."

"Well, thank you. Who would've thought a Hellion could be so considerate? Tripp you're a real gentleman." She says with a breathtaking smile.

Unable to resist, I pull her into me. Her head slams into my chest. I place my arm around her waist and trace circles on the small of her back. Inhaling her scent of ocean and coconut, I put my other hand around her braid. I tug gently, pulling her face to look up at me. Leaning down, breathing against her ear, I whisper to her.

"I'm no gentleman, Doll. No, I'm the man to fuck you seven ways to Sunday. I'm not the man you settle down with or you settle for."

Her breathing now coming in pants, I quickly release her and exit the room.

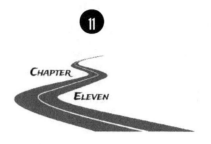

SO CLOSE, YET SO FAR

Tripp lives in Catawba, only an hour or so outside of Charlotte. If we were here under any other circumstances, I would be at Caroline's visiting. As much as Sass and I want to see our friend, it wouldn't be fair to bring our troubles to her doorstep. Delatorre obviously watches us and now is no different. We have other friends here that I would love to see as well, but this trip is not for pleasure. This ride is about safety, I remind myself.

Tripp and Rex slept downstairs last night. Although

I found comfort in his bed, as it engulfed me in his scent, the sandman eluded me. Waking up after only a few hours of rough sleep, I'm on edge and irritable as I begin a busy day of preparations.

Changing over to burner phones is strange for me. My dad has gone on runs before and switched to using one. It's always bothered me to know I can't reach him whenever I want because he doesn't want to be traced. Imagining the stress he is feeling back home brings on more feelings of guilt. My dad has never been in a situation where he isn't able to call me. I may not have been able to freely call him, but he's always had an open line and opportunity to call me. Soon enough, though, that will be our new reality. No longer underestimating the threat from Delatorre, my dad doesn't want us to be traced at all. He has multiple burner phones for me to check in with and switch out throughout this journey. None of us will be using the same phone twice.

All of this, why? Was Delatorre targeting us before the job? Or does this all come down to my fuck up in trying to help that Amy chick? I've wondered why people turn the other cheek when they can see a woman who is obviously abused or in an unhealthy situation. No more questioning why anymore. How do you know if the bitch really wants out, or if she's playing you and gets off on it? Yes, that one deserves what she's getting. Her weakness to stay with that fucker has now shaken my world to its core. My sympathy for her is replaced with anger, hatred, and revenge. Yes, I know my dad and his boys will fuck up Delatorre and his crew. Hell, Delatorre may or may not be breathing when this is over. None of that is my concern, staying safe so I can return to my family is my only concern at the moment. Best believe though, when this shit storm blows over, I'm gonna find Amy Mitchell. She's gonna learn she never should've included me in her sick game with Delatorre.

"Let's go." I hear Tripp call to us from his garage.

Everyone is sure Delatorre is watching our every move. Therefore, we have to act like we are visiting with Tripp and Rex to hang out. We're going to grab some breakfast at a local restaurant and then do some shopping.

After a half an hour of our waitress fawning over Tripp, I'm thoroughly annoyed and no longer hungry. When the waitress asks Tripp for a ride, I want to stab her with my fork. It happens all the time, even when I'm out with my dad. Hello bitches, when there is a lady sitting next to a biker, shut the fuck up and move on. I'm climbing on that bike with him, therefore, there's no room for your wanna be skank ass.

Tripp smiles at the bitch, winks as he tells her. "Sure thing babe, but another time."

What the fuck is there to smile and wink at? She's

some random waitress at a diner! She can't handle a Hellion. Jealousy combines with the emotions already swirling inside me. I want to kick, scream, punch something, or kick someone. I need to do something just to show this bitch she can't handle a ride with a Hellion.

This is not me. I'm delightful Delilah. Not some possessive, cranky bitch. Why am I so bothered by this waitress hitting on Tripp? Hell, my dad has left me at a table to go hook up with a barfly in a bathroom before. The stress must be getting to me. That's it. Certainly, I'm not catching feelings for Tripp this early. It's all the changes affecting me. That's my problem.

Doll is quiet. I can't tell if that's her normal personality, if it's the worry over Delatorre, or if it's my presence. She was all smiles this morning when she was getting ready, but since breakfast, she's clammed up and not had any change in her pouty facial expression.

We're in my sparsely furnished living room. Having just finished pizza for dinner, she and Sass are on the couch with Rex in the chair, all trying to find something on TV. Standing in the room, refusing to sit on the couch, I'm beginning to get stir crazy. No way in hell can I sit on the couch with Doll. It's bad enough she's close to me all day on my bike, and will be even more with this ride coming up. I need some fucking space. Since when do I give a fuck why some broad is quiet all of a sudden?

"Y'all feel like a drink?" I need to get outta here before I do some dumb shit like sit beside her and try to get to know her.

Rex is the first to jump up, "Hell, yeah."

The girls get up and we head to the bar. It's slow tonight from the looks of the parking lot. We get off the bikes and walk in. Tessie is working, smiling when she sees us. Walking directly to the bar, she's already setting out a beer for Rex and me. Doll and Sass are both in jeans, t-shirts, and boots, totally with the casual feel of this dive. I feel a tug on the hem of my t-shirt, looking behind me to the direction the pull came from, I see Doll looking up at me as she's pulling me to her. She's looking around us, taking it all in.

"Are we safe here, Tripp? I'm not used to going out to biker bars without it being Hellion owned and run. I don't see our colors hanging anywhere."

Instinctively, I pull her under my arm and into my chest. She wraps her arms around my waist as we are now chest to chest in an almost intimate embrace. We're so close. Yet, this is so far from where we need to be. I'm protecting her. I'm not supposed to be comforting her at every turn. I put my hands on each side of her face. Making eye contact, I lay it out there for her.

"Doll, I promise you that this place is safe. Please don't be afraid anytime you're with me. I give you my word; you're always safe with me. I won't ever let anything happen to you. Relax, have a good time while we can."

She nods up at me, her eyes sparkling with confidence now that she's had my reassurance. Feeling my chest tighten, I need to get space between us. I pull away and gently push her at the small of her back into the direction of the bar. Too bad I'm driving, tonight is a night I'd love to drown in a bottle of Jack. Finding a way to keep distance between Doll and I is going to be easier said than done.

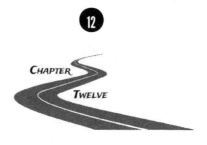

CHAPTER TWELVE

Destination Unknown

ast night was okay. Tessie is a nice enough girl.
Sass and I spent our time at the bar with her. Rex
went off with a barfly to who knows where to get off.
Some chick was pawing all over Tripp, but he ignored
her for the most part. He watched me and stayed where
he could see me at all times. The two guys that did try to
chat up Sass and I were quickly scared off when Tripp

merely approached. The actions of everyone around us made it clear, this is Tripp's territory.

Apparently, Tripp got intel that the business end of the transport to Delatorre is complete. Now we go on the move, while my dad handles the threat. Business is business. Delatorre paid for a job, therefore he will get his transport. He made it personal, or I made it personal when I got involved. Either way, shit's personal now. We've been packed and ready, so when Tripp woke me up at five AM to leave, I wasn't surprised. Good thing Tripp doesn't have neighbors close to his house, the rumble of the two Harleys cranking that early in the morning would've surely pissed someone off.

One thing about traveling by motorcycle, you have to stop pretty often for gas. Tripp won't share our destinations with me. According to him, we may have to change plans in a moment's notice. His last words before pulling out this morning resound in my head.

"Doll, I don't wanna lie to you. I'd rather say nothing at all than lie to you. Accept it as it comes."

Between the promises to keep me safe and not to lie, I'm starting to turn to mush. Sure, I know all the Hellions will do their best to protect me. But when Tripp says it, something inside me wants it to be about me alone, not club duties.

His words continue to tug at me. Deep inside, he's all things good. Yet, he claims he's not. Last night he could've fucked that random chick, but he watched over me instead. When I felt insecure, he owed me no reassurances. He didn't have to explain shit to me about why he won't tell me where we're headed. A simple, "shut the fuck up," or the, "I'll tell you what you need to know and you don't fuckin' need to know," would've been the answer I got from anyone else when questioning where we were going. Either way, he didn't owe me an explanation about not wanting to lie to me. Slowly, the more we are together, the more I can see past his exterior roughness.

Tessie told me he's taken women right there in the pool room, the hallway, or the stock room. That's what all those boys do. She says they're a wild bunch, but loyal and take care of their own. Would Tripp take me in some random bar hallway? What turns him on? What makes him tick?

The bike's vibrations settle between my legs, as I pull myself closer to him. Taking in the mountain scenery as I see the signs showing we are headed towards Tennessee. If this ride wasn't about safety, I'd ask Tripp to take me on The Tail. All Hellions ride The Dragons Tail as their rite of passage. It's the one ride I've never done.

My dad says it's not his place to take me. He calls it the hidden beauty. It's a two lane mountain road with over three hundred curves in an eleven-mile stretch. The

Hellions take an annual ride there. My dad's always giving me the same response as to why I can't go.

"Doll, The Tail is a ride of many things. It's a ride of focus, where a man is forced to clear his mind. It's a ride where a man is forced to accept, own, and become one with his bike, or become one with the pavement beneath him. The Tail has claimed a number of bikes to its gravel top and lives to its curves and drops. Year after year, people don't heed the warnings. If you don't know what you're doing, then the mountain asphalt will own your shit. The curves of The Tail are like the curves of your woman; you hug that shit tight, hold it close, and caress it gently, but with a firm hand. It's a ride to take boys and make them men. It's a ride to solidify trust in your new brother, as you ride two by two, with only feet separating your handlebars, as you slide through each mile of mountain. It's a ride where your ol' lady holds on tight, giving over every part of her trust, body, and heart as she's leaning into the curves with you. Doll, it's the ride for you to take when the right man comes along and earns that level of trust from you. Not one for me to share with you."

Tears prick behind my eyes, thinking about my dad. Thinking about that ride, it dawns on me how little I know about Tripp. Hell, I still don't know his fucking name. Do I trust him to that level? Yes, I do. Being around Tripp stirs so many emotions inside of me.

With every tick of the bike's engine underneath me, the throb between my legs grows. Lust, is definitely something Tripp stirs up inside of me. His body is muscular and clearly defined. The power he could bring to the bedroom plays out in my head. Would Tripp ever share anything more with me than this job where he protects me? He seems so indifferent to having me around. Why do random women get him, but a chick like me, who knows and accepts his lifestyle, can't get the time of day?

Truck stops are great. They're typically crowded with people and usually have a place to eat with a variety of options. Pulling in, I watch the girls head to the restrooms.

"You alright, man?" Rex asks, the look of concern on his face.

Shrugging my shoulders in response, "Yeah, man, shit on my mind."

"More like Doll is on your mind. I've never seen

you this wound up over a broad." Rex says as he jabs me with his elbow in my side, trying to loosen me up.

"What makes you think this is about Doll?" I make a failed attempt at indifference, but saying her name, I can't help but smile.

"Ummm...I don't know fucker. You smile every damn time you say her name. You never fucking smile, Tripp." He replies as he's laughing at me.

"I fucking smile."

"No, you don't. You're mister serious all the damn time. Even when you're fuckin' a bitch, you're still straight faced." He's holding his stomach laughing at me.

"You been in my bedroom watching me fuck? You're a sick prick if that's the case. How do you know I don't smile while I'm balls deep in a bitch?"

The more I think about it, when was the last time I laughed or smiled out of a happy moment or thought. Only when it comes to Doll. Hell, I can't even remember the last time I laughed at a TV show.

I elbow Rex in the ribs for being right. Spotting the girls waving for us, we make our way inside the restaurant.

"We've all fucked bitches in public. Hell, on the last transport, you fucked a random chick against the outside wall of the state line visitor center. Luckily it was a back corner because damn man, kids could've walked right up. You never smiled, Tripp. You're my club Prez, you're my cousin, and damn it you're my best friend. I'm always keepin' an eye out for you."

"Fuck, I wasn't thinking at the rest area."

I rub a hand across my chest as it constricts, getting tighter with these thoughts. Since meeting Doll, I haven't been thinking straight. She was on my mind during that transport. I needed a release, the chick was willing, and I'm an ass for taking her up on it.

"You gotta fuck that one outta your system, man." He says as we approach the girls.

"Damn it, I hate when you're right." I reply as we sit down at the table the girls got for us.

"Right about what?" Sass asks a mischievous look in her eyes. "Rex doesn't strike me as the brains of this operation."

"Got jokes, Sass?" Rex replies, laughing again.

We spend the rest of our meal in easy banter. Since Rex pointed out my seriousness, I've relaxed more. I do smile around Doll. She brings out so much more in me. I'm not sure if that's a good thing.

(Tennessee)

HE WENT TO JARED'S AND NOT FOR JEWELRY

We've long since crossed over into Tennessee. I made sure to have Tripp stop at the visitor center so I could pick up my map. It's a tradition I've had since I was a little girl. My dad always stops at the welcome center, and I get a map. Later, I stare at it and figure out which roads we were on and trace it out. I have maps from when I was six or seven still. Some people take pictures, collect key chains, or other tourist novelties. I collect maps.

Seventy-two hours, that's about how long I've been gone with Tripp. Seventy-two hours that my body has been in overdrive, a constant hum of yearning in my core. Heading to God knows where adds to the adrenaline coursing through me. I'm hyper aware of everything around me because we don't know the situation back home.

Pulling into the next gas station, I climb off.

"You want anything from the store? I gotta use the restroom." I say, pulling off my helmet and looking at Tripp.

He's in his usual jeans, t-shirt, boots, and cut. He has his hair in a man bun knot thing that lies under the half shell of his helmet. And his face is in his usual serious mode.

"Nah, I'll get it myself when I pay for the gas. Wait for me inside."

He goes over to talk to Rex as Sass approaches me.

"You got it bad girl." She says laughing at me.

"Got what?" I try for nonchalance as we make our way inside the gas station.

"You know what! You also know your dad will have his balls. Stop holding on to him so much, it's not like you on a ride. More than that it's borrowing trouble.

You're getting yourself all worked up for something neither of you can have."

"This coming from the bitch that slept with Tank. Pot calling the kettle, much?" I'm unable to stop the sarcasm from continuing to spew out of my mouth. "It's all good for you to fuck a Haywood's Landing Hellion where we live, but I can't tap a chartered brother?"

"Damn, you need to get laid. Bitchy much?" She pulls her arm around my shoulder, half dragging me into the bathroom door. "I'm talking from experience. This isn't something you or Tripp want to deal with."

"I'm sorry, Sass. You're right. It's borrowing trouble to even imagine one night with Tripp."

The more I think about it, the more my irritation grows. Hell, I don't even know his real name. He's shown no interest in me. Why am I still hung up on hooking up with him? He's hot as hell, but there are plenty of hot guys who could get me off without the repercussions that will come with hooking up with Tripp. How am I going to get through days and weeks of being so close to him but not having him? I don't want forever, my dad would never allow that, but I damn sure want one night.

Finishing up, Sass and I silently head back to the bikes. The tension and frustration is building inside of me. I'm putting on my helmet, when Tripp approaches looking pissed the fuck off.

"What part of wait for me inside did you not fucking understand?" Tripp states, pulling my hands away and adjusting my chin strap his way.

"Huh?"

"I fucking told you to wait for me inside. Damn it, Doll. We're not in Hellions territory anymore. You need to be aware. Out here anyone could come along and grab you. Inside the store, where there are witnesses, stuff is less likely to happen. Fuck."

He thinks he's pissed. Whatever! I'm stuck on this damn ride, and now I can't go to the fucking bathroom in peace.

"I'm a big fucking girl, Tripp. I can handle myself." I say, my hands now balled into fists on my hips.

"Handle yourself….handle yourself. Bitch, fucking think straight for two goddamn seconds. Your dad told Delatorre to his face he wouldn't know when or where, but the shit storm was comin'. You would be the ticket Delatorre would need to keep breathin'. Every fucking Hellion is out there scoping shit to bring Delatorre to the ground to keep you fucking safe. And you can't listen to one simple command."

"Y'all are making something outta nothing. Delatorre is all talk."

"All fucking talk, huh? Damn, you are a dumb bitch. Daddy sheltered you to fucking much."

"Dumb bitch. Fuck you, Tripp. Delatorre was in my

office, at my house, and he never did shit. He won't do shit. Having my address doesn't mean he was setting me up for something."

"What about the fucking cameras, Doll? The cameras he watched you cook your meals, change your clothes, shower, and shit with. Oh, I see your eyes are opening now. That's right, that sick fucker had cameras in your house. He watched you lay in that huge bed of yours with that satin red comforter. He knows more than any of us thought, and you've been the target of it all. So yeah, I'm telling you to wake the fuck up, and listen when I tell you something."

Shocked into silence, I don't know how to respond. Delatorre had cameras in my condo? He watched me? My skin is crawling, my stomach churning, my mind is racing. I feel like I'm gonna be sick.

"Get on the fucking bike, we gotta go."

I hadn't even noticed Tripp is now on the bike, helmet on, and ready to go. Rex is back from paying for our gas and ready to ride. I climb on apprehensively. Tripp is pissed, and shit is bigger than I thought. The longer we ride, the more stressed I become.

P ulling in to our stop for the night, I let some of the tension relax out of my shoulders. I didn't mean to drop such a bomb on Doll back at the gas station, but she doesn't realize how serious this is. That fucker watched her for months, not just the time of the transport. Roundman has been keeping me apprised of the information they uncover as they dig deeper into Felix Delatorre.

We've gone a little over three hundred fifty miles today. Trying to be considerate of Doll's comfort, seven hours on the back roads is enough for her ass for today. As the trip progresses, I'll add time and miles and she'll have a better tolerance. Stopping at an old friend's business, I wave Doll off the bike as I pull off my helmet.

She's stretching beside me. Some of her hair has come loose from her braid and is whisking around her face. Damn, she's beautiful.

"*House of Ink Tattoo*?" She's looking at me with a sadness in her eyes that wasn't there before.

"Welcome to McMinnville, Tennessee, Doll. *House of Ink Tattoo* is owned by a buddy of mine."

"Of all the places you could take us, we come here? Why would we come here? You're not seriously going to get inked while we're on this trip are you?" Her irritation is obvious as she questions me.

"Because it's safe, that's the fuck why." My aggravation at her questioning me is something I don't even try to hide. I climb off the bike, stretching.

"I'm sorry. I'm not trying to piss you off. I figured we would be staying at hotels." She steps closer to me with only inches between us; I let out a long breath.

"Hotel? Really? You've been sheltered too damn long, Doll. Hotels want names, IDs, credit cards; all of those mean paper trail."

"We have fake IDs, credit cards, all of that. Hell, you're still wearing your cut. We can't be trying to hide too seriously." She says with a touch of venom in her voice at the mention of my cut.

"We're staying in places that give us extra fucking eyes. Places where I can get a little sleep so I can keep driving. If Delatorre is following us, we don't want it to be obvious why we took you away from the coast. Watch yourself, Doll. My cut is my god damn life, don't you ever fucking go there."

Not one to back down, she's looking at me in sheer defiance. Is she trying to get me going? Does she realize she's playing with fire? Stepping up to me, her breasts are rubbing against my torso as I tower over her because of my height. My dick twitches in my jeans at the feel of her hard little nipples pressing into me.

"How is this place safe to rest? Anyone could come in claiming to want ink."

"Jared won't let that happen."

Pushing into me now, she's wound up looking for a fight. Damn, she's fucking hot when she's all revved up. It's making my dick hard like nothing else ever has.

"Jared? Who the fuck's Jared?"

"He's fucking good people, Doll. I trust him with my life. He's not gonna let anyone get to us."

She licks her lips and I'm done for. The stress and want all tangle together in the form of irresistible desire. Wrapping my hand to cup the back of her head, I run my fingers under her braid, my other hand resting on the small of her back. Tilting her head to face me, I lean down and I kiss her. She melts beneath me with one sweep of my tongue across her lips. Anger, lust, frustration, desire, compassion, yearning, and so many more emotions run a marathon through my system. Pulling her firmly to me, I devour her mouth as if it's my last meal. Leaving no millimeter undiscovered by my tongue, I continue my onslaught. She moans beneath me as her hands reach up around my neck, snapping me back to reality.

Pulling abruptly away, "Now I know how to shut you the fuck up. Get your shit. Time to go inside," I state as I turn and walk away.

FRIENDS

W hat the hell just happened?! How can he walk away after that? He consumed me. He didn't only kiss my mouth, he touched my damn soul. I've kissed a lot of men, but never has a kiss left me that weak in the knees. There was more behind that moment than a means to shut me up. I don't give a shit what he says.

"Tripp, you son of a bitch, I'm not done talkin' to you."

He stops on the spot, but doesn't turn around. Rex

and Sass are standing still by their bike watching everything as it continues to unfold. He's making no attempt to acknowledge me. Frustration running high, I march up behind him. I poke him in the shoulder in an attempt to get him to turn around. When that fails, I jab my finger into the top of his shoulder. Still nothing. Walking around to face him, I'm met with a mixture of laughter and lust in his eyes. He's enjoying this, the fucker.

"You just fucking kissed me. I don't even know your real damn name and you kissed me! You've insulted me, belittled me, taken me from my home to God knows where, and I don't even know your fucking name!" I say jabbing my finger in his chest.

Our eyes are now locked, battling each other in the stare downs of stare downs. My eyes are full of fury and his full of fun, maybe. Is this turning him on?

"If you're running your mouth so I kiss you again, it ain't gonna happen Doll. You're wound up. You need to release the tension. How 'bout we see if Jared can give you some ink?"

"You have lost your ever lovin' fuckin' mind if you think I'm going to let some friend of yours permanently mark my body. Again, I don't even know your name. Yet, I'm supposed to trust some guy you know to tattoo me? Really? I may end up with Tripp tattooed on my ass."

He laughs at me. Not the little '*ha ha you're so*

funny' kind of laugh. No, Tripp folds over holding his stomach because he's laughing so hard at me.

"What the fuck is so damn funny?"

Tripp stands up. The smile now gone from his face, replaced with his ever present serious glare, he looks directly at me.

"Get your ass inside. Shut the fuck up for two seconds so you can meet Jared."

He walks off, heading for the front door. Sass is now beside me, as I stand here with a stupid look on my face.

"Come on, Doll. Let's make the best of it. I'm game for new ink. You should get that tat you've been wanting with another damn bird. We're stuck here until the guys have rested. Jared may be hot or have hot friends. You're way too bitchy, loosen up some."

"Sass, Delatorre had cameras in our house. How can I relax?"

"Fuck! He had what? Come on, let's get inside and figure this shit out." She says, taking me by the hand to the front door.

Walking inside we are surrounded by the designs on the red painted walls. Each intricate piece of work brings something new to life for someone. Hearing the buzzing of the tattoo gun in the back room, I'm immediately itching for a new tattoo. I have a sparrow on my right hip in memory of my mother and a robin on my wrist to represent the bond Sass and I share. Maybe Sass is right, and it's time to get that tattoo I've been wanting on my left hip. Yes, I have a thing for bird tattoos and it drives Sass crazy.

Tripp is leaning against the counter talking to a beautiful lady. She's probably in her fifties, but time has treated her well. There's vibrancy in her eyes as she's chatting with Tripp, her face telling the story of a strong woman. We approach the counter.

"Doll, Sass, this is Momma C. And Momma C, you remember Rex. This is Doll and Sass."

Introductions out of the way, I'm overwhelmed with a sense of comfort. Momma C gives me a feeling of home. Being around her reminds me of being with the ol' ladies of the club. The level of nurturing and compassion that is held in the depths of Momma C's eyes wash over me. I'm smiling and I'm comfortable here even with all the chaos surrounding my life. Tripp was right, I'm safe here. Even without meeting Jared, it's obvious Momma C will protect those around her.

A man with spiky hair, gaged ears, and full sleeved tattoos emerges from the back room. He's followed by a man that walks over to Momma C pulling out his wallet, making it obvious he is a client. Immediately, the spiky hair man greets Tripp and Rex with that man half hug, back slap shit. When he's done, he stares at me momentarily. He extends his hand. When I place my hand in his, he holds it.

"Name's Delilah, but everyone calls me Doll. You must be Jared." I say looking into his eyes. They tell the story of a strong man.

"Beautiful name for a beautiful woman. Tripp's a lucky mother fucker."

I laugh at his comment. "Tripp's not my man."

He pulls me into a hug and whispers in my ear, "With the death glare he's giving me, I think he may disagree, Doll." He kisses my cheek before releasing me.

He greets Sass quickly and escorts us to the back office area. The client is done paying, raises his hand in a slight salute wave in goodbye as he exits the building.

"Mom's locking up. Here's the key to the apartment upstairs. I'll be here the whole time. No one will get to you without getting through me." Jared informs us as he's handing Tripp a key.

We go upstairs to the tiny apartment and settle in. Tripp's in the shower. I update Sass on what I now know on Delatorre. Sass and I are restless, so we head back down to the tattoo shop. Finding Jared at a desk drawing, I smile at his focus. He seems like he's good people, and maybe I shouldn't have doubted Tripp. I need to learn to trust him.

"You need somethin' Doll, Sass?" Jared asks looking up from his design to both of us.

"I'd like a new tattoo."

"Sure thing, whatcha thinkin' of getting?"

"I want an eagle on my left hip, stretching out in flight. Not overly big, but in its talon, I want it holding a very girly heart, not a lifelike heart, a feminine heart and a shield."

He pauses, as a strange look comes across his face. "Doll, why do you want this specific tattoo?"

"An eagle represents the freedom of the motorcycle club world I live in. It's talon holding my heart and a shield for protection. All my life I've been guarded and loved by all of the Hellions, not just my dad."

"You're sure you want an eagle and not the Hellions insignia?"

Irritation consumes me. Why is he questioning me? This is his job. I'll pay for the damn tat. Cocking my hand on my hip, I glare at Jared. "It's not my place to wear the insignia. Look, if you don't want to do the tat that's fine just say so, enough with the bullshit." Looking over at Sass for some sort of comfort as my frustration builds, she shrugs her shoulders like this is no big deal.

Hearing a noise behind me, I turn to see Tripp in the doorway. His hair down and wet. With his arms over his head gripping the doorframe, and his jeans slung low on his hips, I can clearly see the toned 'v' of his lower abdomen peeking out from his shirt. The tattoos on his arms on display, as usual. Holy hell, he's hot.

"What bullshit?" Tripp asks looking back and forth between Jared and me.

"Nothin'. I wanted ink, but Jared's asking eighteen hundred questions like I'm trying to get married or some shit."

"Hold the fuck up, princess. Tripp may be interested to know the exact tattoo you're talkin' about marking your body with." Jared pipes up. Sass backs away from me, leaving me inching closer to Tripp.

"I wanted an eagle with an outstretched talon holding a heart and shield. It's whatever now, you guys seem to know better. I'll get my fucking ink elsewhere. I'm going to bed." As I start to move to the doorway, Tripp moves his arms off the frame. Great, he's going to block my exit. Then, I watch as he removes his shirt. The ink adorning his body is all on display. I see the tats of his forearms go all the way up his shoulders and he has a dragon that peeks on both sides, maybe it wraps across his back. What has my attention though, is the large eagle over his left shoulder blade is coming down with an extended talon holding a lifelike heart and a shield.

He says nothing, as his muscles twitch involuntarily. Before I can stop myself, I'm standing mere inches from him, reaching out I slowly trace the details of the design. I start at the white of the eagle's head, and deli-cately outline the bird. As I reach his talon, Tripp stiffens underneath me. He grabs my hand holding it to his heart, the very place the heart of the tattoo lands. He drops his head, our faces cheek to cheek. His hair has fallen down off his shoulder, tickling my face as his breathing sends chills down my spine.

"My name is Talon Ward Crews. Talon is for an eagle's talon as its tool and its weapon. Ward, meaning guard and protector. The eagle guards and protects my heart." He whispers to me.

Her hand drops at my words. I don't know why she would want the same tattoo as me. I know she's never seen my ink. Backing away, I put my shirt back on. Doll remains silent. Not knowing what to say, I take her by the hand and lead her up the stairs. It's been a long ride and a lot of new information thrown at her. She heads to the bathroom to shower and change.

The upstairs apartment is more like a loft. One open room with a kitchenette, a platform bed against one wall, in the open space is a couch, loveseat, and a small ass television. Since Jared only stays here when the hours are too long at the shop, he doesn't need much. He has a house not far from here for him and his daughter. Jared and I go way back; I know we're safe to rest here.

Doll emerges. Her hair is damp from the shower. She's in an old rock concert t-shirt that is so faded you can't tell the band's name anymore, and some short ass shorts. My cock springs to life as she's watching me. The silent standoff between us is charged with desire.

Rex and Sass come in breaking the moment. Sass heads to shower as Rex grabs a beer from the refrigerator. My phones rings, looking at the caller ID, I nod to Rex. It's a silent communication that this is a private call, I'm stepping out. Answering as I make my way out of the loft and down the stairs, I'm filled with a surge of adrenaline. It's Roundman, he wouldn't call if it wasn't important.

Before I can say hello, he's already talking. "Tripp, head to St. Louis. I'll text you an address, then destroy your phone. Amy Mitchell, Delatorre's bitch, has very little family left. In fact, the only ones we can find are her cousins Ray and Zack Mitchell. They live in South County, St Louis. They're somehow tied to Doll, but I don't know the connection yet. No action needed, look around see what you can put together."

"Got it."

"Stay one or two nights only in St. Louis, find out if

they have families or are in another MC. Whoever the fuck they are, I need to know how they know my daughter."

"Do you want Doll to know?"

"Ask her only if you feel they're harmless and if she seems to recognize something. No need to freak her out more than we have to. Delatorre is on radar; fucker went underground but not deep enough."

"Check in within forty-eight hours."

And with that the conversation ends. Looks like we will rest up here tonight pack up and travel about four hundred miles to Saint Louis, Missouri tomorrow.

WHERE'S WALDO

Tripp and I haven't discussed the tattoo. Hell, we've barely said two words to each other. Getting back on the bike to hit the road, I wish that Tripp and I could be comfortable with each other. There's an underlying sexual tension between us. After that kiss, there's no doubt in my mind he wants me as much as I want him. He's got too much self-control to ever act on it though.

We cross into Missouri, and my ass is numb. Stretching as I get off the bike, I take a moment to stare at Tripp. His serious demeanor is back in place as he settles the bike on its kickstand. He's going to bark orders at me in two point five seconds, I can feel it coming. Wait for it, three, two...

"Take your ass inside, go to the restroom, and get your ass back to the bike. Don't fuck around."

"You can't even say, *'Good Morning, Doll?'* Fuck off, Tripp." He smiles. Not a little smile, but a full, light up his eyes, smile. The asshole likes to get me riled.

"Good Morning, Doll. Now, take your ass inside, handle your business, then plant that pretty little ass of yours back on my bike so we can head out. We've got more miles to cover."

He reaches over and smacks my jean clad ass playfully. Serious Tripp is hot, biker Tripp is badass, but playful Tripp is dangerous. Damn, I want him. Sass and I head to the bathroom. As we reach the corner of the building, I look over my shoulder, sure enough, Tripp is watching me. Well, two can play this game. I blow him a kiss and wink right before rounding the corner out of sight.

We come out of the bathroom and I literally run into Rex. *Oomph.* He reaches out one hand on each of my arms to steady me.

"Distracted much?"

"Why are you standing outside of the women's restroom?"

"Waiting for y'all as usual. We're never far away, Doll." He says with a forced smile.

"I haven't noticed you stalking this close before." I try for nonchalance, but my gut is telling me something's off.

"No need to be alarmed, but we've got company. This is a normal ride to everyone else. No one knows this isn't a vacation. That little stunt you pulled with the kiss sells the reason you're with us. The fuckers will hopefully think you and Tripp got something goin' on. We don't know if they know our play on this road trip or not. So for now, let them think it's a getaway."

"Okay," that's all I manage in a shaky voice.

As we approach, Tripp is putting away his phone. He looks up at me and smiles that panty melting, take me right here, smile he has. He flips up a paper in his hand as I reach him. The smile on his face changes to a lazy half grin that screams seduction. My panties are definitely getting wet staring at this man. Damn, what I wouldn't give for one night. Looking down at the paper, it's my map. He's actually paid attention to what I do at the state visitor centers and picked up a map for me.

Instinctively, I wrap my arms around his neck. No longer wanting to hold back, I kiss him. Gently, I brush my lips against his. He doesn't pull away. Taking my tongue, I glide across his bottom lip. He doesn't move again. Craving more of him, rejection be damned, I pull at his bottom lip with my teeth, firmly making him aware of what I want. Before I can take stock of what's happening, he's laid the map on the gas tank and is pulling me up against him. He's on the bike. His torso is turned to me. He's moving me in a way where I have no choice but to straddle his leg, as he's kissing me back like a caged animal that's finally been freed. My breathing coming in heavy pants as his tongue takes over the dance playing out in our mouths. Reaching up, I pull his hair out of his man bun knot thing, and run my fingers through the long locks. His hands are roaming up and down my spine. As I suck on his bottom lip, he grabs my ass with both hands and rocks me against his leg. Holy hell, I'll hump his leg and get off right here in public if he doesn't stop. Fuck me. Talon "Tripp" Crews can kiss. He groans before he pulls away from me. Once again, kissed into silence, I back away.

Rex and Sass have already mounted their bike. Rex is shaking his head while Sass is laughing at me. Tripp hands me my map. I tuck it into a saddlebag, while he's redoing his man bun knot and putting on his helmet. Neither of us says a word as we settle back in and take off.

K issing Doll was a mistake. Shaking off the thoughts of her body molding to mine, I focus. Knowing the fuckers are following us, I've got to keep my shit straight. The downfall to being followed while you're on a bike, it's hard to watch the bastards following you without making it obvious. Bike mirrors are small and full of blind spots anything more than a car length away. It's a game of where the hell's Waldo. I never have liked games.

Peek-a- mother- fuckin'- boo. I see you Cadillac SVT. Same bastards from before, they have no idea who they're fucking with. Extending my left arm out straight, palm flat to the ground, I make a slight up and down motion to let Rex know to slow down and back off a little. Turning my hand, I single three fingers, then four. Throwing my arm up, bending at the elbow to a ninety-degree angle while balling my fist, then with my index finger only extending I make a circle motion. Rex knows in three quarters of a mile, I'll make a hard right exit, no signal. He's to keep going, let the caddy follow me, while he gets Sass to send the text to the boys to circle around, and back my ass up.

Pulling off, sure enough, the car follows. Hopefully, they take the bait thinking we were riding the two of us and only sent one car to tail. My boys have been following a half hour or so behind us the entire ride making sure to stay out of sight. If there are too many of them, we're fucked. I'll do anything before they get Doll though.

We're on a two lane road that makes a loop. I feel the vibration of my phone cueing me that Rex and crew are heading to the gas station. Officially in BFE (Bum Fuck, Egypt) I pull into the seedy gas station. As soon as Doll realizes Rex doesn't follow the turn off, she holds on tighter. I drop my left hand to squeeze her thigh reassuringly. Hang tight until the cavalry arrives. None of these fuckers are gonna get to her to use as a pawn in some sick game. Not one hair on that pretty little head will be touched as long as I'm fucking breathing.

Pulling in, Doll climbs off. Before I climb off, I grab her hand and swing her to me, snaking my hand around the back of her neck, I pull her in for a kiss. Raw, rough, and real passion flow freely between us as the kiss becomes a tangle of tongues, lips, and teeth. When I pull away, her eyes are glassed over in desire.

"Stay close, and follow my lead, Doll." I whisper to her before kissing her forehead and releasing her.

Climbing off the bike, I remove my helmet. Storing

both our helmets on the bike, I make a point not to touch any of the saddlebags. Knowing we're being watched, I need to make this believable. They may or may not know the real purposes behind this trip. If Delatorre hasn't been taken down yet, they will want Doll to keep him breathing. If Delatorre has been handled, this could be retaliation. Either way, Doll is their target. Time to keep up appearances I smile at Doll to ease her fears.

Walking up behind Doll, I wrap my arms loosely around her waist. Turning her, I keep my body between her and the caddy. Dropping my head, I lightly bite at the sweet spot where her neck and shoulder meet. She softens beneath me. Running my nose up her neck as I inhale her scent, reaching her ear, I whisper to her.

"We've been followed. I need you to do exactly as I say." She nods her head in agreement. "At the bathroom door, I'm going to kiss you. When I do, my body will be blocking their vision. You need to reach in the waistband of my jeans and grab the pistol and tuck it into your jeans. Then you go in the bathroom and lock yourself inside a stall. You don't come out until Sass arrives to get you. If anyone comes inside that isn't me, Rex, or Sass, you shoot them. Hellions cut or not, shoot first ask questions later. My boys are coming for backup but they won't come in here to get you, only me, Sass, or Rex. Got it?" I say, needing her to understand that these men could kill us and get a Hellions cut so she can only answer for people she can recognize.

Once again she nods. I feel her shudder beneath me. I begin pushing us forward, walking behind her, still wrapped around her. The embrace is close like lovers. Under other circumstances it would be intimate, but in this moment, it's about her safety.

At the bathroom door, I lean down and kiss her wrapping my hands around her head. Adrenaline mixes with an unknown emotion as I sweep my tongue inside her mouth. I don't want to ever stop kissing her, but right now I've got to get rid of our problem. I feel the gun being pulled away as she tucks it against her own waist. When she starts to pull away, I pull her head back to me. I kiss her with everything I have in me. If I die right now, I die a happy mother fucker to have shared my last kiss with this woman. Finally, I pull away.

"Be safe, Doll. Remember, no one but me, Sass, or Rex." I kiss her forehead as I release her. Pausing for a moment as I watch her disappear in the restroom, I can hear her lock the bathroom door.

Turning around, I'm greeted by none other than the same shithead from the truck stop.

"Don Juan Mother Fuckin' Pablo. What can I do for you Chico?"

"That was a real nice kiss you shared with your woman. Too bad you won't get to do it again."

His two companions close the distance. The women and men's bathroom doors face each other and I'm being backed against the wall between the two rooms. Seeing Slice and five more of my guys silently approaching, I stand steady waiting for my moment.

Pablo begins laughing at me. "You Hellions. Tsk. Tsk. Is that puta worth dying for? She isn't worth the hassle for you. Walk away, Crews, let us have her and you can live to fuck another bitch. It's good for our business to have her, not you. She's not worth it."

Rage boils inside me. Seeing my boys in place, I step up to Pablo.

"She's worth Every. Fucking. Thing. She's no puta. She's fucking mine. Your mother became a puta the day she fucking conceived you. The only way you or any other fucker will get to Doll is the day I'm no longer fucking breathing."

He reaches for his side, pulling out a knife as I lunge forward. My guys quickly take out his crew. Grabbing his wrist, I yank on the hand holding the eight-inch knife. Pulling his arm around behind him, I move so I'm behind him. Unable to easily grab his knife, I take the blade in my hand. The blade penetrates my skin as he moves against me. Using his position against him, I dislocate his right shoulder where I have his arm pulled behind his back. Taking the knife from him, I use my arm to get him in a chokehold. Getting a tighter grip, he's now gasping for breath. My hand is dripping with blood and throbbing, but I press on. Forcing him forward into the men's bathroom, I nod at my boys to handle the others and call in for clean-up, this one's gonna be a mess. Once inside, I loosen my grip enough to get some information from Pablo.

"Why were you sent for Doll?"

"Damn you're a dumb fuck, Crews. You know she's leverage against Roundman." Pablo is laughing again. His arrogance is pissing me off. "Delatorre is going to make Roundman negotiate business dealings. No worries, though, he'll take care of your precious Doll."

"Do you want to fuckin' die? You're headed to the ground mother fucker, Delatorre too." I grind out between my gritted teeth.

"It's clear, you'll die for the cabrona, but the question is would you kill for her?"

"We'll soon find out. You gonna talk?"

"Don't know shit, Crews. Delatorre is a one-man show, unlike you and your brothers who know too much. Oh that cunt's gonna be sweet. Delatorre's gonna have that bitch on her knees calling him Daddy." Pablo says, no longer fighting against me.

"Then you better hope Delatorre will avenge your death. Not one of you mother fuckers will get to her as long as I'm around. See you in Hell, mother fucker."

And with that, I take the blade of his knife and slit

his throat, ear to ear. Dropping him to the ground, as he falls to his knees, grabbing his throat, the gurgling of the blood as he's choking on it is the only noise around me. I wash my hands, cleaning out the cut in my palm from earlier and wrap it in a paper towel. Walking past Pablo as he bleeds out on the bathroom floor, I drop the knife beside his unconscious body. My boys will have this cleaned up, evidence destroyed and witnesses paid off in a matter of hours. Hellions don't take threats lightly and have no problems eliminating the issues. This isn't the first time and won't be the last time.

Message sent, Delatorre.

Only, you sent the wrong motherfucking goons. I'll kill them all before they take her. Don't fuck with what's mine, and Doll is fucking mine.

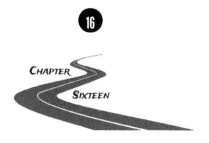

SOMETHING'S CHANGED

F or once, I do as I'm told and stay put. It isn't easy either. Leaning against the bathroom door, I can hear everything going on between Tripp and Pablo. There's a confidence in Pablo's voice. He's cold, calculated. They want me. I need to go out there before they kill Tripp. Just let them take me. I'm leverage to make my dad cut deals on business. This wouldn't be good for the Hellions as a whole. Delatorre would never be satisfied. If we're outnumbered, they will get me anyway. I could possibly save Tripp by walking out and giving myself over. It's me they want and need. The club would suffer being at the hands of Delatorre's dirty business though. My dad won't be able to let me go, so he would do whatever they asked of him in hopes of saving me. This shit is deeper than the Amy Mitchell crap.

Tripp said, *"I'm worth everything."* Those words bring forth such strong emotions in me. My dad has always told me you never settle. Always wait for the man that values you as his everything. I hear a shuffle before it goes eerily quiet. I'm unable to stop myself from crying. The seconds turn to minutes and it all feels like hours.

The knock on the door comes, and to my relief, Sass speaks. "Doll, open up, it's me."

Unlocking the door, I open it a crack to see my best friend. I practically climb on to her as I pull her to me for a hug. I'm sobbing uncontrollably as Rex is guiding us away from the restrooms, and taking Tripp's gun from my shaking hand. Standing by the bikes, I'm anxiously waiting for Tripp. Where did he go? Why wasn't he the one to get me out of the bathroom? Is he hurt? Does he need me?

Tripp comes around the corner of the building. His hair is half out of its ponytail. Obviously he's been in an altercation of some sort. Something in his demeanor has change; he's serious as usual, but there is a hard feeling coming across his features. He nods at Rex before wrapping his strong arms around me.

Looking down at me, his eyes roaming to make sure I'm really here, or I'm okay, I'm not sure which. I reach my hand up and rub my thumb across his cheek. He lets go of my waist to wipe my tears away, saying nothing.

"I'm okay. You kept me safe." I say, trying to convince him.

My words must have given him whatever reassurance he was seeking, as his lips come crashing down on mine. No one kisses like Tripp. He consumes me once again. My knees give out under me. The only thing holding me up is Tripp's grip around my waist. He's kissing me deep into my soul, into the place that tells me, I'm everything to him and he's everything to me. Each sweep of his tongue with mine is another of cupid's arrows landing in the center of my heart. Intense emotions swirl between us, he's giving as much as I'm taking and getting equally in return. In this moment, this intricate, emotional dance of our tongues, something changes, there's a shift between us. I've never believed in fate until this very moment. Fate brought me to this man, and I don't think I can ever let him go.

He slows the kiss and pulls away gently, pulling me

into him. He holds me close, and for few minutes we remain in this silent embrace.

"We gotta go, Doll." Tripp says, as he pulls his hands from my body to fix his ponytail.

"You're hurt." I say noticing his hand. "There's blood on your shirt, Tripp. Do you need to go to the hospital? Where are Delatorre's men?"

Cupping my chin to look up at him, "I'm fine, and don't worry with the rest of the shit. Get on the bike so we can go to a hotel, shower, and rest. It's been a long fucking day."

Clearly in no mood to talk, I decide to listen. He's right. It's been a helluva day.

She's okay. Doll is fine and here with me. They don't know where we are headed. St. Louis was never an intended stop, therefore, we have no choice but to get a hotel. After everything today, I want a shower and a beer. They intercepted us three hours ago. Chances are we're safe for tonight. No one else followed us I feel like I can breathe for the evening.

Shit's gone downhill on transports before. I've done things I'm not proud of. When it comes down to some-one's gonna die, him or me, best believe it won't be me. Does Doll realize this? She's been so sheltered. Does she understand some of the things Roundman, myself, and some of my brothers have done to give her the peace to sleep at night? If Doll found out what kind of man I really am, she wouldn't be kissing me with all the goodness she has inside of her.

Looking around the drab hotel room, my gut twists. Each moment spent with Doll, she chips away at the walls I built around me. I need to know she's safe. I need to see her smile. I need to know she's sheltered from all the danger. I need to know she's carefree and happy. Never before has someone else's happiness mattered to me, not even my own. Happiness is an illu-sion, a simple trick bringing on a high. When it's over, and it always ends, you're left with a desire for more. Like a magician making a trick look simple, happiness leads you to believe things are easy when they aren't. For Doll, I want life to be easy, and I will do anything I can to let her have a carefree happiness.

Our room is simple; two queen beds, a TV on top of a dresser and a bathroom. Rex and Sass are in the room next door. The girls aren't safe until Delatorre is taken down, so we can't leave them in a room together. Imme-diately, I head to the shower. My clothing being put aside to be burned, I climb in letting the water wash away the filth of today's events. Knowing what I did, whether it's for good reasons or not, I'm unable to speak to Doll.

Lost in my musings, I'm startled when I hear the bathroom door open. My gun is on the counter by the shower, I pull back the curtain to reach for it. Looking up, I stop in my tracks, unable to breathe at the beauty before me.

Doll is standing there, naked. Her long blonde hair is cascading down over her full breasts. The pinks of her pointed nipples calling out to my lips, begging for attention. She walks forward, stepping into the shower. Her chest is rising and falling in deep breaths, as she trembles slightly.

"Doll," I say, not knowing what she's planning here.

My eyes roam south to the juncture of her hips. She has a small, neatly, trimmed blonde line of hair leading to her place of heavenly sweetness. I lick my lips in anticipation of all I want to do to this woman.

Moving closer to me, she reaches up with one finger against my lips. She whispers to me, unsure of herself.

"No talking, Tripp. It's been a long day. You need to let go of everything that happened today. Let me be your everything, let me be your escape. Get lost in this moment with me."

Leaning down, I kiss her lightly. In response, she

pushes her chest against me. Taking her bottom lip into my mouth, I nip, then suck gently. Her hands are running through the water coming down off my shoulders onto my chest. Licking her lips with my tongue, I slowly tease my way into her mouth. Wrapping my hands around her, I pull her tightly to me. Moving her hair, I trail kisses down her neck. I suck briefly on the spot behind her ear before tugging her earlobe with my teeth. Kissing my way down to her breasts, I suck hard on her nipple. Her moan in response increases the blood flow to my already hard cock.

Dropping down, I lift her leg over my shoulder. Licking her folds, I place my hands on her ass, holding her firmly against my face. She's rocking against me. Her hands are now tangled in my hair, keeping it out of my face. Kneading her ass with one hand, I move my other to separate the lips of her pussy. Sweeping my tongue across her clit, I take in her unique taste. Craving more, knowing I'll never get enough, I devour her pussy. Flicking my tongue inside her then sucking on her clit, I can feel her body building up. I rub my finger in circles over her clit. Licking circles over the edge of her entrance, I tease before moving to gently nip the inside of her thigh. She rocks forward, her body begging for more. I insert a finger in her core. Instantly her body grips it, as I slowly move in and out, while licking her clit. Increasing my pace, I add a second finger, while I continue to allow my tongue to dance around her folds. Her body quivers over me as she moans. Knowing she's close, I suck on her clit hard, sending her over the edge. Removing my fingers, I rub softly on her folds as she's going through the aftershocks of her orgasm.

Taking her leg off my shoulder, I steady her as she comes down. Kissing my way back up, I knead her breasts, careful not to overdo it on her now sensitive nipples. Pushing her into the shower wall, I kiss her. With her arms around my neck, she wraps her legs around me. My cock is at her entrance as she rocks against me.

"Let go, Tripp. Get lost in me." She whispers between kisses as she bites my neck.

Without a second thought, I thrust inside her. My piercing grazes her clit as I enter her, causing her to shake in my arms. She's so fucking tight. I still, momentarily, allowing her body the chance to adjust to my size. The water is coming down over us as she looks in my eyes. There's an unconditional acceptance in the blue depths staring at me. I'm lost in her right now. She owns my soul completely. I begin to move in and out of her. My piercing rubs the inner wall of her core as I slowly bring myself all the way to the edge of being out of her and then glide back in. She trembles around me at each thrust. She's rocking against me, moaning as she builds up. I pick up speed as she milks me, seeking her release.

Dropping my head, I suck hard on her nipple as I slam hard and fast into her, sending her over the edge. Her pussy is so tight. I slow my pace fighting my own release. Making this last for her, for me, for us, I don't know. What I do know, is this is the closest to heaven I'll ever get, and I want to keep my dick buried in her body forever.

"Taaaaallllllloooonnn," she cries out as her body is shaking around me. Hearing her call out my real name, sends me over the edge, shooting my warm seed deep into her womb.

Letting her ride out her orgasm, I hold her close. Her head is resting on my chest, as we both get our breathing back to normal. When she drops her legs from my waist, I steady her before I pull out of her. She winces, but smiles.

"You're well endowed, Tripp. And your piercing, that's hot." Doll says laughing.

I love hearing her laugh almost as much as my name coming off her tongue. I laugh with her. This is the most relaxed I've been in I don't know how long. She gives comfort to every part of my being.

Putting her under the spray of the shower, I gently clean her up. There is something erotic in seeing my cum run out of her. I have to tell my dick to tame it; she's not ready for round two. Washing her hair and body, I realize this is the first time that I've cared what a woman felt like when we finished.

The water runs cold in the shower by the time we get out. Exhaustion overtaking us, we climb into bed. Doll is lying on my chest, her leg entwined with mine. Easily falling asleep, this all feels right in a way I never imagined.

NOT MAKING SENSE

Waking up in Tripp's arms gives me a secure feeling down to my toes. Maybe it's lust. Maybe it's the crazy circumstances in which we've been thrown together. I don't know. Everything with Tripp feels like so much more, but I don't really know him.

The more I think on this, the more my insecurities creep up. Moving from under his arm, I go to the bathroom. What does last night mean for him? Shit! What does all of this mean? I've only had two semi real relationships and they were from college. Sure, I've hooked up with guys. The walk of shame doesn't bother me. In fact, I prefer it. Not tying myself to someone, means not introducing them to my dad.

The two long term guys I dated in college lasted less than a year each. Regular sex was nice, but the connection was lacking. I need an edge to my man. Tripp has that. Tripp has everything. Damn, I've never been able to have an orgasm during sex until Tripp and that piercing. Sure I've had an orgasm during foreplay or with my vibrator, but never during actual intercourse. That was fucking fabulous. My body tingles at the thought.

Calm down, Doll. You don't even know what Tripp wants. Deciding to keep this casual, I get dressed for the day. When I emerge from the bathroom, Tripp's on the edge of the bed, tying his boots.

"Mornin'," he says with a smile as he looks up at me. His eyes hint to a lust that could completely devour me.

Before I can reply, a tap on the door interrupts us. It's Rex letting us know they are ready. We grab our stuff and head to the bikes.

"Rex, tell the boys to hang back, we're scouting this morning for Roundman." Tripp says as he's securing our bags. Turning to me he smiles.

Damn, I wanna go back to our room and have a

repeat performance. If I knew sex would relax Tripp like this, I would have fucked him in the first hour we left the compound. It's hot to see him chill the fuck out.

Realizing that we were followed by more Hellions through this ride gives me more security. I trust Tripp and Rex to protect Sass and I with their lives, but I've wondered, through the entire ride, who was looking out for them.

"Doll, we have to go to a business and a house. I wasn't planning to tell you, but you may recognize someone and help us figure out why you were targeted. Delatorre has some strange connection to you and Amy Mitchell. Her family lives here. If anyone looks familiar or anything jumps out at you, then tap me." The serious side to Tripp is settling back in his eyes.

"I never met Amy Mitchell before she came in the office with Delatorre. I don't know any Mitchells. I don't see how there's a connection." Trying to relax him, I gently touch his arm.

"Just look around, be aware though. We don't know if Delatorre sent more tails to follow us or not." Tripp tenses at the mere mention of Delatorre.

Unable to resist, I reach my hands up and pull his head down to mine. I kiss him, a quick kiss, but enough to let him know everything's okay. He smiles back at me.

Setting off for our ride, I can't keep the satisfied grin off my face. It's been hell since Delatorre walked into my office the first time, almost a month ago. In the last week, I've relied solely on Tripp for everything. Under normal circumstances, there is no way in hell I could feel the way I do about Tripp. Want, desire, and lust, yes, all those things, but I'm feeling something more for him now. There is an undeniable connection that I can't shake. If I'm honest with myself, I don't want to shake the feelings I'm starting to have for Talon Crews.

W e ride to the last known workplace of Ray and Zack Mitchell. The two cousins work together. They grew up close to each other. Ray was raised by his mom and dad, his mom helping with Zack. Zack was always around because he was raised by his single dad. Zack's mom, although alive, is not part of his life. The shipping yard is nothing spectacular, but definitely a thriving business. We timed our course to arrive at the usual time they do. I point the cars out as they pull in for Doll to know who to look at. She shakes her head no.

Moving on, our next stop is the Mitchell home. The cousins hooked up with sisters from our known information. Pulling up, we park at the house next door, which has recently been put on the market. Hearing voices from the back yard, I tap Doll's leg to get her to climb off.

Following my lead, we walk around the vacant home as if we're potential buyers. Peeking over the fence I see a very pregnant woman, another woman who is obviously her sister, and a toddler running around. Peeking through the fence cracks, Doll gasps. Her reaction alone tells me she knows these people. Connection made, now why do these women and whatever they know about Doll interest Delatorre?

Backing away from the fence, Doll tugs on my shirt. Looking over at her, I ask, "Well?"

"Rachel, I know Rachel. She must've married one of the cousins. We were dorm roommates in college. When Caroline, Sass, and I moved to the apartment, she came with us originally. Eventually she met a guy named Tim. They were in love, so she moved in with him. I haven't seen her in years. Tim took over her life, and she didn't have time for us anymore."

Guiding her back around front, I motion to Rex to

come over. Doll fills Sass in with who's in the backyard next door.

"Rachel wouldn't set us up, Doll. Yeah, she knows our dads are bikers but she wouldn't tie in the transports." Sass says defending their friend.

"Look ladies, the only connection we have between Doll and Amy Mitchell is your college roommate. Who knows what simple detail your friend gave out, think about it? Her husband works for a shipping yard, one Delatorre may or may not use. We don't have details, but this is another piece to the puzzle." Rex says making the girls understand that Rachel's involvement may be unintentional. I step away to call in this detail to Roundman.

After catching him up, I hang up and walk back over to Doll. She's animatedly talking to Sass.

"She looks happy, Sass. She's got a little girl. Her sister is pregnant. It's so domestic. One day, Sass, that'll be us, swollen bellies in the back yard, chasing little hellions." Doll is saying to Sass as they both laugh and hug at the thought.

My chest tightens. Doll wants the happily ever after bullshit. I can't give her that. Little hellions... not happening. I need to walk away now before I hurt her. The things she wants I sure as hell can't give her.

We spend the night outside of St. Louis in a different hotel. Holding Doll fills me with mixed emotions. She feels so right being with me, beside me, and behind me. Yet, she wants things I'm not capable of giving her. I can't get comfortable with this. Roundman's gonna cut my dick off when he finds out. We want different things and we have two different lives.

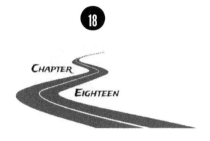

MILES KEEP PASSING BY

Tripp's been quiet. More quiet than before since we pulled out of St. Louis. Crossing the Nebraska state line, he doesn't even stop at the visitor center. I will have to get my map somewhere else. He's shown he knows the maps are important to me, why wouldn't he stop?

The miles tick by as Tripp tenses under me. Something is definitely bothering him. We settle in at some cabin in the outskirts of some tiny town. Using the washer and dryer in the cabin, I begin doing laundry for all of us. Tripp takes off to the bathroom to shower. I feel like he's avoiding me.

He comes out, hair wet, shirt tight across his chest, jeans loose, and barefoot. Walking up to him, I reach out. He steps away, so I grab him. Turning to me, his eyes are cold. Long gone are the looks of desire and want that I would get lost in.

"Tripp, what's wrong?"

"Nothin'. Go shower and rest. We have a long ride tomorrow." He's void of emotion in stature.

Boldly, I step up. Running my hands up his chest, he stiffens beneath me. I pull him down to kiss him. He does nothing. Absolutely not one fucking thing. I separate his lips with my tongue, and he makes no moves. Rejection stings as tears prick behind my eyes.

Pulling back, I look at him. "What is it?" I ask in a whisper, trying to contain my emotion.

"Fucking you was a mistake. One that won't happen again. I can't give you what you want." I flinch at his words. Anger consumes me as he claims what we shared was a mistake.

"What I want? What is it exactly that you think I want?" I ask trying to keep my emotions at bay. The rejection he's dishing out stings.

"You want it all. Kids, house, husband, a permanent place on the back of someone's bike. That's not me. My club comes first. I can't give you that. Make no illusions about where we stand. You're another piece of ass warming the back of my bike." His words cut deep, and I stalk backwards from him.

"You think you have me all figured out? I've known you, like really known you, two weeks. Let's get some shit straight. I'm not your average woman. I'm not out to bag a biker. I'm not out to warm the back of a bike. My validation doesn't come from an ol' lady cut. Tripp, you're hot. We're stuck together. I wanna fuck, not get married. I was born a Hellion, I'll breed little Hellions one day, and then I'll die a damn Hellion. ONE. FUCK-ING. DAY. I want a good time, not a fucking ball and chain. Nothing more, nothing less right now."

With that, I storm off to the bathroom. Showering, changing, and going to bed without a single word to anyone else.

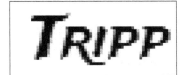

The walls are closing in. Being so close to her, but keeping my distance fucking sucks. It's for the best that she hates me. One day, she does want the happily ever after and I'm not that man. I'm thirty-three years old. I don't live a lifestyle that promises me thirty-four.

Hooking up with her was a mistake. I crave her body like a heroin addict craves a needle to put in their vein. She's my paradise. She consumes parts of me I never knew I had. Compassion, concern, and comfort, those are things I never had for anyone outside of my club brothers and I only have so much for them. With each mile that passes by, I worry more about Doll's comfort and her needs. Never has a bitch gotten so deep within me.

I'm not good for her. I'm a bastard kid that grew into a bastard man. She's a Hellion with or without tying herself to a brother. Roundman wouldn't want her with me. He knows what I've done for the brotherhood, the risks I take with each run. That's not the life I'd ever want for my daughter, if I had one.

Internal conflicts wage war in my head all night long. I wake up after little to no sleep, feeling no better about the situation with Doll. On one hand, I want nothing more than endless nights sated inside her body. On the other hand, the more serious hand, I'm no fucking good for her. I'm no fucking good for anyone.

HOW IT'S GONNA BE

Another state behind us, South Dakota is a beautiful place to ride. Once again, Tripp didn't stop at the visitor center, I have no map. I have an old map from my first time at the Sturgis bike rally. Motorcycle clubs come to the different rallies throughout the year to meet. Sometimes it's to reaffirm allies are still intact, other times to negotiate business in a public way so to speak. Authorities would question twenty or more bikers rolling into a small town with no event calling them into the area. At a rally, as they all come together, it's expected to have an over-abundance of bikers in one place. This makes for an easy meeting place to discuss future dealings.

Missing home, missing my dad, and spending all this time on the back of a bike, I've realized a few things. Maybe I'm not meant to be with Tripp, but I am meant to be an ol' lady one day. Seeing Rachel with her daughter, I'm certain that one day I do want kids. One day, though, not now. I still have a lot to sort out.

The first thing being my dad. He's not going to let me be with anyone freely. How does my dad feel about me being an ol' lady? We've never discussed it. Pretty boys won't do. My dad laughs that off because the pretty boys can't handle me, he claims. I could meet someone like Dina and Maggie. Once they got married their husbands prospected and eventually patched in. Would an outsider really understand the lifestyle I've grown up in?

The thoughts swirling in my head make me dizzy. I don't know what the future will bring, but I belong on the back of a bike. I belong with a man that will never consider one moment with me a mistake. I deserve a man that knows I'm worth everything and shows it every chance he can, not hiding behind a façade of bullshit.

After a long day of riding and almost five hundred miles under us, we stop outside of Sturgis. Sass is lost in her own thoughts today as well. I can see on her face that she's homesick. My mistakes are what put her in this situation. My very best friend, now along for the ride, in a life she's decided she no longer wants, and now she's stuck in twenty-four-seven. At every turn, I'm fucking everything up for everyone. As my thoughts consume me, I want nothing more than a shower and a bed.

We're staying at an affiliate owned house tonight. It's an off the compound house for the bikers to keep their mistresses and club whores away from their ol' ladies. From the outside it looks like every other house in the neighborhood, nice two story white house, red shutters, a red front door, and a front porch with a swing.

Pulling around back, I park the bike. Doll climbs off. The separation immediately tugs at me. Walking in the back door, we enter through the kitchen.

The kitchen is a decent size, no upgrades, nothing fancy. Everything about this house is meant to blend in.

Sitting at the small four-person round table, coffee mug in hand is, Carmine. Her dark brown hair falling down past her shoulders in waves. She's wearing an off the shoulder sweater falling far enough to expose the top of her rounded breasts cupped in a lace bra and tight black leggings leave nothing to the imagination of the tone body that is beneath the clothes.

Walking over to me, she wraps her arms around my neck, pulling me down so she can place a chaste kiss on my lips. My body stiffens at the contact.

"Tripp, it's good to see you again." She coos.

"Only here for the night, Carmine. Need a room." I bark.

"One room for the four of you. Damn, Tripp, I knew you liked kink, but I never thought you to be one to share."

Glaring at her, "Don't fuck with me bitch. You were given the heads up. Which room?"

"All worked up, Tripp, it's kinda hot." She's tracing a finger over my chest around my Hellions cut. Grabbing her, I pull her up to me and whisper.

"Which fucking room, Carmine?"

"Upstairs, second on the left. Anything you need, just call."

"Won't be needin' a damn thing." I reply, releasing her roughly.

Yes, I brought Doll to a house that's sole purpose is

for hookups. One that I've been to before on a Hellions run. One I've spent more than one night with Carmine in. Carmine is the house mom. She was once a hooker whose pimp sold her to pay off a debt. Using her brain, she convinced the club that got her to use her skills to keep their women on the side away from the club. No longer a prostitute selling her own body, she runs this house. She's a beautiful woman, and our mutual attraction has led to a couple of hookups when I'm on the road. Never anything serious.

Knowing this house has lookouts from the club that owns it, I can breathe for a minute that Doll is safe. As soon as we are in the room, Rex takes off to find a whore. This may be the longest he's gone without a piece of ass. We won't see him again until morning.

Sass settles in and Doll goes to shower. Feeling on edge, I decide I need space. Frustration consumes me at wanting Doll but knowing I'm no good for her. I exit the room, tension and conflicting emotions rolling off me.

Finding Carmine in the hall, I yank her to me. No words are shared between us. Pushing her up against the wall, I move her hair off her shoulder, exposing her neck, I suck hard. That's gonna leave a mark and I don't give a shit. She knows what I need right now. She's pulling at my belt buckle. I pull her shirt off her and throw it down the hall. Roughly, I tug her breasts from the cups of her bra, releasing them. Taking them in my hand, I twist and pinch her nipple. She moans as her excitement builds up. Her hand moves down into my pants, stroking me. I tug her pants down, only removing one leg. Reaching in my back pocket, I remove the condom from my wallet. Carmine is stroking me with one hand, while reaching down and playing with her pussy with her other. Pulling out of her grasp, I move my pants enough to expose my dick and roll the condom on. I pull her other hand away from her pussy and replace it with my own.

"So wet. You dirty little cunt. Your pussy is always so wet and waiting for any cock to fill you."

And with that, I pull my fingers out and pound into her. Taking one of her legs I wrap it around my waist as I thrust vigorously in and out of her. The pace is furious and leaves me sweating. Roughly, I pull her hair to the side, exposing her neck, as I suck hard again. Yeah, I'm gonna mark the bitch up. She likes it rough; fuck she likes it any way she can get it. I'm pounding so hard inside her that my piercing is painfully pulling on my dick. I don't give a fuck.

My mind is on the blonde taking a shower. The water washing over her full breasts. Her tongue licking the lips that were made for me to kiss. Is she washing her thighs? Thighs that were made to wrap around me. Is she washing that sweet pussy? The pussy that hugs me like no other pussy has ever before. It's not because

I fucked her raw either. I wrap up every single time. Doll is the only one I've ever had sex without using a condom. Shit felt good, too good. I growl my frustration as my balls tighten, my release soon coming.

"Kiss me, Tripp." Carmine whimpers bringing me back to reality.

As I explode into the condom, I pull back. "I don't kiss the bitches I fuck."

With that, I pull out of her. Pulling off the condom, I knot the end and toss it to the floor. The bitch can clean it up. Tucking my junk in my jeans, I turn to go back to my room. Looking up, I find I'm face to face with one enraged Doll.

CHAPTER TWENTY

IN MY FACE

W hat the hell am I watching? Unable to move, I continue to stare like an idiot. It's the train wreck you can't take your eyes off of. Looking around, I see Carmine's shirt on the ground with a condom wrapper.

Shit! Tripp and I had unprotected sex. It hasn't crossed my mind until this moment. I'm on the pill so I'm not worried about an unplanned pregnancy. Damn it! How many bitches has he fucked? Looks like I need to get checked when I get home from this ride. Oh what wonderful souvenirs, chlamydia, crabs, and genital warts, oh my! Fuck Me!

Tripp's so rough and cold with her. Completely different from how he was with me. Did I imagine the passion and kindness he shared with me? He's finished and is now looking at me. Out of the corner of my eye, I watch Carmine putting her pants back on. Rage consumes me.

"You mother fuckin' piece of shit, bastard." I say as Tripp walks to me.

As soon as he's within arm's length, I slap him hard across the face. He steps forward again, rubbing his cheek. Needing to release my aggression, I ball my fist and swing. Right as my arm is coming up in the upper cut, he grabs my wrist. Pulling me into him, he growls into my ear.

"That's your one pass. You wanna hit me like a man, be ready to take it like a man." He says in a cold tone with his eyes looking down into mine with a faraway gaze.

Tensing under him, I yank my wrist away. "It's good to see your true colors come out. You're right, Tripp. You can't give me what I want. I deserve better than you. Fuck your whore against the wall. Fuck your life away for all I care."

"Sleeping with you was a mistake, Doll. Tame your shit before this gets outta hand." His cold stare sends ice through my veins.

"A mistake. Bastard, I'm no one's mistake. You don't deserve a woman like me for even one night. I only wanted one night of fun. I got it. Lesson fucking learned to think there was more to Talon Crews than bikes and bitches. My bad for thinking there was a heart behind the man. Or for thinking for two goddamn seconds that you could respect someone you were balls deep inside two fucking nights ago. Do what the hell you want, but I never thought you'd throw it in my face. I see the real you now, I know the score. Fuck off."

Storming back inside the room, I slam the door in his face and lock it. Once inside, Sass immediately rushes over. My body is trembling as the adrenaline is running through me. I'm confused, angry, homesick, and hurting. Tripp and I aren't in a relationship. He's never promised me anything. He said I was worth everything though, and I can't get that out of my head.

It's all too much. The shit with Delatorre, leaving home, and being stuck in such close quarters, it's messed with me. Tripp isn't worth all this bullshit, no man is. Finding a new resolve, I'm ready to get through the rest of the ride and go home. When I get back home, this will be nothing but a memory.

W alking past Carmine, I say nothing. I'm numb. Finding Rex, I send him back to the girl's room while I crash in another bedroom. Tossing and turning, I'm unable to sleep. My phone rings around midnight.

"Crews," I answer, not looking at the caller ID. Only three people know I have this phone today and tomorrow I will have a new one.

"The threat's been dealt with." Roundman says.

"You want the girls on a plane home then?" I ask sitting up in the bed. Roundman sounds stressed. The threat may be handled, but something isn't right.

"Not yet, head on to Broadus, then go west. Don't care where you go, you know the checkpoints. When we're sure there's no blow back, you can send the girls home."

"Everything alright, Roundman?"

"Tank took a hit. He's in the hospital. Don't look good. We've got two others in critical that probably won't pull through. We lost Bull and Perry." His words slam into my chest. It's a risk we all take in this life-style, but it stings no less when you face it.

"Fuck!"

"Yeah. Check in after the Shifters and take care of my Doll. I'll call her in the morning and make sure she knows her place tomorrow. Letting her in my clubhouse is one thing. Having her in someone else's makes me fuckin' twitchy."

"She's fierce, but she won't fuck over the Hellions by startin' some shit tomorrow. No worries, Roundman."

"I don't like havin' women around this shit. She's safer with you than here though, so I ain't got no fuckin' choice."

With that our conversation ends and I plan our route after our stop in Montana.

CHAPTER
TWENTY ONE

KNOW YOUR PLACE

Tripp slept in another room the last two nights, which is fine by me. I never had any expectations of him. Having expectations of people only leads to let downs. We had a good fuck, moving on. Carmine has stayed clear of me too, which is in her best interest.

Talking to my dad this morning, my stomach tightens. I miss home. Hell, I even miss chasing down people over storage shit now.

Lecture after lecture from him about going to another motorcycle club have me on edge. He doesn't want me to fly off at the mouth to the other club. The shit I may get by with in his club is one thing, but these other bikers don't know me, and none of them owe me a damn thing.

Toto, we're not in Kansas anymore, I think to myself. I fucking get it. I'm not in the safety of the Hellions' compound. No popping off at the mouth to the bikers. I'm not an ol' lady. I may be Roundman's daughter, but I'm on my way to Shifter's territory. They don't know me, and they don't give a fuck who I am. They've earned their cuts and my respect, period.

'Know your place, Doll.' My dad's voice reverberates through my head. We have an agreement with the Shifters, but at the end of the day, agreements can be broken in a moment's notice. For whatever reason, my dad likes these guys and trusts them, so I will know my place, be seen, not heard, and nowhere near business.

Thinking about the many rallies and trips I've taken with my dad, I know I've opened my mouth one too many times before. Bikers are brash, blunt, and rough around the edges. I know these things, but approaching me like a club whore never ends well. Sass and I have never been degraded in our own club, but it happens when we're out. It usually ends with us cussing someone out, a Hellion either stepping in to pull us off, or to kick the ass of whoever offended us.

Keeping my mouth shut is never easy, but the club needs less drama right now. Pull it together, Doll. I'm twenty-five years old, I hate when they act like I'm seven-damn-teen. I've been sheltered, that's fuckin' apparent in this trip, but I know how to act.

Tripp is at the bike ready to go when I get outside. Without a word, I put on my helmet, and climb on. Keeping as much space between us, we silently ride. Another state line crossed with no map. What the fuck ever, I don't really feel the need to memorialize this trip anymore anyway.

Traveling normally doesn't bother me. Outside of the club I've got no roots. That's why I was given the name Tripp. I'm always ready for the next ride, the next trip out of town and my next moment to escape the ordinary day to day. When no one has been truly solid in your life, there's nothing holding you down. Outside of my club, no one cares if I'm in Carolina or California.

Rex and I make sure his mom, Jolene, doesn't have to work as hard anymore. She checks in on us, but the connection never has been strong. We've always been too much for her to handle. She smiles, cooks us a meal every so often, and calls every few days to check in. She doesn't like taking our money, but she does use it to keep flowers on our grandparent's grave and keep up their old house. I'm pretty sure she helps my mom. She's never admitted to knowing my mom's where-abouts to us or my grandparents, but she always acts funny when you mention her sister.

This trip with Doll is weighing on me. Once we get back to Carolina, I'll be forgotten. She can settle down and find a man to make her happy. For her sake, and that of her future little hellions, I hope it's not someone in this life.

Tank's in a coma, hooked up to who knows how many devices to keep him going. Machines are breathing life into my brother. Two shots to the head, four to his abdomen. We're lucky he's even semi stable now. The last update this morning is no news is good news. They don't know what he will be like when he's healed enough to be pulled out of the drug induced coma, or if he will pull out. We lost two brothers already and two more are in critical condition, not expected to pull through. A few others banged up, but not in life threatening situations. Delatorre's crew suffered more loss, but that's not something I'll lose any sleep over.

Arriving in town, we pull into the cabin we are staying in for the evening. My boys are not far behind and will get some food for when we get back from the compound. Dropping off our bags, I let the girls stretch, change and rest for an hour before we head out again.

CHAPTER
TWENTY TWO

THERE'S NO PLACE LIKE HOME

The ride has been uneventful. Tripp and I only exchange casual pleasantries. We pull over not far from the Shifter's compound. I make no move to get off. Tripp removes his cut. Looking over my shoulder, Rex is taking his off and tucking it into a saddlebag as well. Seeing the confusion on my face, Tripp gives a half smile and squeezes my thigh.

"It's okay, Doll. It's a sign of respect. We're in their territory, my colors don't belong here."

His touch, his voice, send tingles through me. As pissed as I may be, I'm not immune to Tripp.

Pulling up to the gate, I look up into the security camera. We all have them, nothing to be shy about. Get in, handle business, and get out. Normally, we wouldn't be allowed to come along as females, but given the nature of this ride, I'm sure my dad has made them aware, Tripp can't leave me behind. After a few minutes waiting, a huge man comes to the gate. He's tall, taller than Tripp who is already over six feet. He's got dirty blonde hair with some crazy design shaved into it on the sides. He is by far the wildest looking biker I've ever seen. He approaches. He's got ink down his right arm that's in a detailed design that I don't want to take my eyes off as he's moving around.

As he's opening the gate, he looks over all of us. Walking up to Tripp, "Hellions," is all he greets glancing over at me and Sass with questions dancing in his eyes.

"Kraze, this is Delilah. And that's Savannah, over with Rex." Tripp answers as he's pointing to us.

The gate is opened, and we pull in. Parking the bikes, we get off. Nervous energy consumes me. I've been to rallies, events, but never to another compound. Walking in, it reminds me of our clubhouse. The building is different, but the feeling is the same. Against a bar, I can see a couple making out, the little I can make out of the woman, she's an exotic beauty. Boys are off to the side talking, drinking beers. Everything is just as it would be on any random day at our clubhouse.

"Dyson, Tripp's here." The guy referred to as Kraze calls out.

A hand comes off the beauty's ass, to lift up one finger. Well, that's Dyson then. Still looking around me, I see a man with a stone cold look to him. He's got that serious demeanor that Tripp carries around. After a moment, he seems to sense we're no threat and walks off down a hallway off the back of the room.

The room feels charged with a different kind of energy. It's like they are following our emotions and sensing things because although watching us, everyone seems to settle quickly with our presence. It's like they know something we don't or they are that confident in the hold they have over the Hellions. My dad doesn't give other clubs that kind of power, so I'm thinking they sense this visit doesn't affect them negatively, that it's business.

A woman walks in with short hair that is brown on top and pink on the bottom. Her confidence rolls off her in waves. Her clothes are skin tight, hugging every luscious curve of her body. She's a pin up model walking. She walks over to Kraze, who immediately grabs her waist pulling her to him for a kiss. This is common at our club too, but right now it nags at me. Clawing at my insides, to stand here and know that I'll never have that. It's obvious in the features and actions of these men, those women aren't club whores. No, those are ol' ladies. Club whores are man handled and wouldn't just be kissed, by now they'd be on their knees sucking someone's dick.

The first couple take a breather, breaking apart. Taking in Dyson, it's obvious he and Kraze are twins only his ink adorns his left side versus the right of his brother. Dyson nods to Tripp as his sign that he should make his way over. I don't move at first, unsure of where I'm supposed to be to stay out of the way. Tripp takes two steps, when I don't follow suit, he grabs my hand, lacing our fingers together. The act comforts me and pisses me off as he pulls me close to him.

Never releasing my hand, he gives a quick greeting to Dyson. Rex and Sass are right beside us. The serious man comes back to the room, showing no signs of any emotion whatsoever.

Looking to me, Dyson introduces, "This is my ol' lady, Siofra. Stay out here with her and Nikki, they'll keep you company." He's pointing over at the pink haired woman as she smiles over to me.

"Dyson, this is Delilah and Savannah." Tripp makes quick introductions, pulling me closer. Kraze walks over, as does the serious faced man, who is introduced as Thorny. The atmosphere and members of the Shifters Pack all remind me of home and my Haywood's Hellions.

"Let's take this to the office." Dyson says. The guys all start to move away.

Tripp pulls me to him, leaning down he brushes his lips against mine before sucking on my bottom lip. Frustrated, I fist his shirt at his chest. Normally, his cut would be there to grab, this feels so foreign. Pulling my mouth away from him, he brings his head down on my shoulder.

Gritting my teeth, I whisper, "What the fuck are you doing?"

His hand now rubbing my ass, he whispers, his breathing is heavy on my ear. "Tame it, Doll. Right now, I'm going in an office where I can't watch you. The other assholes here need to know you're taken. Behave yourself until I get back." The last sentence ends with a pat on my ass.

"Rex isn't kissing Sass. You gonna pee on my leg to mark territory that isn't fucking yours, Tripp?"

Grabbing my head with both hands, he leans in forehead to forehead. "Tame it, Doll. I'll be back. Don't fuck around with anyone out here."

I push him off me and turn to Sass as he and the others walk out of the room and off to wherever.

Siofra and Nikki are smiling at me when I turn to face them.

"You can call me Fry and Nikki is Sparkles." Siofra informs us, still grinning at me.

"Fighting it hard." Nikki says with an all knowing smile.

"Nothing to fight. There's nothing there." Shrugging my shoulders, I try for nonchalance.

"Tell yourself that all you want. When a biker sees a woman he wants, he stops at nothin' to get her. And that biker wants you. With that small display of affection, he made sure none of our boys got any ideas while he's tucked away. Whether you want to believe it or not, that one is claiming you." Siofra says with a slight laugh.

"He fucked some bitch just the other night in a hall-way. He's far from claiming anything other than a new piece of ass." I retort, the hurt building back inside me.

"He could fuck some bitch right here in front of you, that doesn't mean he doesn't want you. It's the world we live in. Until they know they have you, really have you, any willing whore is free game. Deep inside, you have to know this Delilah. Don't kid yourself, there is some-thing there whether you own up to it or not." Nikki says walking to the kitchen to get a bottled water for each of us.

Tripp claiming me, oh if she only knew what he really felt, or didn't feel as it may be. We spend the next hour chatting. It feels like we've known each other for years, not just an hour. 'Fry' has been through a lot and came out on top of it all. There is a strength to both of these women that make them just as tough as the men of their pack.

Seeing these girls happy as ol' ladies solidifies that, yes, one day I do want this and I could have this. Would my dad be okay with me being with a Hellion? If Tripp really did want me, how would my dad handle that? Deny it all I want, part of me really does want something with Tripp, but I'll never admit it.

Walking back out to the common area, my chest tightens when I see Doll. She's smiling and looking completely at ease here. This is what she knows, so of course, this is where she would feel most settled.

A Shifter walks over to her and the other girls. He says something that causes her to playfully smack his arm. Jealousy, like I've never known before, courses through me. Picking up the pace in my stride, I wrap my hands around her waist from behind. Pulling her to me, her back to my chest, I nuzzle into her neck. Waiting for her to stiffen or reject me, I still. When she does neither, I rub my hand gently in circles over her belly.

"Told you." Siofra says to her and all four women fall into a fit of laughter.

Dyson leans over Siofra kissing her, before taking her by the hand to pull her away. She stops quick enough to hug Sass. Doll pulls out of my arms to say goodbye to her new friends. I feel empty. Doll brings out things in me I've never felt before.

The meeting with Dyson is cut and dry. They have the details for the job and the payment. Another task on this trip is handled. Delatorre down, the tie in with the Mitchell bitch becoming clearer, the Shifter Pack paid, and Doll still safe.

After the typical goodbyes, we climb back on the bikes and leave the compound. As soon as we cross the gate, I reach in my saddlebag and get my cut back on.

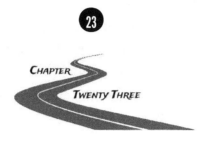

TAKING IT ALL IN STRIDE

Tripp has a different look in his eyes now. He's his usual serious self, but there is a void in his eyes when he looks at me. Something is going on back home because both Tripp and Rex are calling in more often. I wish they would give us an update, but even my dad hasn't slipped me any information.

As we cross another state line with no map, things are beginning to bug me. Okay, we fucked. I thought we had a deeper connection. Was I wrong? No, I didn't misread what is going on between us. Tripp and I have an attraction there. Obviously, the thought of a long term relationship spooked him. Hell, up until I met Fry and Sparkles, the thought of a long term relationship would've sent me running.

Tripp doesn't want an ol' lady. I get that. Why can't we move past all this and be friends? I'm stuck on this ride with him. I don't want to hate him and I'm sick of the distance between us. Fucking Carmine in the hallway was a good thing. It makes sure I have no illusions about a future with Tripp. He's a good time, and this ride is a chance circumstance. When I get home, it's time to settle down and get serious about my life.

My dad will handle Delatorre. Once I'm safe, I can return home. Time to put my big girl panties on and have the talk with my dad we have both avoided. Can my dad accept if I want to be an ol' lady? He's chased away every guy I've ever brought home. It's time he let go and realize I'm not a little girl anymore.

Pulling in, I realize tonight we are staying in Yellowstone National Park. If I could feel safe, this would be a nice stop. Road trips are always nice to take in scenery and such. On a bike it's even more of an experience because you feel it surround you.

I'm off the bike waiting for Tripp to finish his conversation with my dad. My worry must show on my face because he's staring hard at me before he pulls me up against him.

The smell of leather, gas, road, and Tripp mixes together in an aroma of comfort for me. His voice brings an ease over me, as he reassures me.

"You're safe, Doll. Things are being handled. Relax, that's why we came here. Let the tension go."

With that, he pulls away. Grabbing my backpack while he grabs his bag from inside the saddle bags, I take a moment to breathe. Tripp will keep me safe. After the run in before, I know he won't let anyone get to me. He takes my hand in his, interlacing our fingers, as we check in to the cabin we'll be staying in.

The cabin is small, more like a motel room, but in a separate building instead of wall to wall. Sass and Rex had to get their own cabin to share because the four of us wouldn't fit comfortably in just one. The cabins are a basically one open room. Each cabin has one queen bed, a small living area, a kitchenette, and a bathroom in each. Not even a Jacuzzi tub, amenities may be lacking but the views are breathtaking. Immediately, I take a shower. Road grime does not feel good. I love the back of a bike, but the wind and air dry out your skin. Once I'm done, Tripp follows suit.

We're both in the sitting area. Tripp's in the low slung sweat pants he usually sleeps in. His hair down and wet. His face is now sporting the rough look of days on the road without shaving.

Rather than sit idle in awkward silence, I decide to do laundry. Going over to our bags, I remove the dirty clothes. There is a small stacked washer-dryer unit in the cabin, so I get started. Being on the road, I don't know how often we will have access to washers so each stop that I can catch up, I do.

"You don't have to wash my clothes, Doll. I can do it when you're finished." Tripp says looking over at me.

God, he's hot. His tan skin, the dragon tattoo that wraps around his back and both his sides, they're all screaming out to me. The dragon's head comes up facing the eagle over his chest. The body coming across his back as the tail climbs up his ribs on the other side. The dragon's body wraps under his Hellions insignia back-piece. The eagle's talon holds his heart and shield directly over his heart, but its large face and body come over his chest and shoulder. The intricate details leave a fierce look to the eagle's eyes. It's a look that draws me in. The longer I stare, the more I feel I'm drowning in the very being of Talon 'Tripp' Crews. Unable to take my eyes off him, I take in the tribal design covering his right shoulder and going all the way down his arm. Every piece is interwoven together, all protecting him in some way. Why, in all this time together, have I not taken the time to absorb the many details of the ink covering this sexy man? His left arm is covered in chains that are broken in places. The first broken place holds a baby rattle up by the eagle's beak on his shoulder, the second broken place holds a pocket watch on his bicep, the third broken piece holds a heart with an arrow through it on his fore arm, and the final broken piece comes to the top of his wrist with a coffin.

Lost in my thoughts and taking in the details, I don't take in what Tripp is saying as he once again tells me not to do his laundry. He gets up and walks over to me. His pants hanging low, show the words that adorn each side of the 'v' that is the joint of his legs and hips. His right side says 'take chances' with the left saying 'no hesitations'. The words catch me off guard. Before I realize it, Tripp's in front of me, his hands on my hips. I shudder at his touch.

"Doll, about the hallway...with Carmine...I'm a jackass." His eyes look directly at me as I gaze up to meet his stare. They hide his many emotions, and I wish I knew what was really going on in his head.

"Tripp, it's okay. I overreacted. We had a good time. We're not in a relationship. You're free to do what you want." I manage to get out in a whisper.

"Are we good? Friends?" He asks.

"Friends." I confirm with a small smile.

He backs away and goes back to the small couch. We spend the evening chatting like old friends. He tells me about being a kid and going hunting with his grandpa and Rex. He never mentions his mom or dad, but talks about his grandma and Aunt Jolene. Before we realize it, we're both yawning and trying to stay awake, as it's after midnight. Going over to the bed, I climb in. Tripp is way too tall to fit comfortably on the couch.

"Tripp, come get in the bed." I invite turning the covers down on the other half of the bed.

"Doll, that's not a good idea."

"Why not? We're friends, Tripp. You need sleep, real sleep, not tossing and turning barely resting. Your legs hang way over the end of the couch. Quit being stubborn and bring your ass to bed." I smile over at him, as he gets up and makes his way to bed.

At some point in the night, Doll ends up wrapped in me. I'm not sure if she climbed over me, or I pulled her onto me. Either way, I wake up with her blonde hair spread across my chest, as I lay on my back. Her arm is wrapped around my torso, her leg entwined in mine. I have one hand on her back and the other on her bare thigh from those damn short ass shorts she sleeps in, with the scrap of fabric that one might call a tank top covering her top.

We agreed to be friends last night. Waking up like this, friendship is the last thing on my mind. I want my cock buried balls deep in her tight little cunt. Fuck! Tame it, Tripp. I've got to stop thinking of how good she felt, how tight she was, or how her body molds perfectly to mine.

Shifting slowly out from under her, I get up. Taking a cold shower, I'm awake and my dick is only semi hard now. To get her mind off Delatorre and the drama, we're going to spend the day taking in the sites here at Yellowstone, then head out tomorrow.

Checking in with Roundman, Tank is stable, but still in a coma. The two others didn't make it. The club is making arrangements to provide for the families of the four lost brothers, as well as the service arrangements. From what I gather, it was not easy to get to Delatorre and blood was shed on both sides. The blow back seems minimal as Oscar Delatorre comes to terms with his son's transgressions. Roundman has the Amy Mitchell chick in one of our safe houses, unsure as to what to do with her. Getting off the phone, my orders are to take my time coming home. Take Doll out to see some sites before we head back to allow more time for any consequences to come down before the girls return.

CHAPTER
TWENTY FOUR

FEELING COMFORTABLE

S pending our day on the trails, we were able to take in the geysers and all their natural beauty. Everything about being out with Tripp, Rex, and Sass today, felt so normal. We all laughed, joked, and had a good time. Putting aside the reason we're here, it was as if we were four best friends on vacation together.

Seeing Rex and Tripp together in a relaxed setting is fun. They razz each other much like brothers do and challenge one another in everything. The close bond the two share is obvious.

After dinner, we head back to the cabins for an early night. Once we're inside, Tripp brings in another bag from the bike. I'm sitting on the bed when he opens the bag and brings over a large clasped envelope. Handing it to me, I stare at him in confusion.

"Open it." He commands with his hands on his jean clad hips. His black t-shirt is stretching tight across his chest where his cut is resting comfortably.

Doing as I'm told, I open the envelope. Dumping out its contents, I find the maps for Nebraska, Montana, and Wyoming. Tears prick behind my eyes, but I refuse to cry.

"We can't be predictable, Doll. We can't make it a habit of stopping at each visitor center or at each state line somewhere. I know the maps are your thing, so I picked them up at the gas stations when paying for our gas while you used the restroom. I'm an ass, but this means something to you. I'll always make sure you have what's important to you."

Left speechless, I climb off the bed and hug him tight. His hand rubs my back gently as I enjoy the connection in this moment with this all-consuming man. He frustrates me in a way no one else ever has. He can hurt me quicker than anyone has ever been able to hurt me. He can make me smile in a way no one ever has made me smile before. There is something about him that I don't think I'll ever be able to let go of.

Friends. We're just friends I remind myself. My traitorous body wanting so much more from this man in my arms. He hugs me back, his head dropping to the crook of my neck. As he inhales, I feel like he's breathing me in. Sucking my soul further into him, I'll never be the same again. We may never have sex again, but Talon 'Tripp' Crews will, forever, hold a piece of me.

There were so many moments today where I wanted to reach my arms around her. Times that I wanted to kiss her, hold her hand, to be more than I can really be for her. Long term, there's no promise of a future. Therefore, I can't lead her on as much as it kills me to restrain myself.

It was relaxing to let my guard down and hang out today. Usually, when we travel it's for a transport, and I have business on my brain. The club needs are always on my mind. To make sure my brothers all have what they need to provide for their families and stay safe is my priority. It's been years since I've been somewhere and taken in the moments and the memories created. Memories, that's what all of this will become once we get back to North Carolina.

I once asked my grandpa how he could go on without grams. He said, *"Talon, you live on with the memories you make. Cherish the times you have with those you love to push you through the times when they're gone."*

This is a time I'll forever cherish. Doll has gotten into a place no one has ever been before. I don't know how to handle this. I don't know what I'm feeling. Everything about her is suddenly important to me and not because Roundman ordered me to protect her. She's everything because she's Delilah. She's the doll I treasure and value. A doll to protect and cherish.

After she finishes tracing the route we took on the new maps, we decide to sleep. After clearing off the bed, we both lay down. Rather than fight what I'm feeling, I pull her over to me. Wrapping her arm around my waist, pulling her leg over mine, and placing her head on my chest. Warmth, comfort, security, and acceptance all surround me as I fall into an easy sleep.

CHAPTER

TWENTY FIVE

NEVER

Waking up in Tripp's arms, rather than an empty bed, brings a smile to my face. It's comfortable to be with him like this. I run my fingers over the chains of his tattoo. Tracing the rattle, Tripp grabs my hand to still me.

"What's it mean?" I ask, leaning up to look in his eyes. He sighs before beginning.

"The chains of our pasts always hold us back until

we die. The first place I was broken, was as a baby. My mom left me and never looked back." He states as I trace lower to the pocket watch. "Hands of time. My grandparents were taken when I was much too young. We never know when our clock will stop." He answers with sadness in his voice. My finger tingles as I trace lower.

"Someone broke your heart?" I ask as I reach the broken heart. He laughs under me. "No, Doll, I've never had my heart broken. But there is heartbreak in loneliness. And there are people who aren't meant to have love like that." He answers with a tone that is devoid of emotion.

"Have you ever been in love, Talon?" I ask, now curious about why he feels he's not meant to have love.

"No, Doll, I've never experienced the feeling of being in love. I have love for my family and for my club. As for a woman, I don't lead a lifestyle that is conducive to having love and a long lasting relationship." He stiffens under me.

Sitting up in the bed to look at him, I reply. "Why do you feel you can't be loved? Don't give me that lifestyle bullshit because there are ol' ladies that freely accept what their men do."

"I never said I can't be loved. I've never been in love. I won't put a woman in the situation to face my lifestyle. It's not fair to them to wonder where I'm at or whether I'll make it home."

"That's a bunch of bullshit, Talon. This life isn't an easy one. But damn it, when you find someone and it means something, you make it work. The good times outweigh the bad. Tomorrow isn't promised for anyone. Why shut yourself off from happiness for a club?"

"It's not just a club, and you fuckin' know it. The club comes first; you tellin' me a woman would understand that?" He sits up abruptly, now face to face we sit on the bed.

"Not every woman would, but there are some that can and do." Instinctively, I bring my hand up to run my fingers along his cheek and follow his jaw. "This is my world, Talon, I don't know any other way. Don't close yourself off when you could have it all." Pausing before I continue, knowing in this moment, I'm opening myself up in a way I never have before. "And all of it could be sitting right in front of your face." I whisper.

The words come out of my mouth before I can stop myself. This is a risk, exposing my feelings to him. Feeling vulnerable, I lean in to kiss him, soft, slow, and with passion. What starts out tenderly, quickly becomes so much more. His arms come up, pulling me to straddle him. His tongue devours my mouth as I run my hands up into his hair. His hand grabs my ass, grinding me on his erection. The sensation sends fireworks through me.

I want him. Pulling away, I lick his neck before sucking his earlobe gently. His hand comes up my shirt, cupping my breast with his palm as his fingers tweak my sensitive nipples.

"Talon, please," I beg, already worked to a frenzy in need of release.

He removes my shirt, immediately taking my nipple into his mouth. Taking his hand, he runs up my thigh and under my shorts. Rubbing my mound through my panties, I rock against him needing more. Pushing the lace aside, he rubs my pussy. His thumb now making circles on my clit brings me to the edge. He continues sucking and blowing on my nipples, then tracing his way to gently nip at my collarbone and neck. When he inserts his finger in my tight, wet heat, I am ready to combust. His pace steady, I'm so close. He inserts a second finger. Rocking into him, I lose myself to his fingers. When his thumb rubs my clit, I go over the edge, calling out his name.

"I love hearing my name come off your lips." He growls against me, before I kiss him with everything I can give.

He removes his fingers, sliding off my shorts and panties. Pulling him to me and rolling us over, he's now over me. He stops and stares at me for a moment. I run my fingers over his jaw.

"Talon." Before I can finish my sentence, he's

kissing me hard as I wrap my legs around him and try to remove his pants.

Pounding on the door stops both of us. Tripp drops his head to my breasts. "Fuck!" He groans getting off me gently with a chaste kiss. He stalks over to the door with no way to hide the tent bulging in his pants. I lay back on the bed, wanting more time with this man.

"Shit better be important," He says looking in the peephole of the door. I hear Rex on the other side.

"Fucker, you're late. I've been calling, shit-head. Put your clothes on and let's ride."

"Ten minutes." Tripp answers never opening the door.

He runs his fingers through his hair as he turns back to face me. "Come on, Doll, we gotta get dressed and go." The frustration is evident in his voice as his muscles tense with his body's need for release.

"We have ten minutes." I say with a wink.

"Darlin' I'm no ten-minute man with you. If we continue, I'm not stopping until you can't walk right."

He walks over to me. I get up on my knees on the bed as he reaches me. Kissing me wildly, I moan into him, as I rub my hand over his cock. Pulling away, he smiles down at me, while he moves my hand off of him.

"I'm going to take a very cold shower. You get dressed so we can leave when I get out."

Before I can entice him to stay, he kisses my forehead, and heads to the bathroom. When I hear the lock of the bathroom door, I get dressed knowing that I need not be a further distraction.

The cold water runs over me as I try to calm my raging hard on. Damn it! I've never shared so much of myself with anyone. She stirs so much inside of me. Rex came to the door at the right time. Otherwise, I'd be balls deep in her right now. If I'm honest with myself, I'd be a happy man to wake up talking with her every morning.

Fuck! I'm no good for her. No more sleeping with her. We need space between us. She wants things I can't give her. Even if she can accept my lifestyle, I can't tie her down to waiting for me to come home from a run or a transport. Thinking of how much I'm away, easily reminds me why she's better off without me.

When I can't take the cold water anymore, I get out of the shower. Still semi hard, but manageable, I get dressed. Today, we will head through Utah. The time on the road will be good for me to gather my thoughts.

Self-control is something I've always had until Delilah 'Doll' Reklinger walked into my life. With her, I can't stop myself even when I need to.

Walking out of the bathroom, I wasn't a hundred percent sure Doll would listen and actually get ready. Part of me wanted to walk out to her naked and waiting. The responsible, serious side of me is thankful she's dressed and packed.

We walk out of the cabin and secure our stuff on the bikes.

"I knew you were a five-minute fucker." Rex yells over to me laughing. Doll's face blushes before she responds.

"Five minutes promises me two orgasms and that's just with his fingers. You gave us ten minutes, Rex. I'm still working through the aftershocks. Now, I'm gonna ride this bike to wherever we're headed with my panties soaked waiting to give Talon the ride tonight. By tomorrow I won't be able to walk straight. Question is…what can you do for your woman in ten minutes, Rex? Can you make her crave you all fuckin' day? Can you make her soak through her panties in want for you in a mere five minutes? No, babe, you can't. So put your helmet on, climb on your bike, and next time you come knocking, bring coffee."

Rex and I both bust out laughing, as she walks over and high fives Sass. We forget Doll grew up around bikers and our brash language. We get settle on the bikes and pull out. The ride to Utah does nothing to calm my need and want for the woman on the back of my bike. If there's one thing I don't need to do, it's have sex with Doll again.

CHAPTER
TWENTY SIX

ONE STEP FORWARD, TWO STEPS BACK

The weather stalls us once we cross over into Utah. We're under an overpass waiting for the rain shower to move through. Tripp steps away to make a phone call. I'm unsure where things stand between us. Determined not to overthink all of this, I've decided where Talon 'Tripp' Crews is concerned, I'm going to go with the flow.

Rex is wiping down both bikes, leaving Sass and I

waiting around. She is standing beside me as the cars pass us by.

"Okay love, we haven't had our girl time lately. Spill it, bitch." Turning to face me, she's smiling.

Laughing at her, I reply. "I don't know. Tripp triggers so much inside of me."

"You've got it bad, Doll. Never has anyone gotten you this smitten."

Pushing her playfully, "smitten? Did you really call me smitten?"

"Sure did. If the shoe fits, wear it Cinderella." She puts her hands on her hips as she is holding in the laughter that's threatening to pour out of her. I've never been the one to get hung up on a guy. For her this is better than reality TV.

"I. Am. Not. Smitten. We're in extenuating circumstances." She nods at me with a 'know it all' smile. "Damn it, okay, I'm smitten. I'm head over heels in lust with Tripp. There. Happy now?"

"You're more than in lust with him. Admit it. There's a whole lot more going on then raging hormones."

Unable to bring myself to admit it, I look at her with pleading in my eyes. She wraps her arms around me knowing I need the comfort of my best friend right now. What if this is all one sided? We don't really know each other. Do people develop feelings this quickly? Am I setting myself up for heartbreak? Pulling back to face her again, I respond.

"Sass, what if it's not real? Look at the chaos surrounding us. I can't say that I love him because that would seem like a fantasy to fall in love so quickly. I'm not stupid enough to say that I don't have feelings for him. Yes, I'm attracted to him. Beyond the physical though, I want to know him. What makes him tick? What makes him smile? The man inside his soul calls to me to go deeper and find him."

Her face draws serious. "Fate has a way of giving us exactly what we need, when we need it. Tripp's your protector at the time you've needed it the most. He's also been your security in all of this. Whether you make the emotions swirling around you last a day, or a lifetime, you live in the moment. Whatever you're feeling right now, don't you dare turn your back on it out of fear. Doing so will leave you with a lifetime of what ifs."

She's right and I really hate it when she's right. Guarding my raw emotions once again, I look over at Tripp before returning my gaze to Sass.

"He may not feel anything for me anyway. I'm an order, remember? Protecting me, this ride, the charade we're all putting on here is a direct order from my dad."

"Doll, cut the shit, it's me you're talking to. Your dad certainly didn't give Tripp the order to kiss you, fuck you, or worry about your comfort. The order was to take you on a ride and keep you safe. There is an attraction for both of you, whether you want to pussy foot around it or not. Keep dancing around each other or get real. Be an adult, own what you're feeling. Rex has even said Tripp's never been this relaxed with someone. Don't fight what's meant to be."

Rex walks over, ending any further conversation. The expression on his features when he looks at me is one of knowing. Rex sees right through me.

"Talking about Tripp, huh?" He asks, handing Sass a rain jacket to put on.

"What? Tripp? No way. Why would you say that?" I try to cover my tracks.

"Whatever, Doll. Anytime he thinks of you or talks about you, he smiles. When you talk about him or think of him, you get all serious. Opposites attract they say, but you two bring out the opposite in each other." He says shaking his head and grinning lazily.

"He smiles when he talks about me?" I question innocently, stunned by Rex's candid statement.

"Yeah, Doll, he does. Y'all need to quit fighting it and see where it goes."

"Where what goes?" Tripp interjects approaching.

"The love, lust, fucking crazy ass attraction you two have." Rex answers bluntly. Shaking his head, Tripp doesn't reply. Instead, he hands me a rain jacket and gets us ready to get back on the road.

Apparently, Doll is as conflicted as I am about the magnetic pull between us. After a miserable few hours riding in and out of rain showers, we are finally settled into the guesthouse we're staying in tonight. We're on the Steel Riders motorcycle club Prez's property. He has a pool house he's opened to us for the evening. It's an open room with a small bathroom, one bed, the sofa that pulls out into a bed, and a chair.

We each take turns showering. Sass has taken the couch, Rex is settling into the chair, and Doll is curled up in the bed. I lay down beside her without a second thought. I hear her whispering.

"One step forward, two steps back."

"What the fuck does that mean?" I whisper back to her, rolling her over to me.

"Exactly what I said. We take one step forward only to take two steps back."

Is she that blind that she doesn't see it. Tipping her chin up to make her look me in the eye, I reply.

"Don't be a bitch Doll. Am I not here in bed with you?"

"Yeah, you are, but what are we doing? One minute, you're ready to ravage my body, the next you act as if you're merely tolerating me." She says struggling to keep her whisper low.

"You can't possibly believe that. Where am I right now, Doll? In. Fucking. Bed. With. You."

I can see the tears pooling in her eyes out of uncertainty. I've given her no reason to have confidence in me, or in us. Those tears are pooling because I'm not man enough to give her the reassurance she needs.

"You're in bed with me because the only other option is the floor." She replies dryly.

"What do you want from me? Obviously, you expect something and I haven't delivered." My irritation is clearly evident in the grading in my tone.

"I don't fucking know Tripp. This morning, you couldn't keep your hands off me. Then today, you barely acknowledge me. Now you're in bed with me actually planning to sleep."

I can't stop the laugh that slips out of me. She's frustrated because she wants me, and she thinks I don't want her.

"Do you want me to fuck you in an open room with your best friend and my cousin here to watch?"

She shakes her head no. The realization of what she's wanting is dawning on her face. I decide to have a little fun and help her relive the tension.

"I can strip you down right now." I rub my hand ever so slightly up and down her leg, feeling the goose bumps erupt over her flesh as I continue to whisper in her ear. "I can take my tongue and start right here at the sweet spot of your ear." Gently, I lick the bottom of her earlobe before nipping it with my teeth. Moving my hand, I trace her neck with my fingers, working down to follow the line of her tank top. "Then come down and take your perfect pink nipples in my mouth and suck hard until you are squirming beneath me."

Trailing my hand lower I rub circles on the belly of her tank top without going under her shirt. "I can lick my way south," I say as I slide my hand under the waist-band of her shorts. As my hand finds her folds, she rocks into me, seeking more. "Using my tongue, I could tease this spot right here." I say as I firmly circle her clit. Her body is coming alive under me. I insert one finger, "I can lick inside you and taste your sweet essence. You're my drug of choice, Doll, and I'll never get enough." I begin slowly working my finger in and out of her as she's building around me. "I want to bury my cock so deep in you. I want to hear you scream my name over and over as my piercing hits the walls of your pussy, baby." Her panting becoming faster, I add a second finger, stretching her. I increase my pace as she's rocking on me. As she reaches her climax, I kiss her with everything I've got. Silencing her moans in my mouth, I take in this moment.

She is my addiction. There's no way I can walk away from this ride the same man I was going into it. She's claimed a piece of me. I'll never get it back. Truth be told, I don't want to.

She reaches over to stroke my erection. "No, Doll. If you do that, I'm going to give Rex and Sass a show they'll never forget. My self-control can only take so much, darlin'."

She looks at me searching for the reassurance that I'm okay with this. I'm more than okay with this. My woman is in my arms, in my bed, satisfied, and safe. This is a moment to treasure.

"Sleep, Doll." I whisper before kissing her gently and tucking her against me for the night.

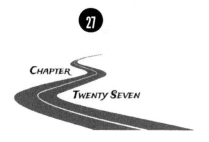

LET LOOSE A LITTLE

D on't get used to this, I remind myself. This is a ride. Tripp has promised me nothing. Eventually, I will return to the coast and Tripp back to his home. Whatever it is we're doing here, it won't last. My chest tightens at the thought of not having Tripp with me. How will all of this play out?

We get up, dress, and head out. The road time is beginning to wear on all of us. No one is overly talkative this morning as we go through the motions and get back on the road.

We cross into Nevada. After a brief stop for breakfast, we're on the road again. Wondering where we are heading, I can't contain my wild desire to venture away from the plan. Stopping at a gas station, I can't help myself. Climbing off the bike, I try for innocence when asking.

"Tripp, can we have one night in Vegas?"

Smiling at me, Tripp asks as he's getting off the bike and stretching. "Did you just bat your eyelashes at me?"

"Depends. Did it work?" I laugh. "I promise not to get you drunk and take you off to the little white chapel. And no marriages done by an Elvis impersonator either." I joke as I watch a serious expression cross his face at my words.

"Drunk or sober, this is one man that won't be getting married anywhere, Vegas or not."

"I didn't mean anything by it. I'm sorry. It was a joke in poor taste obviously." I say barely above whisper, feeling deflated. "It was a dumb idea, forget I mentioned it." And with that I walk away, going to the safety of the restroom.

Does he ever let loose? The only time Tripp seems to relax is when we're fucking or he's in bed holding me. How does he relax? All work and no play isn't the way to live life. Even my dad knows how to unwind.

Going back outside, I silently get back on the bike. We pull away off to who knows where, since Tripp obviously didn't take my request seriously. The day is winding down as we reach our destination. Pulling into the hotel, I'm stunned. In the distance I can see the lights of sin city. It's so close, yet so far.

Getting off the bike, I gather my things quietly, refusing to hide my disappointment. He could take us a little farther in and I would be there. We check in and take the elevator to our rooms. Tripp pulls Rex aside as I go in the room. Annoyed with Tripp, I go straight to the shower. When I finish, I come out to see Tripp laying clothes out on the bed, my clothes specifically.

"What the fuck are you doing?" Crossing my arms over my towel covered chest.

"We're going out. Wear this." He states, walking past me. He tugs at my towel, leaving me naked. He smacks my ass playfully before heading to the shower himself.

Going out? Where is he taking me tonight? Adrenaline rushes through me, as I dress in the short halter topped number with the matching red lace bra and thong Tripp picked out. Smiling as I think I'm glad I packed this.

Tripp exits the shower. His hair is down and his ink glistening as his skin is drying. Walking over to him, I reach up to touch him. He quickly stops me.

"You wanted to see Vegas. We're gonna see the lights and have a night in sin city. You start something now and we won't leave this room."

Tripp easily gets ready, pulling on his jeans, a t-shirt, boots, and his cut. Sass and Rex meet us in the hallway, ready to go out. As we approach the strip, the lights illuminate everything around us making it feel larger than life. I see why it's called sin city. The atmosphere sucks you in. I feel wild, reckless, and on fire to be as big as the buildings surrounding me.

Parking, we get off and make our way through the crowds. Tripp is tense beside me, his arm wrapped securely around my waist. Entering a nightclub, I'm ready to drink, dance, and let loose. Going to the bar first, Sass and I throw back a shot quickly. Lining up the next round, we are getting ready to let the fun begin. Tripp and Rex realize we plan to enjoy the evening for a while and order a beer each. We take our third shots, as a woman is already hanging on Rex.

Hello, do they not see that he's here with us? I get it, he's hot. Well, they're both hot because he and Tripp could easily pass for brothers, their family resemblance is striking. Rex has long hair like Tripp's but lighter in color. Where Tripp has golden flaked hazel eyes and no visible piercings, Rex has blue eyes and a tongue ring that peeks out when he talks. Do women typically throw themselves at Tripp like this? I'm sure they do.

Hell, I tried in my own subtle way the first time we met.

Tugging on my arm pulls me out of my musings. Sass is guiding me away from the bar and to the dance floor. Tripp grabs me, halting my forward progress. Pulling me up against him, he growls in my ear.

"Where do you think you're going?"

"To dance," I answer crossing my arms over my chest.

"No."

"No! You don't fucking own me Tripp. I'm going to dance with my best friend. We're in sin city. Drop the control. Let loose for one night. Quit taming the wild inside of you and let everything go. For tonight, be in the moment. Be here with me, Tripp." I go from anger to pleading. Truth is, I don't want to dance with anyone but Tripp.

Before I can finish my ramblings his mouth crashes onto mine in another one of those kisses that I get lost in. He consumes me with every touch, every kiss, and every word. I groan against him, liquid courage coursing through me as the earlier shots hit my system. Pulling Tripp to the dance floor with me, I grind against him as he kisses and sucks all over my neck. He's not really moving as much as he's keeping his hands and mouth all over me, as I keep the rhythm of the songs going with my hips. He allows me four songs before taking me back over to the bar. Leaning over, he gives Rex some sort of information, then Rex gives a slight nod before smiling at me. I blush as Tripp is now eagerly guiding me by the hand out of the club. He doesn't say anything. Have I pissed him off? Was someone there watching me? Are we in danger?

Unable to take one more second of her grinding her ass against me, knowing that skimpy red thong is begging to be removed, I decide we should leave. Rather than give her an opportunity to stay longer I pull her out with me giving no explanation.

As soon as I get the door shut and locked to our room, I scoop her up and back her into the wall as she wraps her legs around me. Pushing the scrap of fabric of her dress up over her ass, I pull hard on the small side thread of her thong, ripping it off. Rubbing my finger between her folds, she's drenched and ready for me. I bite into the skin of her shoulder as I undo my jeans, releasing my hard cock.

"Take me Talon. Now." She rocks against me.

Without another word, I sink into her. She trembles at the contact, crying out in satisfaction. Pounding into her with no restraint, her head falls back banging hard into the wall. I brace my hand behind her head, pushing her ass into the wall hard with every thrust.

"Harder, Talon." My name coming off her lips is the sound of pure bliss.

No longer able to hold back, I crush my lips to her mouth. Her nails are digging harshly into my shoulders even through my shirt. Taking my hand from her head, I take both her thighs and push her into the wall as I pull almost completely out and slam back into her. Thrust after thrust she's taking everything I'm giving her and demanding more. The buildup in both of our bodies is climbing higher and higher than anything I've ever felt before. She's squeezing my cock like no one has before. My piercing hits the spot. She's shaking so hard she's unable to hold herself onto me anymore. Wrapping one arm under her ass, the other to her back, I cradle her to me, as she milks my dick with her aftershocks. My balls tighten, my release closing in.

"Talon, you're worth everything." She whispers sending me over the edge, spilling my seed deep inside her. I've not been anything to anyone since my grand-parents died. Gently, I pull out. Setting her legs on the ground, I make sure she's stable before I remove her dress.

Leaning down, I kiss her before guiding us over to the bed as I remove my clothing. Laying her down, I stroke my thumb over her cheek. Having her naked under me, her words on repeat in my head, she's my angel. She's a heaven sent treasure, the light in the darkness, the calm in the chaos, and she's damn sure everything to me. We may have nothing beyond this ride, this night, but this is a moment that will forever be ours and one I will never forget.

Kissing her slowly, I run my hand down her side lightly, just grazing her skin. At her thigh, I work my way back up, she raises up seeking more contact. I kiss her neck, running my teeth gently against her shoulder, as I continue feathering her skin with soft touches. My cock quickly becomes hard again. Her hands are pulling at my hair as she's begging for more. I lick around her nipple, then blow, causing it to come to life further. Taking it in my mouth I suck hard.

"Talon, please," she whimpers.

Settling myself between her thighs, I enter her slowly. She's everything, this is everything. Gliding in and out of her, I take in every inch of her body. She's reaching up, trying to speed up seeking friction and release.

"Give me this, Doll. If tonight is everything, give it to me slow, baby. Take in every second and every breath with me, darlin'." And with that, I kiss her with everything I have in me.

There's nothing left of me that she doesn't own whether she knows it or not. No matter what the future holds, Doll will always have me in a way I will never be able to give to anyone else.

After treasuring her body for a few hours, we clean up in the shower and go to bed. How will I sleep without her when we return home? She belongs in my bed, in my arms, and with me. She deserves better than me, but I can't let go. She's gonna walk away at the end of this ride and I'm going to be forever lost, as she takes pieces of me with her.

CHAPTER
TWENTY EIGHT

I COULD GET USED TO THIS

Since Vegas, our ride has been one of ease and comfort, for the most part. Long days, back to back, on a bike are not comfortable and leave you stiff and sore. We've passed through Arizona, New Mexico, Texas, and Oklahoma. Tripp and I have since shared five nights of passion. He's even adjusted some of the accommodations to ensure we have our own private room. I can't get enough of this man.

The more I get to know him, the more I crave everything about him. I find myself looking forward to our evenings alone. He's taken my body through highs I've never felt before. It's more than sex though. We talk every night as he holds me close.

He shares little pieces of himself with me each day. He's told me how my dad made him get serious. My dad taught him not only how to run a club but to run a business.

The love he has for his grandparents. His mom took off the first time when he was only days old. His grandparents stepped in and took care of him. When his mom came back months later, they tried to give her the space to be his mom. According to his Aunt, his mom was young and she didn't have the patience to raise a rambunctious little boy and would take out her frustrations on him. He was just a toddler. His grandparents made the hard decision to put his safety first and kicked her out to save him further abuse after she broke his arm when he was two years old. There are so many pieces to the puzzle that make up Talon Ward Crews. Every little detail adds to the depth of my feelings for this man.

Stopping at a truck stop for dinner, Sass and I head in first to use the restroom and get a table. Just like every other truck stop in America, it has a gas station, open area for kiosks to sell a multitude of items from cell phones to truck accessories. There are showers inside the restroom, an internet café, and a full restaurant serving everything from Chinese, to Mexican, to Pizza. We settle ourselves into a booth while we wait for the guys to finish pumping gas.

"Okay girl, I love seeing you happy, but damn I miss our girl time." A sad expression is in her eyes.

"I know Sass. I can't help it. You know when we get back home this is all over for me." I say fighting to keep my tears at bay.

"Doll, are you prepared to let him go?"

"What choice do I have? Prepared for it, hell no. I'll deal with it when the time comes. There is no other option but to let him go." I reply, looking across the table at her trying to reassure myself that I can walk away from Tripp at the end of this ride.

"You love him, don't you?" Pausing, I'm unsure if I'm ready to answer this question.

"Yes." I whisper. My admission settles on my chest like a pallet of bricks. How does someone prepare to say goodbye to the first person to make them feel truly alive? When the time comes I'll have no choice but to say goodbye. Tripp's life is in Catawba, not at the coast. I may be accepting of his lifestyle, but that doesn't mean I actually fit into his life.

Someone touching my hair, tucking it behind my ear, brings me out of my musings. Looking up, I'm met with crystal blue eyes. The man before me is handsome enough and his confidence makes him all the more attractive. He's tall with broad shoulders, and the build of a working man. His blonde hair is not long but definitely shaggy. Any other time, I'd be ready to turn on the charm.

"Hello, beautiful." He speaks breaking into a grin that shows his perfectly straight teeth.

Before I can respond, he's being yanked backwards away from me. I watch as Tripp lets the stranger loose.

"She's taken fucker." Tripp shoves the guy.

"No ring on her finger, she didn't tell me to leave." The men are eyeing each other.

"I'm telling you she's fuckin' taken. Walk away while you can still manage to walk." Something in Tripp's tone let me and the man know this isn't an idle threat.

With one last look over his shoulder at me, the stranger walks away. Tripp slides in beside me, draping his arm around my shoulders like nothing happened.

"What the fuck was that?" I ask, pissed off at his macho display of ownership.

"He had no business over here. It's been handled. Moving on," Tripp says looking at me with what I see to be a mix of possessiveness and pride.

"I'm capable of sending someone away, Tripp." Knowing I'm playing with fire, but too irritated to care, I add, "or giving him my phone number."

Leaning in, Tripp whispers, "Last night, was my cock not the one filling your pussy so deep you could feel it from your head to your toes? Is it not my name you call out as you come? You think he's man enough to give you what you need? Darlin', do you think that fucker could handle having your nails rake his skin to the point you draw blood? All because you're so lost in the sensation, you can't stop yourself. Then, by all means, go give him your number."

My expression is one of heated desire and surprise as he moves out of the booth waving a gesture of come on. Thinking about the waterfall scratches down Tripp's back, I begin to realize Tripp causes me to get lost in him every time we're together. I've never been so consumed in passion that I've scratched someone hard enough to mark their skin.

He's challenging me. In case he hasn't figured it out, this bitch doesn't back down, fucker. Time to learn that real quick. Sliding out of the booth, I'm standing up. I take two steps before Tripp reaches out to grab me.

"Think about what you're doing. I don't play fuckin' games. You want him, go get him. I don't share, Doll. You go after him, we're done." He releases me. His stare is one of loss and a new distance between us.

Once again, Tripp has me on a rollercoaster of emotions. On one hand, it's nice that he says I'm taken. On the other, we've made no commitments to one another. I'm perfectly capable to send someone away on my own, that was my point. I never intended for it to be such a serious matter.

Sitting back down, I say nothing further. I've messed things up. Know your place, Doll. Damn it, I know how bikers are. Some people may find it degrading, but it's not like that. To stake a claim that I'm taken means I'm his. He will take care of me, protect me, and be there for me.

Our waitress comes over, smiling at Rex as she takes our orders. Sitting here, I watch as Sass is fidgeting nervously. What's going on with her? Is she upset about what transpired between Tripp and me? I don't know what I think of what's going on between us much less understand what it looks like to everyone around us. I'm sure she's homesick because I feel it too. I don't have to wonder long as she looks over at Tripp and asks.

"Have you heard from Tank by chance?" That is what's on her mind, what she's left behind. The longing on her face as she asks shows she is desperate for even a crumb of acknowledgement from Tank.

There is a flash of sadness that blinks across Tripp's face as he shares a knowing glance with Rex. He stiffens beside me as he responds.

"No, Sass. I haven't talked to Tank." She seems to sense they are hiding something.

"Look guys, I'll be honest. I've been texting and

calling Tank on the burner phones. Usually I can reach him at least once a day. It's a simple reassurance he's okay and for him to know we're okay. I haven't been able to speak to him or get a response from a text back in more than a week. Do you know something?" Her concern is genuine.

"Sorry, Sass, I don't know anything." The somberness of his tone has me on alert. There is definitely more to this. Tripp won't lie, he's said that many times over. What is he leaving out?

The saddened expression on my best friend's face hurts my heart. She has deep feelings for Tank, on what level I don't know. His safety is important to her. His friendship has always been one she's kept close. Regardless of their hookup and subsequent fighting, she still needs that connection with him.

The rest of our meal passes in strained but casual conversation. Tripp doesn't touch me once. The weight of what's gone wrong weighs heavily on my heart. Getting back on the bikes, we leave to find our place for the evening while here in Arkansas.

T ension rolls off me in waves. The situation with Doll today reminds me soon enough this will be done. Only a fool would get comfortable and make something out of this. She wants to fuck around, fine, moving on. She didn't go to him though. Wait and see how things play out between us has been my recent thoughts, but this has been a good reality check to remember there's no real future between us.

Once we all get checked into our rooms, I call Rex out into the hallway. Leaving him there to keep a watch over Doll and Sass, I go downstairs. Needing space, I stay in the parking lot sorting things on my bike. An hour later, I'm no more at ease than I was before.

Going back upstairs, I nod to Rex to say thanks for watching out, and head inside my room. Doll is curled up on the bed facing away from me. Deciding not to face anything, I go straight to the bathroom and shower. When I come out, Doll is sitting up in the bed waiting for me.

"Are you mad at me?" She asks with sadness in her voice and a look of dejection on her face.

Moving over to her, I climb into bed. Lying down, my head propped on a pillow up against the headboard of the bed. Pulling her into my arms, I lay her leg across me and rest her head on my chest. Running my hands through her hair I contemplate how to explain myself.

"I'm not mad, Doll. We both have a lot going on right now. Things are stressful. It's not you, okay."

She nods her head against me. Her fingers tracing over my tattoos like she's come to do every night when we lay in bed talking just like this. I've found it unwinds me and I sleep better after our chats.

"Something's wrong with Tank, isn't there?" She asks.

"Doll, let it fuckin' go." She looks up at me. The depths of her blue eyes draw me in.

"He means a lot to Sass. I know the code, Tripp. I get that there are times you can't tell me things, but Tank is important to my best friend. Is he okay?"

"Doll. You need to go to sleep."

Not telling her what's going on is killing me. I won't lie to her. It's not club business or information that would harm her, but I can't tell her about Tank. She would feel obligated to tell Sass. I may not know Sass well, but I know her enough to know she'd flip her shit. It's not something we need on this trip.

Things are safe and settled back home. Telling Sass now, she'd want to be on the first plane home and Doll to go with her. Roundman gave me the all clear to head home. I could put the girls on a plane, I'm sure. Selfish bastard that I am, I'm not ready to ride without Doll yet.

My business and my club need me back in North Carolina. The quicker I get back the sooner things will fall back into place. I should be walking away from Doll, putting space between us. I can't though. Thinking of it, I pull her tighter against me. Kissing the top of her head, I continue playing in her hair until she finally falls asleep.

ACCEPTANCE

Waking up with Tripp is a calming deep inside of me. No matter how hard I try to stay awake, when I'm in Tripp's arms I find the worries wash away as I drift off to sleep. This morning, I'm slightly unnerved. Tripp's avoidance at answering questions about Tank last night lets me know something is going on. My anxiety is in overdrive about all the boys back home. I wanted to question him further when we settled in for the evening, but didn't get any real answers. As he stroked my hair, the sound of his heart beating under me, and the comfort of his hold, I couldn't stay awake long enough to push the issue.

Not much is said as we head out for the day. We cross into Kentucky. Instinctively, I know we're headed to Bowling Green. We've met up with the boys of Heaven Hill MC before.

Pulling in, I see we are staying in a hotel that's in their territory. Passing through on a run, our club has stayed here before. Getting off the bike, I stretch. My body is aching from the hours on the bike. We check in and shower.

Taking my cues from Tripp, I keep my distance. Really, I want to push him on the bed and ride him, giving us both the opportunity to release all the pent up frustrations and unshared emotions between us. He's not showing any signs of being in that kind of mood. Instead, he seems restless, almost like a caged animal. Maybe that's why he's named Tripp, he doesn't like when things get routine or common. I've become common to him and he's ready for a change of scenery. I'm sitting on the bed as Tripp is staring out the window, when a knock at the door breaks our silence.

Going to the door, I open it to find Rex and Sass on the other side.

"Let's go grab a beer, man." Rex says as Sass nods

her agreement. Tripp looks over to me. A strange look comes across his features before he agrees we need to get out.

We're at a local dive. It's a small, crowded bar and one that's definitely crawling with Heaven Hill members. The space is full with pool tables to the right, a modern digital jukebox on the back wall between some dartboards. A few tables and a bar to the left, the restrooms are off the back wall, as well as, what I assume to be, their stock room.

Going straight to the bar, we order four beers. No taps here, take your liquor straight or your beer in a bottle the bar keep tells us. I like it. It's small and a reminder of hanging out back home in one of the local places.

We aren't there an hour and Rex is off with some barfly in the bathroom after we watched them devour each other openly for a good twenty minutes. At one point, I was sure Rex was going to take her right there in the chair. She came over to say hi, I never caught her name before he pulled her on his lap and started making out with her. Since her mouth was full of his tongue there was no point in asking her name, she wouldn't be able to answer. Hell, the way they're going at it, I'm surprised the bitch can breathe. That tongue ring of his must be fun to play with.

A biker with long black hair waves Tripp over. He's

a Heaven Hill boy, so Sass and I stay put. Know your place Doll, I remind myself. If the other biker wanted us in the conversation he would've approached the table, not nodded for Tripp to join him. Leaving me and Sass to our own accord, I sit back, taking a pull on my beer.

"You okay, Sass?" She shrugs her shoulders. Taking a drink herself before replying, she seems more determined now.

"I talked to my dad. He said Tank's not avoiding me, but unable to talk to me. Fuck 'em all. My dad's even sticking up for the bastard blowing me off now. It is what it is. I've talked to Nick a few times. He's waiting for me to get back. He wants to take me out on a real date as soon as we get home. After all the traveling, I'm ready for something normal. I want to feel safe. Nick is secure."

"Nick is not Tank, Sass. Nick can't give you the rush you need in life."

"Tank is my friend. He'll always be my friend. The older we get and the more we deal with, the more I don't want this. Hell, I can't even call my fuckin' friend right now and him answer me. It's not for me, Doll. My question is….Doll, is this for you? Can you handle Tripp going on transports and not being able to reach him?" She asks, but before I can answer another Heaven Hill member approaches. I don't catch his name as he snakes his arm around my shoulders. I brush him off me.

"Oh don't be shy. The women who come here, come to hook up. Let's go, baby, I'll be gentle the first time." He has a seedy grin spreading across his face.

"Not these women." I say gesturing to Sass and myself. "We're not here to hook up. I'm here with someone."

The cocky bastard continues. "You've got no property patch. In these parts you're fair game, no need to be a prude, we can share. I can satisfy you and your friend. The man you came with can even watch."

Tripp approaches. His face serious, but I can tell he's not sure what's going on since the man isn't touching me anymore and is casually leaning over the table. Standing, I reach out, grabbing Tripp by the waist and pull him to me. Snaking one hand up around his neck, I bring his face down to mine and kiss him. When I pull away, the serious look in his face has changed to heated desire. I tuck myself into him as I look over at the stranger.

"Like I said, I'm here with someone. I'm no bar bitch, so move the fuck on."

Anger passes over his face at my tone with him. I'm sure very few women have given him lip before. When his eyes make their way to Tripp, he throws his hands up in defeat. I can hear him muttering as he passes us by.

"Not worth the hassle, plenty of other pussy."

"You okay?" Tripp asks, now understanding what happened. I wrap my arms around him tightly, resting my head on his chest.

"Perfect now, babe." I answer, relaxing in the moment. For the first time in my life, it felt good to say I was someone other than Roundman's Doll.

We hang out for a little while longer as I meet Tyler, Heaven Hill MC VP. He's the biker that called Tripp over earlier. I'm introduced to Liam, the club Prez and his ol' lady Denise. We meet a few other Heaven Hill members before we leave for the night. It was comforting to be in Tripp's arms all night. If I was sitting, then it was on his lap. If I was standing, then it was with his arm around my waist and his hand down in the back pocket of my jeans cupping my ass cheek. I'm not used to having someone on me like that, and if it had been anyone else, it would have annoyed the shit out of me. With Tripp, though, shit felt right. It felt good, so much so, I could spend my lifetime in that man's arms, by his side and never get enough of him.

Waking with Doll tangled in me after a night making her body tremble beneath me is a happiness I've never had. As a kid, my grandpa always talked about the love he and my grandma shared. Every moment he had with her was a treasure. He always told Rex and me, *"Treasure your women when you find them. Make sure your woman knows that she's the center of your world. There is no better feeling than waking up to the person who accepts everything about you. The moment she climbs into your arms, when she seeks you out as her comfort, her protector, and her love. You carry that moment for a lifetime."*

Last night, Doll came to me. She could've shut the guy down without claiming herself as mine, but she didn't. Pop's was right, there's no better feeling than waking up with Doll after she's climbed into my arms. Choosing me, she's choosing me.

The thoughts of having her like this for my lifetime brings warmth deep inside of me. Today, I bring her back to my house. Tonight, I will have her in my bed. Tomorrow, I return her to her world. Tomorrow, I say goodbye to my lifeline. Tomorrow, I say goodbye to my heart because when I leave, I leave it with her. As much as it's going to suck, I'm going to leave her. It's going to crush me, but I'm going to walk away. The other thing Pop's always said, *"Don't give your woman unnecessary pain."* My life would be unnecessary pain for Doll.

I have all of today, tonight, and tomorrow's drive to make sure Doll knows she's my treasure. Starting in this moment, when I gently rub the back of my hand against her face. Knowing she's asleep, I share what's on my mind.

Whispering to her, "You're everything, Doll. You're the good in me. When the days get long, you'll be what pulls me through. I'm gonna let you go, but I'm always gonna carry you with me." I watch her breathing.

No longer able to contain myself, I move to kiss her forehead. Rolling her over, I kiss her cheek, then her neck. She's waking up under me. I take my time trailing kisses over her neck and collarbone. She reaches up, running her fingers through my hair. Our eyes meet. The words are on the tip of my tongue, but unable to come out. I see the love this woman has for me in the depths of those piercing blue eyes. Does she see what I feel for her? Does she see the man behind the bike? Rather than speak the words, I spend my morning making love to her body. Taking in every second of this and committing it to my memory in a way to last me a lifetime.

Tomorrow, she'll be home. Tomorrow, our ride will

end. Tomorrow, I'll be man enough to walk away. We're in too deep. I never should've let this happen, emotions and entanglements are things I don't do. Today, I'll give her all of me. Today, I'll take everything I can. Today, I'll let my weakness for her consume me.

ONE LAST NIGHT TOGETHER

For a moment, I almost slipped and told Tripp how I feel about him. What we shared this morning goes beyond orgasms. He claimed a piece of me that I don't want back. I gladly walk away knowing a piece of me is with him. We get up and shower together. It's like Tripp can't get close enough to me. I take in every second of it, knowing we are headed home and our future is uncertain.

We're on the road again. Crossing over into North Carolina, my chest tightens. I don't know what tomorrow brings. Pulling in to Tripp's house, I'm so grateful to be off the bike. My body is sore from spending almost a month on the back of a motorcycle.

Once we unpack the bikes, Rex is itching to go out. Tripp looks at me, trying to gage whether we're going out with Rex or not. Deciding it would be nice to hang out with his boys, I get ready so we can go. It's strange riding in a truck with Tripp. Sass is riding with us and Rex took his bike. The danger has been eliminated. I'm sure his plans for the night don't involve returning home.

Walking into the bar, I look over and see Tessie working tonight. Tripp is stopped immediately by one of his club members wanting to chat. Sass and I leave him there and make our way to Tessie. She smiles and places our beers in front of us as we settle onto the stools.

"Good to have y'all back." She smiles.

The last time we were here, we got to know her a little bit and she's genuinely a nice person. If given the time to hang out, I know we could be good friends. We're chatting away, catching up on the drunken escapades she's seen while we were away. Sass and I told her about seeing the sights and the weather while on our trip. Tessie doesn't know why were gone and she's doesn't need to either.

Tripp comes up behind me, his hands coming around my waist as he drops his head down to my neck. His hair is down and brushes against my bare shoulder causing me to shudder.

"This is a first." Tessie says with a smile that lights up her entire face. "Never thought the day would come where Tripp was tamed. There's hope for all you Hellions yet."

Surprisingly, Tripp hears her, but doesn't deny being tamed. My heart wants to latch on to this and go with it. My head knows it's unwise to have any expectations or desires outside of what Tripp is willing to give me today, and today only.

Rex has been wondering around the bar. For once he's ignoring all the barflies though and only talking to his brothers. Hmm… I wonder what's going on with him. Tripp is casually wrapped around me, never letting go as his boys come and go, stopping to catch up before leaving. Rex makes his way over to us. Initially, I think it's for Tripp, but when he turns and goes behind the bar, I'm surprised.

Turning around, Tessie runs right into Rex's chest. Before any of us register what's going on, Rex is leaning down and kissing Tessie. Her arms go around his neck as he's pulling her up against him. I don't know what to think. Tessie told me they have a history. This is not something in the past though, no this is a kiss shared between lovers. Quickly becoming a moment that they should consider getting a room. He pulls away abruptly. Her face is flushed. He knew what he was doing getting her worked up with that kiss. Apparently, incredible kissing is in the Crews genes because one kiss from Tripp can melt me into a puddle. The look on Tessie's face makes it apparent she's become a puddle. Slapping her jean clad ass as he tells her that he'll meet her at her place after work and walks back over to the room in the back with the pool tables. Well, I know what he'll be doing later.

Tessie's shock is apparent as Rex leaves her standing there. She shakes her head at me as Tripp is whispering in my ear his own surprise at Rex's behavior. He's the man of no repeats, except maybe where Tessie is concerned.

After exchanging numbers with Tessie to keep in touch, we leave the bar. Back at Tripp's, Sass immediately takes off to Rex's room. We go to Tripp's room. I watch as he removes his boots, socks, and then his cut and shirt. The ripple of his abs, the details of his ink, and the 'v' of his hips, and every inch of this man's body is consuming me. Walking up to him, I remove my shirt and jeans as I go.

Standing before him in my black satin bra and panties, I look up at him. Reaching out, I grab for his jeans, unbuttoning them. I unzip them and push them off with his boxers. He's naked in front of me as I drink him in.

"You want something, Doll?" I nod my head in agreement as I bite my bottom lip. "Then take it babe."

Take it I do. I push him down on the bed. Stepping back, I stand in front of him. I do a circle roll of my hips as I turn around putting my back to him. I slowly hook my thumbs into my panties. Teasingly, I remove my undergarments. Turning back around to face him, naked, I cup my own breasts, pulling at my erect nipples. Looking down, his cock is rock hard and standing at attention. Climbing over him, I slide onto his shaft. I still for a moment, taking in the sensation of him filling me to the hilt. Looking into his eyes, I feel joined with him completely, our souls entwined. As I lean over and kiss him, I begin to move. Slowly, I ride him. Leaning up, he takes my nipple in his mouth, sucking. I clinch my core around him as the energy zings through me. His hand comes down. His fingers finding our joined bodies, he rubs my clit, pushing me higher to ecstasy. I'm trying to stay in control here, but the more he touches me the more I want to let go and release everything. I'm so close, but I'm holding back. I want this to last because I know tomorrow he's going to leave me and not look back.

When he's had enough of my pace and my tight rein on my orgasm, he rolls us over. Now he's in charge.

Pinning my arms above my head, he begins pulling all the way out and slowly sliding back in as his piercing grazes up the front wall of my core, causing me to tremble. He leans down, breathing heavily on my ear as he continues to keep his strokes in me slow and measured. Sensing my overwhelming need for release, he kisses his way to my breasts, as he finally increases our pace; no longer teasing my impending climax, he's now slamming into me. He comes down and sucks my nipple then nips it sending me over the edge. As my aftershocks milk him, he follows me, his warm seed exploding into my womb. He pulls out of me and holds me silently for the longest time as we both come down from our orgasmic bliss. Eventually he goes to the bathroom, returning with a washcloth to gently clean me up. He curls up in bed with me. Laying there in his arms, I don't want this night to ever end.

Holding Doll in my arms, it's time to have the conversation I've been avoiding. Sighing, I don't know where to begin.

"Don't say goodbye, Tripp, okay." Doll starts before I have to. Her head is on my chest as she traces my tattoos with her finger. "I know what tomorrow is. I'm well aware this was a fling. Let's just enjoy the time we have and tomorrow we part as friends."

Friends, the word cuts deep coming from her. "Doll, I don't want to hurt you. My life is surrounded in chaos. I'm never home. Hell, I can get a call at noon and be on the road by two, gone for weeks at a time. That's no way for you to have to live."

"*Hell raisers demanding extreme chaos.* That's what my dad always says about the Hellions. I get it Tripp, okay. Don't ruin tonight by making this about why we won't work. I know your lifestyle. I also realize we live five hours apart. Now is not the time for the explanations for something I know and accept. Enjoy what we have while we have it."

"I'm always here for you, Doll. One call, that's all it takes. I programmed my number in your regular cell phone that's now back in your purse. Day or night, you need me, you fuckin' call."

"Okay, Tripp." She whispers as she snuggles closer. Much more and she'll be sleeping on top of me tonight. "Tripp, we haven't used condoms. I'm clean and on birth control. Since I don't know when I will see you again, is there anything I need to worry about."

I knew she was on birth control, I saw them in her

bags, and I've never worried about her having anything. "Doll, I've never been with anyone else not wrapped. I knew you were on the pill. With you, I can't seem to hold back and I don't want to. Nothing between us ever, baby." I reply, pulling her tighter and hoping to give her the knowledge she's someone different and special to me.

Not knowing what else to say, I kiss the top of her head and lay back. We lay together lost in our own thoughts for I don't know how long. She continues tracing my tattoos. When she thinks I'm asleep, I hear her whisper.

"Nothing between us ever, baby." She pauses, in an even lower whisper, "I love you, Talon."

I feel the wet warmth of the tears, as they fall on my chest. Remaining still, I let her think I'm asleep. I don't want to tarnish the memory, the moment of hearing her say she loves me. If she knows I'm awake, she'll try to back track. Saying goodbye is hard enough. Having her try to take back those words would kill me inside.

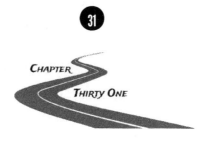

CHAPTER THIRTY ONE

HOME SWEET HOME

Waking up, my eyes are puffy from crying into Tripp's chest last night after he fell asleep. As I move around, I realize Tripp's already out of bed. Guess I need to get used to waking up alone. It's time to put my big girl panties on. He never promised me anything. By dinnertime, I'll be back on the compound. Sass and I decided we didn't want to live in the condo anymore, after the camera thing. We're staying in one of the duplexes until we decide where we want to move next.

We pack up our stuff. Rex is staying behind to catch up on stuff while Tripp makes the drive home. Holding in my tears, I load my bag into his truck. If I had known yesterday would be my last ride with Tripp, I would've held on tighter or something. This feels awkward to know our time is over.

Sass settles herself in the back of the crew cab Silverado. Tripp climbs in, once we're on the road, he takes my hand in his and spends the entire drive rubbing circles over my hand with his thumb. God, this sucks. I don't want this to end.

Outside of the chatter Sass and I share about housing possibilities the ride is relatively quiet. Tripp's phone rings quite a few times, some he answers, some he doesn't. Pulling into the compound, my chest hurts. Physical pain consumes every inch of me. Is this what a panic attack feels like? I can't do it; I can't let him go.

A few of the guys are standing out front with my dad, Danza, and Frisco as we get out. Tripp grabs our bags as I rush over to hug my dad. I get the usual grunt response. He's not the most affectionate man. Before I can say anything else, I hear Sass ask her dad.

"Where's Tank?" All the guys tense as Danza responds. Everything I thought I knew changes in an instant.

"Sass, there was an incident."

Putting her hand on her hip, her face reddening in anger and frustration, "what the fuck do you mean there was an incident? Where the hell is Tank?"

"Sass, calm the fuck down." Danza says trying to tame the outburst building in his daughter. Tripp is suddenly beside me, his arms wrapped around my waist.

"He's in the hospital. He's been shot. He's in a coma and it's not good." Danza says immediately dropping his head in anguish.

My knees give out from under me, and the only thing holding me up is Tripp. Sass falls into Danza's chest crying. Leaning back into Tripp, I realize he knew.

"You fucking knew." I say turning to face him as he drops his hands from my waist. "You fucking knew and you didn't tell her."

My dad steps over to me to pull my shoulder back. "It was my call not to tell y'all, not his."

Hurt and scared for Tank, I can't see past my tunnel vision that I was blindsided. All this time, Tripp knew. Yet, he let us walk into this. I need to get away from all of this. I need to get my best friend to Tank. We need to see him; she needs to see him.

"Where's my fuckin' car?" I scream walking over to Sass. Tripp reaches out for me and I shrug him off.

"Get the hell off me. Don't you dare touch me! You

knew damn it. You fuckin' knew. All of you fuckin' knew."

Sass is crying on my shoulder as she starts to straighten up. She's pulling herself together, realizing we need to get out of here and go see him. He's one of the brother's we're both closest to, especially Sass. My dad pulls my car keys out of his pocket. I grab them from him.

"What hospital?" I ask. Frisco steps up. Reaching out to grab my shoulders, I pull away from him. I'm pissed at all these shit-heads for keeping this from us.

"Doll, calm down. I get your fuckin' pissed. I'll tell you where he is but you gotta calm down, honey."

"Calm down. What the hell?" Sass says staring each one of these large men down. "Tell me where the fuck he is so I can see for my damn self what '*it doesn't look good*' means."

Frisco takes my keys, offering to drive us and fill us in on the ride. Without another word to anyone, we turn and climb in my Camaro. To hell with all of them, there was no reason to keep all of this from us.

W atching Doll walk away crushes me. She never looks back as she gets in the car and leaves. No goodbye, no see ya around. No, she got in her car and left. I spend a few minutes talking general business with Roundman. Handing off the girls bags to a prospect to put in their place to stay, I'm officially done with this task.

"You alright, Tripp? Anything you need to tell me?" Roundman asks, looking at me as if he knows everything. He's looking at me like he reads me. He knows I fucked his daughter. I don't like feeling exposed.

"Nah, Roundman. I'm tired, gotta get back to Catawba." I say getting ready to turn and leave. His voice stops me.

"She'll come around, Talon. Give it time. Then you and I will have a talk." Without another word, he turns away from me, conversation over.

I climb in my truck, absolutely deflated, and make the return drive home. It's after midnight before I pull in. Ten hours on the road round trip, and all the emotions and craziness of the day I want nothing more than to shower and sleep. Climbing in my bed, her scent engulfs me. Knowing I won't be able to sleep, I head down stairs and crash on the couch. Managing a few hours of shuteye, even if it was filled with dreams of Doll, is better than none.

Morning comes. My first morning in a month without her, loneliness is already creeping in. Calling to check on Tank, I find out the girls stayed at the hospital all night by his bed. The doctors can't say if he's going to pull through or not. Life's short, too short. If I don't make it to see another day, I experienced the unconditional love of a woman once and that's more than some people ever see.

Heading into my office the paperwork is piled up. Rex walks in with coffee in hand.

"You okay?" He asks sitting in the chair in front of my desk.

"Yeah, why wouldn't I be?" Not looking up from my desk, I continue the mundane task of sorting papers.

"I don't know fucker, the broad you're in love with is gone for good. After a month of steady pussy, that you couldn't get enough of, you're left with your hand and some fantasies."

"Fuck you, Rex. You ever talk about her pussy again, family or not, I'll beat the shit outta you." I look up this time to find his face full of amusement, as mine is full of rage.

"You got it bad, man."

"Shut the fuck up and get to work." I throw a set of keys at him for his next job.

"Jolene wants us over for dinner tonight. Says it's important."

"Alright, what time?"

We map out the rest of the day so we can make it to his mom's for dinner. Not how I planned to end my day, but whatever. Catching up keeps me busy and before I know it, Rex is walking in reminding me we have plans.

Arriving at my grandparent's house, my gut twists. This is the place full of my happiest memories. Well, my happiest memories before Doll. Pop's was always big on memories and making moments last. Aunt Jolene has the house now. She's given it the modern upgrades, and added her own personal flare. Walking in the front door, I hear two female voices. Going past the living room that's painted turquoise with a beach theme that includes huge sand dollars on the wall, we head to the sound of the voices. I stop in my tracks at the woman beside my aunt, the resemblance is uncanny.

"Talon." The woman says looking at me with the same eyes I see in the mirror every day.

Her hair is lighter than mine. She's tiny. Only five feet tall or so, skinny, and her face full of wrinkles. Time has not done her well. She looks fragile and broken. She may only be forty-nine years old, but she looks to be in her late sixties.

"Lucy." I reply as the ice runs through my veins.

"I'm glad you remember who I am." She says never looking away from me as Rex goes and hugs his mother.

"What the fuck do you want?" Might as well cut to the chase, she's not here for well wishes.

"I'm moving back home. I want to get to know you son."

I laugh. I can't help myself, after all this time. "Nothin' to know. I go to work, I come home. I got a club that's my family. When I need to fuck, I got bitches to fuck. Nothin' more to tell. Nothin' more you need to know. I'm a grown man. You want to know me? That time was long before now."

"You've got a business. You've traveled. I want to know about all that. Do you have a wife? Do I have grandchildren?"

"Some things come too little, too late. You want to move in here with Aunt Jolene, fine. Y'all sort that shit out. I'm outta here."

And without another word, I leave. Tomorrow, I pull out for a transport. I'll find a way to stay gone for a while.

IT'S BEEN A WHILE

Forty-eight days. That's how long I've been back home. Forty-eight days that I've picked up my phone to call or text Tripp and haven't done it. No one will tell Sass and I everything, but what we gather is the Hellions went to Delatorre's warehouse. A fight ensued. Delatorre and his crew were eliminated. We lost four guys and Tank's in the hospital fighting for his life, while machines take each calculated breath for him. I've paid my respects to the families of our lost brothers.

I'm in my office staring at the computer screen. I could email him, or should I text him? Leaving so many things unsaid between us, over time, is pulling at me. The more I think on it, the more I decide not to contact him. He knows my number, and he hasn't called me. The pain cuts deep, the hole in my heart growing with every passing day that Tripp's not in my life. Is he okay? Is he on a transport?

Brought out of my musing by my office door opening, I look up to see the bitch I've been waiting for. Standing, I walk straight up to her. Balling my hand into a fist, I rear back and punch her in the face. She stumbles back at the unexpected force. Immediately, her hand goes up to clutch her rapidly swelling eye. I missed her nose. Damn, I'd love to break that. Give her a bump that will make her think of me every damn time she looks in the mirror.

Frisco runs in from where he was outside. "Doll, what the fuck, babe?" He asks staring me down.

"She had it coming." I say shaking my, now sore, hand out. "Been waitin' to get a hold of her."

She looks at me, tears streaming down her face. "I deserve that and more. Doll, I'm-"

"Name's Delilah." I interject with my hand on my

hip now. "My friends and family call me Doll. You aren't my family and you sure as shit ain't my friend."

"Delilah, I'm sorry. Felix, he threatened Alyssa, she's Rachael's daughter. He wanted me to be friends with you, using Rachael as a connection. I couldn't do it, though. I pretended I was talking to you on the phone. When he told me he was bringing me to meet you at your office, I knew I was busted because you didn't know me. He beat the shit out of me and still made me come. I was supposed to talk to you while they were in the office, but I didn't want to put you in danger. I'm sorry, Delilah. I can't say that enough, but I was protecting my cousins and the people that mean the most to them. I did just enough that he would leave them alone and took the beatings for not drawing you in. I worked at the shipping yard with Ray and Zack. Delatorre offered me money to handle getting some shipments through. That was just the beginning. When he did a background check on me, he found my only remaining family. He tied Rachael to you. He wanted me to be a pawn in his game to push the Hellions to do more than transport. He wanted them to sell the drugs he's been shipping too. I got in too deep and I brought you down with me. I'm glad you're okay and I wish I could go back and change so many things."

This woman got her ass beat multiple times for me. A stranger. She let that man hurt her so that she wouldn't drag me into the mess. Loyalty like that is rare, but I'm still pissed. I can forgive, just not easily.

"I don't know what to say to you." My tone is now one that is calm and collected.

"You don't have to say anything. I needed to apologize to you. The trouble is gone. I'll be going home soon. I wanted to face you and tell you why."

Frisco steps up, pulling her against him, "Told you, babe, ain't goin' nowhere until the nightmares stop and you know you're safe."

He's my dad's age, she's my age. Yet, seeing them together doesn't seem awkward, rather it seems he's exactly what she needs. Frisco's wife left him years ago, saying he was never gonna grow up. He always took care of her, like the rock star situation. It wasn't enough and when it came to club or love, Frisco wouldn't walk away from the club. Do I want Amy Mitchell hangin' around? No. But after feeling the fear of Delatorre being after me, I can understand the need to help her be secure once again. Frisco will make sure she feels safe and get her back on her feet.

"Water under the bridge. You stay outta my way, I'll stay outta yours. You fuck over my club, I'll cut a bitch. Know that." I say before retreating to my dad's office. Okay, so I probably wouldn't cut her because I don't have it in me, but she doesn't know me well enough to know I'm bluffing.

Hearing the door open and close, I go back to my desk. Well, I guess if I can attempt to move past things and put up with Amy then I should face the situation with Tripp. Pulling my phone out, I type and this time I actually hit the send button.

Thinking of u. Take care Talon. <3 Doll

Deciding that waiting to see if he'll respond would kill me, I turn my phone off. He's moved on. Someone else is warming his bed. Hell, he may not recognize the number or given the way he left, he may not even respond.

Being on the road usually relaxes me. Not this time. I've made sure to stay gone as much as possible the last six almost seven weeks, since taking Doll home. It's done nothing to help my mood or keep Lucy off my back. She calls daily. I ignore them. She leaves messages. I've contemplated changing my number, but this is the number Doll has. If she needs me, I made a promise to be there.

On the last run, I met a chick named Danielle. Her

shoulder length black hair, her brown eyes, and her curves all reminded me she wasn't Doll. She was pretty enough, she wanted me bad, but in the end she wasn't Doll. I couldn't do it, so 'Dee' and I parted ways almost as quickly as we began. So, it's also been almost seven weeks since I've fucked. Although I'm not Rex, this has been a long fucking dry spell.

Pulling into my drop off point, I unhitch the trailer. Finding my hotel for the night, it's after eleven, and a bed's never been more inviting. Well, any bed with Doll is more inviting, but that's done. I fall into the same restless sleep I have every night. Consumed in dreams of her smile, her kiss, and each one ending in her walking away, it's the same dream night after night.

Getting up the next morning, I shower to try and bring life back into my exhausted body. Sitting on the bed, I turn my phone on so I can check in with Rex back home. The phone lights up as her name appears on my screen. Well, fuck me, she sent a message yesterday. Sending a quick reply, I type.

U need something?

What do I say? The only reason she should be reaching out to me is because she wants something. Before I have a chance to finish gathering my stuff, my phone pings alerting me to a new message, I look down to see it's her.

I need 2 know ur ok <3 Doll

Fine. U good?

I reply. And so it begins. We spend the rest of the day texting here and there. Soon, one day turns into one week. One week turns into one month, and now two months.

It's been almost four months since I've seen her now, and for the last three weeks, we've talked daily after we've been texting regularly. Tank is stable, but there is no guarantee he will ever wake up from the coma. Sass visits him all the time according to Doll.

Listening to her tell me about her day makes the long hours on the road manageable. I've never looked forward to talking to someone before. I'm heading back home tonight and Doll is supposed to be there when I pull in. I don't know where we go from here. Tonight though, she's gonna be in my bed where she belongs. In the morning we can sort out our shit once and for all.

CHAPTER

THIRTY THREE

NOT ENOUGH

Having had enough of only having phone time, I want to see Tripp. He's on his way in from a transport. I agreed to be at his house when he arrives home. Making the five-hour drive wasn't terrible. Stopping by his office, I plan to run in real quick and get the house key from Rex.

"Doll," he greets, stepping from behind the desk. Standing in front of me, he hands me the key. "I'll be out for the night so the house is yours." He adds with a wink.

"Thanks, Rex. It's good to see you." I say, getting ready to leave.

Something in Rex's face changes as I turn to see what has his attention. I'm lost on the little woman in front of me. Time has not treated her well, her skin looks like leather that hasn't been oiled. She's shorter than me, around five feet tall. Her clothing is well worn, having seen better days. Her hair is shoulder length golden color that looks brittle. Everything about this woman looks easy to break. She smells like alcohol and stale cigarettes. It's the middle of the day, why does she smell like she's spent her time in a night club or bar? My eyes come to meet hers. One look, my chest tightens as I recognize those eyes.

"Rex, when is Talon due back?" She asks. Her voice gravelly from what I assume to be too many years of smoking.

"Lucy, I can't tell you that." Rex says stiffening beside me.

"Then I'll just sit on the front porch of your house until he returns." Moving in closer to Rex and me as she speaks, I'm at a loss as to what to say or do. Tripp didn't tell me his mom was in town.

"Lucy now's not a good time. I'll talk to Tripp for

you, but honestly, you need to give him space." Rex says, as he's guiding her by the elbow to the door.

"No, I'm not leaving Drexel Devon Crews and you can't make me. Talon needs to talk to me. If I can fix this with him, then I can fix me, Rex. Y'all don't understand. I have to fix things with my son before I can fix myself." She pleads, now crying.

My heart breaking for her and for the man I love. His mom is a mess. The years of drinking and obvious guilt have made their marks.

"Give it time. Tripp will open up. You being around and wanting this is still fresh." I find myself saying before I realize it.

Shit! I've stuck my nose in something I shouldn't have once again. The look on Rex's face lets me know I crossed an unspoken boundary and Tripp will not like this.

"You Talon's woman?" She turns around to face me coming back toward me and away from the door.

"Doll, don't go there. This is between the two of them." Rex warns, reaching out to turn Lucy around to the door again.

Jerking out of his grasp, she faces me once again. "You tell my son, I love him. I'm sorry. I want to fix this. I'm sorry. Tell him that please. I'm sorry. I can't say it enough." Her words feel like they are more than drunken ramblings. They feel heartfelt and real.

Unable to control the tears now freely falling from my face, I can only nod my head in agreement. I hear Rex muttering cuss words under his breath as Lucy finally leaves. If only I could have a second chance to be with my mom. She's gone. I can't forgive anything even if she was to mess. Surely, Tripp can see that nothing can be that unforgivable. She's making the effort to be here that should count for something. He's got to talk to her.

Parking the truck in the back lot, I enter the office. Rex let me know earlier that Doll arrived safely. Walking in my office, I'm ready to sign off on this transport and get the hell home.

"Rex, you got everything covered for tomorrow?" I ask, signing the paperwork on my desk.

"Yeah man. Tripp, you need to know. Lucy was here today." Suddenly, carefree Rex is serious.

"What's she got to do with anything?"

"She was here while Doll was here." He says meeting my stare.

"Was she wasted?"

His face gave me all the confirmation I need. My mom can't lay off the booze. She's been out of control since I was born. According to Aunt Jolene, she was so young. Having a baby was overwhelming. My dad bailed on her. She was lost and went wild. Being too young to be responsible she blamed me, an innocent child, for every problem she had. When she started taking her frustrations and anger out on me, my Pop's stepped in and sent her packing. She had nowhere to go and sunk into a deeper hole. She's trying to get her life together, but feels like she can't do that without me. All these years later, she's still blaming me. Her problems still rest on my shoulders. Without my forgiveness, she can't move forward and get sober, she claims. At what point will she own her shit and fix herself?

"Doll react to it?" I ask as the tension builds inside of me. Doll had her mom when she was young. Maybe not long enough, but she had her from the beginning. Doll has always had Roundman. He's a rock, someone you can depend on.

"She's gonna try to fix it knowing Doll. Head's up man, she was cryin'. I tried to explain it, but Doll was muttering about her own momma. I don't know what you're walkin' in on at home. I'll be at Tessie's tonight if you need me."

Shocked by his choice of sleep arrangements, I'm quickly drawn out of my own problems.

"Man, why the fuck are you going to Tessie's? She's got Axel. He doesn't need to see you there. Tessie ain't like that, bringing men around her boy. You got her wrapped, damn it. She's incapable of tellin' you no, and has been for years. So, she ain't gonna tell you not to be around her boy. Pick a barfly. Hell, get a hotel. Don't go to Tessie's house."

"It's all good, Tripp. Axel will be at her mom's tonight. You know Tessie won't let me or anyone else near her kid. She knows the deal, it's all good. You get your ass outta here, your woman's home waitin'."

Rex and Tessie is something I'm not getting involved in. He's gonna fuck her over. That's their deal, I'll always be there to throw her an extra few bucks, but she gets her head and heart wrapped up in Rex, that's on her. We've known Tessie for a while now. She knows Rex better than most. This dance they're playing though, it ain't gonna end well for her.

Leaving the office, my excitement from earlier is now turning to anger. Lucy won't go away. Doll met my mess up of a mother. What am I coming home to?

Pulling up, my irritation is building more. Walking in, I'm expecting weird tension between us. I haven't seen Doll since she left without saying goodbye. Entering through my kitchen, she meets me at the entry to the living room. She looks amazing. She's in a navy blue, knee length dress with these red, fuck me heels. Her blonde hair is down with one side pinned back with a flower. The gloss on her lips makes me lose focus on everything but kissing her. Leaning down, I wrap my arm around her waist, pulling her into me. My other hand snakes through her hair as I crush my lips down on her. She moans against me, her body relaxing into my hold. Our tongues and lips in a tango, the passion is burning between us as I pull away.

"Hello Darlin', miss me?" The smile that comes across my face causes my breath to hitch. Damn, she's everything. Her hands come up on my t-shirt as she pulls at me.

"Kiss me, Tripp." She says looking up at me.

Leaning down, I whisper against her ear. "Say it."

"Kiss me, damn it." Doll demands.

"Not till you say you missed me." I say running my nose along her jawline.

"I missed you. Kiss me, damn it." Laughing, I take her head in both of my hands now.

Brushing my lips against hers, I slowly tease her. When she stomps her foot down in frustration, I devour her mouth. Pulling her out of the entryway and into the kitchen, I push her up against the kitchen wall. Having the wall behind her, she wraps one leg around me as she tries to climb up my body. My hands roam, cupping her ass as I rock her into my ever growing erection. I want nothing more than to take her to my room and fuck her until she can't walk in those fuckin' shoes. Gathering my self-control, I pull away. We're both breathing heavy as Doll looks at me. My forehead resting on hers, the depths of those crystal blue eyes consume me.

"Babe, I've been on the road. I need a shower and a meal. Then I'll give you everything you want, okay?"

She bites her bottom lip. Sexy as hell, I'm fucked. One of her legs still wrapped around mine and her hands fisted into my shirt. She's not letting go. Her face flushed in her want. Unable to resist, I use my tongue to sweep across her lips causing her to stop biting at her bottom lip so I could suck on it. When I pull away this time, she's smiling at me.

Fuck it. I lift her up as she wraps her legs around me. She's kissing my neck, reaching my ear she tugs at it gently with her teeth. Laying her back on my kitchen table, I push the bottom of her dress up and pull her panties off. My fingers immediately begin moving between her wet folds as she rocks into me moaning for more. She pushes herself to the edge of the table, and reaches for my belt. Quickly, she's released me. The look in her eyes, as I stare down at her, is one of heated, irresistible desire. She's taking another piece of me with her as I join my body to hers. Her tight cunt squeezing around me after so long is the real homecoming for me.

Never breaking eye contact, I look down at her. Watching as she tries to control her body and hold out. Reaching between us, I rub circles over her clit sending her over the edge. Unable to hold back any further, I release into her. Something about watching her lose all control under me pulls at my emotions. She's mine. For a moment, I keep us connected as I come down and kiss her with all the unsaid feelings between us. Pulling out, I tuck my dick in my jeans and bend down to retrieve her panties.

"Do you want me to cook for you?" She asks shyly, putting her panties back on and sliding off the table.

"No babe, we'll go out for dinner. You cookin' in my kitchen in those shoes will not motivate me to get a shower or get us fed."

A devilish smile comes across her face. "I can take the shoes off." She starts to step out of them.

"Oh no, you keep those shoes on." Leaning down to her ear, I breathe against her. "Later, I'm gonna fuck you for hours in Just. Those. Shoes." I feel her nod against me.

Pulling away without another word, I go take a very cold shower. She cleans herself up and my kitchen table. Just thinking of fucking her again, I'm getting hard. Doll is here. Damn, she twists me up in a way no one has before.

CHAPTER

THIRTY FOUR

I DON'T DATE

Tripp walks out in a charcoal gray shirt, jeans, and his motorcycle boots. His hair still wet from his shower is pulled back. The look on my face must have given away my appreciation because Tripp is smiling at me.

"Like what you see?" He says, stalking over to me.

"You clean up well." I smile up at him. He places a

quick kiss on my forehead then takes my hand and leads me out to his truck.

We get to the restaurant, are seated, and order. Catching up over our meal, I update him on Tank and my day to day stuff. As much as I want nothing more than to be home, lost in bed with Tripp, I need to talk to him about his mom. I don't want to ruin our evening, but I can't get her out of my thoughts. As we're waiting for our dessert, he seems to notice my head is all over the place.

"What are you over there lost in thought about?"

"Your mom." I answer honestly. Sadness quickly washes over both of us. Damn it, Doll, learn to shut your mouth.

"Lucy isn't your problem Doll." His eyes meeting mine with a stern stare.

"Hear me out, please." I pause giving him a chance to stop me. His silence allows me to continue. "My mom is gone. I can't know what you feel because I had her for a while, but I do know what loss feels like. The difference is you don't have to have the loss. People can change. Give her a chance. Don't look back and miss something great because of pride or inability to forgive."

"Doll," He starts.

Cutting him off, I continue, the tears prick at the back of my eyes. "Life is short. Tomorrow isn't promised. Look at Tank. At least give her a chance to say what she needs to say before you close her out completely."

"Doll." He starts again, but I put my hand up in protest.

"I don't claim to know her or what you've been through. She needs help, and maybe you could give her what she needs to get that help. She had you young and weak. I don't think she knows herself, Tripp. I was given my dad to be strong for me. Maybe no one has been strong for her." A single tear escapes as I whisper my last sentence. "You were strong for me with Delatorre. Be strong for your mom and help her."

Without a word, he moves to be beside me. His arms wrap around me, pulling me into him. Something has changed. He pulls back, wipes my tear away and whispers, "okay" before he kisses my forehead.

Feeling at peace, I smile at him. Taking my hands, I place them on each of his cheeks and pull him into me for a soft, slow kiss. The waitress bringing our dessert interrupts us. Tripp stays sitting beside me as we share dessert. Taking care of the check we walk back out and head home.

D oll gets to me. I can't say no. I'd lay the world at her feet if it meant her happiness. I don't want to bring tears to her beautiful face. She wants me to hear Lucy out, fine. It won't change anything but it will give Doll peace of mind, so be it.

Once we're home and in my bedroom, all thoughts of anyone else evaporate. My woman is in my house, and soon she'll be in my bed. This is how it should be. Taking Doll by the hand, I walk us to my room. Turning around to her, I cup her face as I lean down and kiss her. When she moans into me, I trail kisses down her neck while I unzip her dress. She's pawing at my shirt. Breaking away, I pull her dress and my shirt off. Looking at her standing before me in a red lace bra, matching panties, and those shoes, I growl. My erection is painfully pressing on the zipper of my jeans. I unbutton and unzip them to give myself some room before I begin kissing her again. Pushing her back as I kiss her, we make our way to the bed. Laying her down gently, I quickly untie and remove my boots and socks.

Starting with her right leg, I massage up her calf as I brush my lips against her ankle, then her knee. Going to her left leg I do the same. At her thighs, I open her to me, trailing my tongue on the inside of her legs. Stopping at her core, I breathe in her scent. She's relaxed under me as I graze her mound with my teeth over the lace covering her. She rocks up seeking more. I push her panties aside and insert one finger as I let my tongue lick between her folds. She's drenched and rocking into me. I circle my tongue over her clit and then suck. Inserting two fingers, I kiss along both of her inner thighs. Nipping at her hips, I work my way slowly up. Keeping a steady pace as I finger fuck her, I pull her breasts out of the cups of her bra. Swirling my tongue over her erect nipples, I then blow across them. Their peaks are calling out to me. Her hands on my head are threading through my hair. Doll is rocking hard against my fingers, as I begin rubbing my thumb over her clit. I suck hard on one of her nipples, sending her over the edge.

"Talon, fuck me now," She cries out reaching down she's attempting to push my jeans down. I help her out and remove the last of my clothing. Hooking my thumbs under the sides of her panties, I slide them off of her as she's unhooking her bra. Skin on skin, she was made for me as she fits perfectly to me. Her legs come up, wrapping around me. Rubbing the head of my piercing against her core, she's pushing into me, as I tease her.

"Talon," She pleads. My name off her lips is heaven.

Still teasing, I kiss her as I finally slide into her. She's tight, wet, and gripping me. I still myself, wanting to absorb every sensation. I begin to bring myself in and out of her making sure my piercing rubs her inner walls with each stroke. The spiky heel of those shoes dig into the backs of my thighs as I pick up my pace. The feeling of being in her, while her nails rake down my back, as she's arching up to meet me thrust for thrust, is every-thing. No one will ever fuck me the way Doll fucks me, matching my every move. Leaning down, I nip at her shoulder and lick her neck and the spot right behind her ear. As she gets tighter around me, I feel her getting close. Reaching between us, I rub her clit, giving her the climax she's been working for. The aftershocks of her orgasm grip me and milk my rock hard dick. No longer able to hold back, I release, filling her. Once I'm drained, I gently pull out of her.

We lay together for a while as I run my hands gently over her body, allowing us time to get our breathing back to normal. Once we both recover, I take Doll to my shower, where I make sure to not only clean her, but give her another orgasm. With her, I can't seem to get enough.

Waking up after a night with Doll, I realize there's no way I can let her go. Nothing's the same without her. I kiss her forehead. She's stretching beside me. Looking up at me, I smile at the innocent face she's making. Her eyes say she's in complete bliss. This is a look I could wake up to every fuckin' day for the rest of my life and never get tired of seeing.

"Thank you Talon." She says as her arm comes across my waist and her legs tangle back in mine.

"For what?" I ask.

"For our date last night."

I stiffen under her. "Doll, I don't date." I reply with all honesty. The disappointment crosses her face at my response.

"Oh." The smile she had now gone.

"You wanna do this, we do this. I'm not gonna chase you. I'm not gonna wine and dine you. If this is what you want, we do it. You get me. I get you. I don't share and you don't either. The distance thing, we'll figure it out. Your dad, babe, I don't know, but we face that too. You gotta know though, I don't date. You get me when I'm not on the road and can work it out. We gotta eat, I'll take us to eat, but I'm me. I'm not gonna kiss your ass, buy you gifts, and worry about making a good impression. You get me and I get you for what we can work out."

Her expression is unreadable as she takes in my words. She's climbing over me before she's kissing me. My dick comes alive at her touch.

Muttering between kisses, she replies. "We'll figure it out." And at that she grabs my shaft and slides onto me. She sets her own pace as she rides me. Her eyes never leave mine as she is moving up and down, rolling her hips on me.

"I get you and you get me. That's everything I need, Talon." She whispers before biting her lip. Using my thumb, I pull her lip out from her teeth.

"We'll figure it out." I say before pulling her to me for a kiss.

With that we're both quiet as she rides me until we both reach our orgasms. We shower and dress. Doll packs to go back. She has to be at work the next day and needs to return to the coast. Saying goodbye sucks, but we're going to find a way to make this work.

35

CHAPTER
THIRTY FIVE

WHEN IT COMES DOWN TO IT

Getting back to the coast, I'm left empty. Tripp consumes me. I want him here or me there. For a moment, I thought I was reading too much into things. Tripp's not one to romance me, I knew this, but hearing the words *'I don't date'*, stung. He has me though, and I have him. I don't know what the future holds, but I have him for now and that's everything.

Going to bed without him leaves me tossing and

turning, missing the feel of him beside me. Waking up without him burns. I've never needed someone the way I need him. His presence calms me, commands me, and consumes me. Being apart from him, I feel empty.

Moping about it won't change anything, so I ready myself for the day after my restless night. I'm at the office trying to work. My dad walks in. His face is one of determination and conviction.

"Doll, my office." He orders walking past me. Fuck, this isn't good.

Following him in, I take the seat in front of his desk as he sits down.

"You got something to tell me?" He asks or states, I'm not sure which. Obviously, he thinks I have something to tell him.

"Dad, what are you talking about?"

"You went to Catawba. You got something to tell me?"

"Yes, I went to Catawba. I stayed with Tripp as you clearly seem to know." I say avoiding eye contact.

"You gonna tell me what the fuck that's about?"

"Ummm…" I don't know where to begin. "I have feelings for him. We're exploring things."

"Exploring things? What the fuck, Delilah?!" He roars. "Either he's gonna man up and do right by you or not… and NOT is not a fuckin' option. You don't explore things with my fuckin' daughter."

Shit, this is not coming out right. "Dad, he's doin' right by me. We're takin' things slow. He's committed to me."

"So you're an ol' lady now and neither of you fuckin' told me?" He slams his fist down on his desk.

"No, no, no. I'm not Tripp's ol' lady. We're trying to sort things out dad. Please, let me have this. He's good to me." Looking in his eyes, pleading for him to see how much I want this.

"Damn it, Doll. This ain't the life for you." He states back in his normal tone.

"This is all I know, Daddy. This is what I want. Anything less than a biker won't do. Tripp's a good man. He respects you. If you are against this, I'll lose him."

"He said that to you?"

"Not exactly, but I know him. Don't make him choose his club or me. Not when we don't know if we can work things out without the added club pressures. Look at Tank, tomorrow isn't promised for anyone. Tripp makes me feel alive. He shows me in his eyes and the ways he treats me different that I'm everything. Don't make me choose him or this club. You may not like the answer you get."

"Doll, you love him?"

"Yes, Daddy, I do." I say matching his gaze and refusing to back down. "I've never asked you for anything like this. I've done what's been expected of me and asked of me. You wanted me back home after college, I came. You wanted me to go on that ride, I went. Let me have a chance at this."

"Doll, he hurts you, I'll break him."

"Daddy, everyone knows this." I smile at my dad as I make my way over to hug him and kiss him on the cheek. He never moves from his sitting position behind the desk.

"Enough of that. Go on. I got shit to do."

I walk back out front. I'm pretty sure the 'shit' he's got to do involves Tripp now.

Roundman has called me to the coast. Doll and I start to make plans when I tell her I'm on my way there. She warns me, her dad knows and that's what I've been called for. He's gonna have my fuckin' balls, but I can't stay away from her, so he can have 'em.

Pulling in, I climb off my bike. I don't make it to the door before Doll is in front of me. She wraps her arms around me and pulls me down to kiss her.

"Hello, Darlin'," I greet, unable to stop myself from smiling. Yes, this precious doll makes me smile.

Before we can say more, Roundman is walking out. He nods to me and points to his office. I kiss Doll's forehead before following him to his office. His gun is out on the desk. He earned his name from being a one round man. One bullet. One round. One shot. One kill.

"You fuckin' my daughter?" He looks at me and asks. He points for me to sit in the chair by his desk as he leans against it.

"It's not like that Roundman."

"Then enlighten me." His head cocks to the side, the sneer evident on his face and tone. "What the fuck is it? She's not your ol' lady. She's been to bed with you. Yet, you're not taking care of her. So, tell me, what the fuck is it?"

"It's everything. She's everything. You want me to give her my property patch, done. You want her to move to Catawba, I'll take care of her. You want me to marry her, then take me to a courthouse, a church, or the god damn back yard. I'll put a ring on her finger and give her a new last name. All that, I'll do gladly. I'll give her my fuckin' world."

"You spouting off at me boy. You're fuckin' my daughter, and trying to feed me bullshit about what you'll do. You gonna do all that shit for her or for me? You say you'll give her your fuckin' world...what if I don't want that world for her? You gonna give up your patch for her. You gonna give her the world I want her to have."

Standing up out of my chair, he follows suit. Eye to eye. "Fuck the world YOU want her to have. Doll's a Hellion by your choices, not mine. This is the world she knows, accepts, and lives for. Get a few things straight, I won't do any of that shit for you. I do it all for her. If she wants a property patch, hands down she has it. If she wants a wedding, I'll give her the white dress and the goddamn suit. You want me to choose between her and my club...I choose her because she'll choose to support my club and be with me in it."

Waiting for him to reach for his gun or at least punch me, I'm on edge. Never breaking eye contact, I watch as a grin slowly moves across his face.

"Got balls, Tripp. Always been a tough guy. You've met your match in Doll."

"We good, Roundman?"

"As good as we're gonna get since you're fuckin' my daughter." He hands me a small box. I open it to see the bullet. "One round, Tripp, that one's got your name on it. You fuck her over, you take that bullet. We clear? She's had enough loss in her life. You do this, you don't get to leave her. She lost her momma way to fuckin' young, she doesn't lose you too."

"We're clear."

"Go out there and take care of my daughter. Sort your shit."

He takes the box back and moves it to his safe. There's no doubt in my mind that bullet will be waiting for me, if or when I fuck this up.

THINGS CHANGE FOR US ALL

Tripp comes out of my dad's office. That's a good sign in itself. He leaves to go visit Tank with the promise to be back when I get off work for the night. How am I supposed to get any work done now with Tripp in town? I want to be with him, not sitting in this office. I'm drawn out of my musings when my dad's office door opens.

"Until you and Tripp sort your shit, you got work to do, Doll. So do it."

And with that he leaves. Left to my own thoughts, I get no work done. Sort our shit, what does that mean? What are Tripp and I going to do? While I was away at college, my dad had an ol' lady of one of the guys that did the regular bookwork, answering the phones and such. Maybe he'll do that again so I can go to Catawba. Does Tripp want me to move there? It would be nice to be closer to him.

Caroline would let me stay with her. I could live with her and get a job. Maybe Ryder needs a girl Friday for his garage or Dina could use a secretary for her company. I have opportunities there and don't need to depend on Tripp. Forming a plan in my mind, I'm lost in thought when the front door opens. Sass is walking in, looking tired and depressed.

"Hey." I greet standing up to hug her. "Did you come to look at new places together?" I ask nervously because I'm no longer sure I plan on staying here.

"No, I came to talk to you about that." She says settling in the chair in front of my desk.

"Okay, what's up?"

"You know I've been seeing Nick since we got home." Yes, I knew this. I tried to ignore it, but she was out with him all the damn time, except her early morning visits to Tank.

"Yes, I know who you've been seeing." Looking at her, the confliction is written all over her face.

"He wants me to move in with him."

"Are you going to? How does he feel about you being in love with another man?"

"Don't be bitchy, Doll. He understands my feelings for Tank. He's not once tried to stop me from going to be by my friend's bedside. He gives me the calm I need. I can't get wrapped up in all the Hellions stuff."

"Is this really what you want?"

"This is my chance at normal. I want to know what normal feels like." She's pleading with me to let her go.

"Sass, I'm always here for you. If this is what you want, then go for it."

Tears streaming down her face, she comes over and hugs me. After a few minutes she straightens back up. She never smiles, though. How can this be what she wants if it doesn't make her happy?

"If you're gonna move in with Nick, then I think I'm going to take a chance of my own."

"I see that look in your eyes, Doll. What are you up to?" She's my best friend, and of course, she knows my recent trip to visit Tripp.

"I'm going to see if I can get a job with Ryder or Dina and stay with Caroline until I can set up myself. If Tripp and I are really gonna do this, I don't want to be five hours apart."

She squeals in delight for me and hugs me again.

"You two are made for each other, Doll."

"He's everything, Sass. I can't describe it other than to say that. He makes me feel like I'm the only woman in the world. And when he kisses me, it's like time stands still. I know it sounds like all that cheesy romance bullshit, but he brings that out in me." I'm unable to keep the smile off my face.

"You know he doesn't normally kiss his women, right?"

"What are you talking about? He kisses me all the damn time."

"Not you. The women he fucks, he doesn't kiss them. Rex told me once after we saw you two kiss. Tripp doesn't kiss unless it's someone he cares about. Maybe it's the intimacy, I don't know. To Rex, it was a big deal every single time Tripp kissed you."

"Hmmm..." I say trying not to think of him with Carmine and saying he won't kiss her. He's mine now and all that's in the past. We both agreed to try and I'm going to give this my all with no baggage.

"I'm happy for you Doll." Sass smiles over at me.

We chat for a little while longer making plans. Once she leaves, I start getting my ducks in a row to give things a real chance between Tripp and me. I call 'Vida', she's Ruby's wife. They have three kids, and he works in the Hellions garage. She agrees to come take my position in the storage office. Talking it over with my dad, he agrees to let her replace me if I want to move to Catawba. My ducks getting in a row, I've got to talk to Tripp and see if this is what he wants.

T he smell of the hospital makes my stomach churn. It's clean, like the smell of disinfectant, not one of clean, crisp, fresh air. Entering the building I feel suffocated. The walls feel like they're closing in as I look around the room.

Tank's lying in the bed, tubes everywhere. His head wrapped, his face swollen, and all life seems drained from him. The steady hiss of the ventilator reminds me that my brother can't breathe for himself. The constant beeping of the machines keeping the rhythm of his heartbeat isn't soothing. Every sound is a distinct reminder that every second that goes by is another moment missed. Tank is fighting to either wake up or succumb to the dark angel of death.

Sitting beside the bed, I stare for the longest time. The nurse comes in and says to talk to him. She claims he can hear us. According to the nurse, the only time they see any change in him and it's subtle, but it's something, is when his one lady friend visits each morning. There is a slight change in his vitals, but nothing bringing him out of this state. No doubt in my mind that special visitor is Sass. The nurse leaves and I'm still staring. Memories invade of the good times I've shared with Tank. He's made a lot of runs with me for the Hellions.

"Tank, damn it, wake up." I begin speaking before I can stop myself. "Sass is missing you man. Don't make her stress. Hell, I'm missing you. Wake up and shake this off." Nothing. No movement, no change.

I continue to sit there and blankly stare at my friend. Thoughts invade of the brothers lost in the Delatorre fallout. We can't lose Tank too. Thinking of Sass sitting here day in and out trying to bring him back to her, my chest hurts. Time is short, tomorrow isn't promised as Doll tells me constantly.

Making the call to Lucy isn't easy, but doing it with Tank here, in his situation keeps it in perspective. Deciding to forgive my mother isn't an easy task. The conversation isn't long. It's straight forward. It's an agreement that she goes to rehab to get sober, and I will to get to know her when she's cleaned up. I want to know my mom for who she is, not the person she's become because of the alcohol.

Finishing the call, I sit back. Is Doll willing to leave Haywood's Landing for me? Is what we're building strong enough for her to leave what she knows behind? The more I ponder, the more I look over at Tank unmoving in the bed. Watching him lifeless like this, and being helpless to do anything is killing me.

"You're stronger than this. You're a mother fuckin' Hellion. Wake your ass up and let's ride." I say over him, hoping for something. He's got to pull out of this.

Leaving the hospital, I'm lost for my brother, but I'm completely sure of what I want in life.

WE GONNA DO THIS

Tripp spent the night with me. Waking up with him feels right. In a wild moment of passion last night, I almost slipped and told him I love him. It was on the tip of my tongue. As much as I may feel for this man, I don't know if he's there with me yet. Tripp is obviously giving me more than he's given any other woman, but that doesn't mean he's in love with me.

Insecurities build inside of me. What the hell am I

doing? Walking away from everything I know and rely on for a relationship that's one sided. At least I will have Caroline there for me. Moving from the bed, Tripp stirs beside me.

"Go back to sleep, babe. I have to get ready for work." I say, trying to settle him back into his slumber. Without a word, his arms snake around my waist, pulling me naked over to him. Leaning over I kiss him gently. "I have to go to work, Tripp. This will make me late, you're not quick."

"You want it quick, darlin', I'll give it to you quick." He says with a smile full of unspoken orgasms.

Maneuvering out of his hold, I jump up. "Meet me in the shower and let's see if you can make it quick."

After our shower together, I make my way to my office. I'm still feeling insecure. Things are going on around me, everything is changing rapidly. Sass is moving her stuff to Nick's today. Danza met him. Given the situation with Tank, he'd rather Sass be with Nick than in this lifestyle.

Settling in for the day, I get organized to train my replacement. Jenna Mariella Castillo de Natera, 'Vida' arrives not far behind me to start her first day. She's Ruby's ol' lady. Her dark hair, natural tanned skin, and dark eyes all add to her Latina beauty. She's twenty-seven, but looks more like twenty-one, and you can't tell from looking at her that she's had three kids.

We start going over everything right away. She's a quick learner and great with the computer. Considering my dad hates the thing, this will be good. With Jenna here, I don't feel like I'm abandoning him quite so much.

Around lunchtime, Tripp stops in. I stand to meet him. Immediately, he pulls me into one of his all-consuming kisses. Forgetting everything but being in his arms, I moan as I melt into him. He pulls away leaving me breathless. He laughs, breathing on my ear as he whispers to me.

"Doll, you're at work. As much as I'd love nothing more than to take you right here in your office, on your desk, we have company. No more moaning like that or I won't give a fuck who watches as I take what I want."

Smacking his chest playfully, I pull away and purposely sashay my way to my desk. I'm in jeans that hug my every curve, a tight fitting, scoop neck black shirt that shows cleavage, and my black heeled boots give extra swoosh to my swinging hips. I feel him come up behind me, his arm snaking around my waist to pull my back into his chest.

"You're playin' with fire, Doll. You feel what you do to me?" He asks pushing his hips into me so I can feel his erection in my back. "Apparently, I didn't work you over good enough last night because you can still strut those sexy ass hips of yours. Tonight, babe, tonight, I'll make sure you feel me for days to come." He whispers against me before sucking hard on my neck.

I want nothing more than for him to bend me over my desk and take me now. He loosens his grip around my waist.

"I came by to tell you that I'll pick you up after work so we can go for a ride. Gotta go back tomorrow, Rex needs me for a run."

Turning to face him, I nod my head. The thought of goodbye, even for a few weeks, saddens me. He leaves after a quick kiss.

"You two are caliente." Jenna says to me, her Spanish accent and words coming out.

Smiling at her, I can't help myself. "Look at him. It's because he's hot."

"He's hot for you." She says to me smiling from ear to ear.

"You think?" I ask, my insecurities showing their face.

"Doll, that man looks at you like you're the only woman in the room. You're his vida, his life."

"Is that why Ruby calls you Vida? You're his life?"

"Yes."

Jenna and I spend the afternoon talking about work, men, and life in general. She's amazing as a mom, wife, and ol' lady. Before I realize it the day is done and Tripp is here picking me up.

D oll on the back of my bike is exactly where she's supposed to be. Nervous energy runs through me as we make the ride over to Cedar Island. We stop for a quick bite to eat. Then I take Doll down to the beach. In boots, it's not an easy walk for either of us, but I need to talk to her without any distractions.

Finding a spot, I sit down. Pulling Doll to sit between my legs, her back to my chest, I wrap my arms around her. We watch the ocean silently for a while. Inhaling the scent of her hair, I lay my head into her neck.

"We gonna do this, Doll?" I ask as she leans back further into me.

"Do what, Tripp?"

"This Doll, us? We gonna do this?"

"What are you asking me Tripp?" She turns forcing me to look up and meet her eyes.

"I leave tomorrow, Doll. I don't know when my schedule will allow me a trip back. We got shit to sort out before I leave. I'm asking if we're gonna do this?"

"Yeah, Tripp, I wanna do this."

"You gonna move then? With my business and club, I can't leave Doll."

Her face breaks out in the biggest smile. She entwines her fingers in mine. "What are you smiling about?"

"Well, I've sort of been thinking. I didn't want to be so far away from you. Jenna was at the office today training. I talked to my dad and she's gonna take over my job." My smile must give her encouragement because she doesn't sound as insecure as she continues. "I talked to Caroline and I can live with her. I'm gonna check with Dina or Ryder about a job." I lift my finger up to her lips to quiet her.

"Doll, you wanna move to Catawba? For me?"

"Well, for us, yeah."

"You ain't livin' with Caroline. You wanna work that's on you, but you don't have to. You wanna do this, you live with me."

"Rex?" she questions.

"He's been talking about getting a place of his own for a while."

"You sure?" Her face is one of panic.

"I've never been more sure of anything in my life, Doll."

I lean down and kiss her with all the love I feel for her but can't ever seem to bring to words. The thoughts clutter my head as I continue to kiss her. She's been working on finding a way to be closer to me. She's done all this because I mean something to her, being together means something to her. Pulling away, I rub my thumb across her bottom lip.

"We gonna do this, Doll? You gonna live with me? You gonna be my ol' lady? You know the club is part of me."

"Yes to everything." She says in a whisper. Tilting her head to me, I bring my forehead down to hers. Eye to eye, nose to nose, I say what I've known for months now.

"Love you, Doll."

"Love you, Talon."

ONE RIDE FOR LIFE

A fter the confessions of love on the beach, Tripp took me home and showed my body just how much he loves me. He was true to his word, I felt him the next day. I wasn't sashaying my ass around anywhere. It was a sore so good.

Tripp left the next morning to go back. I had to stay behind to tie up loose ends here in Haywood's Landing. I spent two weeks training Jenna. Rex moved out while

Tripp was on a transport. My stuff was packed and moved for me by some prospects.

I've settled into Tripp's space pretty well. It's been six months of living together and I can't get enough of him. He's been open to changes around the house, as long as I didn't put flowery girly shit everywhere; his words not mine. The French country blue kitchen is now a light gray and upgraded to stainless steel appliances. Dina offered me a job, but Tripp offered me one at his office as well. I took the second offer because he's gone quite a bit and I love the extra time together when he's home.

Rex is still man-whoring around. I've become close with Tessie. She is done holding out hope for Rex to change. It's going to be a challenge but she is trying to break free of the hold he has on her. She is trying to move on in life for her and for her son.

Tank is still in a coma. He's stable, his body healed, but he won't wake up. The doctors say it's up to him now. He's got to find the reason to wake up. Sass visits him every day still. She's living with Nick, and although the light is gone from my feisty friend's eyes, she seems as happy as she's gonna get without being with a biker.

Tripp and I spent last weekend riding the Dragon's tail. It was everything my dad said it would be and then some. Being an ol' lady is different. Those women who always looked out for me and nurtured me were an important part to my life that I overlooked until becoming one. Now, I'm looking out for the newbies that come in with one of the guys or helping with the little Hellions they have. They've all taken me in here quite well and I love my extended family.

I've got a special dinner planned tonight since Tripp has been gone for the last week. He walks in looking edible himself. I smile at him, as I walk over to the kitchen entryway. Snaking my arms around his waist, I rest my head on his chest. His arms come around me as he moves to tilt my head to him. Then he devours me in his kiss. I don't care if it is fifty years from now, a kiss from Talon Crews will consume every part of me because he is everything that makes my heart beat. After a few minutes, we break apart.

"Something smells good, babe." Tripp states as he drops his bag in the laundry area. "What's the occasion?"

"I missed you." I smile innocently at him.

"Doll, what's going on? I know you missed me, but this is something more."

"Well, Caroline has been having some troubles with a guy from work. I sort of asked Rex to help me out and look out for Caroline. That being the case, they haven't officially met even after all this time. Rex has been on the road or Caroline was busy. I doubt they even remember their first meeting at the barbecue." I say looking down.

"Why didn't you tell me that Caroline needed something?" He asks, lifting my chin forcing me to make eye contact.

"You were gone when she called. This guy at work is being a bit aggressive. Having Rex on her arm for a few work functions may deter him."

"Is this why Caroline stayed over a few nights while I've been gone?"

"Maybe."

"Is this maybe because she's afraid of the fucker?"

Saved by the bell, the doorbell rings and I bolt to answer it. Caroline is having some troubles and I don't know what to do for her. Rex will though. He and Tripp protected me and I know they will protect my friend.

Caroline is helping me set the table when Rex walks in through the back door. He and Tripp do the handshake, half hug, back slap thing guys do for a greeting. He waves over to me and then he faces Caroline. The smile on his face is one of seduction and surprise.

"Rex meet Caroline, again." I say in introduction, as Tripp moves over putting his arm around my waist.

"Nice to meet you, Lux."

Caroline's face distorts in annoyance. "Lux?"

"Lux, as in deluxe. You're the deluxe model. High class and shit." Rex says settling into a chair at the table.

Caroline's face is pleading with me to save her. I stifle a giggle at her reaction. We eat dinner as Caroline fills us in on the details of what's been happening. Rex is pissed in a way I've never seen before. After dinner, Rex and Tripp go and talk in the shop, while Caroline helps me clean up.

"Are you sure about this Doll?"

"Caroline, I'd trust Rex with my own life. He's not going to let this Chad guy get to you or keep bothering you. He'll handle it and you can feel safe again."

With a few more reassurances, she is feeling better about leaning on the Hellions to help her. Rex follows Caroline home. Tripp is sitting on the recliner in the living room. As I walk by, he grabs me and pulls me to his lap. Nuzzling his face in my neck, I sigh.

"I love you, Talon."

Rather than respond, he kisses me. He's moving around under me. Breaking the kiss, he pulls away and looks in my eyes as if he's searching for an answer to an unknown question.

"Doll, we gonna do this?"

"Babe, we are doing this." I answer, not understanding.

He moves a small black velvet box in front of me. "Doll, we gonna do this?"

Tears already falling as I ask, "What is it you're asking me to do exactly?"

"You have my babies. You have my name. You keep that pretty ass of yours on the back of my bike for the rest of our lives. You be my everything. You be my wife. One more time and then I'm not askin' again, we gonna do this, Doll?"

"Yes, Talon, we're gonna do this."

The End
Until the next ride …

AFTERWORD

Thank you for going on *One Ride* with Tripp and Doll. For those of you curious as to what took place at the warehouse with Delatorre, it's coming to you in Book 2, *Forever Ride*, out now!

The characters of the Shifters Pack in Broadus, Montana were brought to you courtesy of author Theresa Marguerite Hewitt and her Broadus Supernatural Society Series.

The characters of Ray and Zack Mitchell were brought to you courtesy of author Cat Mason and her Broken Roads series.

The characters of the Heaven Hill MC in Bowling Green, Kentucky were brought to you courtesy of author Laramie Briscoe.

I hope you enjoyed *One Ride*! I would love to hear

what you thought about *One Ride (Hellions Ride 1)*. If you have a few moments to leave a review, I'd be very grateful. Don't want to miss a single release or update to my schedule, sign up for my newsletter here! I promise I won't spam you. I send out a monthly update on my release schedule and a quarterly Steals and Deals email full of bargain books waiting to fill your library.

ABOUT THE AUTHOR

USA Today and Wall Street Journal bestselling author Chelsea Camaron is a small town Carolina girl with a big imagination. She's a wife and mom, chasing her dreams. She writes contemporary romance, romantic suspense, and romance thrillers. She loves to write about blue-collar men who have real problems with a fictional twist. From mechanics, bikers, oil riggers, smokejumpers, bar owners, and beyond she loves a strong hero who works hard and plays harder.

Chelsea can be found on social media at:

Facebook: www. facebook.com/authorchelseacamaron

Twitter: @chelseacamaron

Instagram: @chelseacamaron

Website: www.authorchelseacamaron.com

Email chelseacamaron@gmail.com

Join the fun in my reader group here: Chelsea Camaron Biker Broads

ALSO BY CHELSEA CAMARON

Love and Repair Series:

Crash and Burn

Restore My Heart

Salvaged

Full Throttle

Beyond Repair

Stalled

Hellions Ride Series:

One Ride

Forever Ride

Merciless Ride

Eternal Ride

Innocent Ride

Simple Ride

Heated Ride

Ride with Me (Hellions MC and Ravage MC Duel with Ryan
Michele)

Originals Ride

Final Ride

Hellions Ride On Series:

Hellions Ride On Prequel

Born to It

Bastard in It

Bleed for It

Breathe for It

Bold from It

Brave in It

Broken by It

Brazen being It

Better as It

Brash for It

Boss as It

Blue Collar Bad Boys Series:

Maverick

Heath

Lance

Wendol

Reese

Devil's Due MC Series:

Serving My Soldier

Crossover

In The Red

Below The Line

Close The Tab

Day of Reckoning

Paid in Full

Bottom Line

Almanza Crime Family Duet

Cartel Bitch

Cartel Queen

Romantic Thriller Series:

Stay

Seeking Solace: Angelina's Restoration

Reclaiming Me: Fallyn's Revenge

Bad Boys of the Road Series:

Mother Trucker

Panty Snatcher

Azzhat

Santa, Bring Me a Biker!

Santa, Bring Me a Baby!

Stand Alone Reads:

Romance – Moments in Time Anthology

Shenanigans (Currently found in the Beer Goggles Anthology

<u>She is ...</u>

The following series are co-written

The Fire Inside Series:

(co-written by Theresa Marguerite Hewitt)

<u>Kale</u>

Regulators MC Series:

(co-written by Jessie Lane)

<u>Ice</u>

<u>Hammer</u>

<u>Coal</u>

Summer of Sin Series:

(co-written with Ripp Baker, Daryl Banner, Angelica Chase, MJ Fields, MX King)

<u>Original Sin</u>

Caldwell Brothers Series:

(co-written by USA Today Bestselling Author MJ Fields)

<u>Hendrix</u>

Morrison

Jagger

Stand Alone Romance:

(co-written with USA Today Bestselling Author MJ Fields)

Visibly Broken

Use Me

Ruthless Rebels MC Series:

(co-written with Ryan Michele)

Shamed

Scorned

Scarred

Schooled

Box Set Available

Power Chain Series:

(co-written with Ryan Michele)

Power Chain FREE eBook

PowerHouse

Power Player

Powerless

OverPowered

EXCERPT FROM FOREVER RIDE

Forever Ride

(Hellions Ride Book 2)

Prologue

"Oleander, you didn't possibly think bringing your boy here would save your sorry ass, did ya?" the tall, over-powering man asks my dad with a smirk of pure evil.

"Jones, give me a minute. I wasn't expecting you. Lewis said we were meeting tonight," my dad says with a look of fear crossing his features.

At the man's slight nod, my dad turns to face me.

When I look in his eyes, the worry, stress, and tears are all present as he's trying to push them back.

"Franky, my boy. I need you to go on over to the bagel shop. Get breakfast for your mom and sisters and then head home. I've made some mistakes, son, but none of those are your fault. You're gonna be the man now. Take care of home. Go on. And no matter what you hear, don't come back. You've seen nothing here today!" He orders firmly before turning me around and sending me on my way.

I barely make it a block away when the sound of repeating pops fills the air. *Crack. Crack. Crack.* No one has to tell me what has happened, and I know better than to turn around or question anything. My dad runs with bad people. Mom has always told him it was only a matter of time before it caught up to all of us.

Whether they will come after me or not, I don't know. However, I have to get home to my mom and sisters, step up and take care of what my dad has never taken care of. At eleven-years-old, the innocence of childhood has never existed for me, but a man is what I've become on this unexpected, cold winter day.

Going home, I make a decision not to tell my mom what I've seen today, though the cops arriving later does not surprise me. They inform her that a passer-by found my dad's body in an alley. They tell her there will be an investigation and ask if she has any information that may give them a lead. She doesn't know anything, so I know the case will go cold quickly, or I hope it does.

When they leave, Mom takes the news as a turning point, deciding it's time to get out of the place we are in.

———

Life sometimes hands you opportunities in the craziest of moments. It has been five years, and Mom has moved us from the inner city of Detroit to be with her family here in coastal North Carolina. She claims having the help to keep an eye on my sisters and me is the reason why. However, I think the weight of my dad's associations in Detroit were inescapable, so she retreated.

She has found herself a decent enough waitressing job at The Shell Shack, though. It's a small diner, specializing in local seafood. I bus tables there on the weekends. We manage to make ends meet, but it's only barely, so I've been known to steal here and there to bring in a few extra dollars. It's still better than the danger and the pace of life in Michigan.

I have made some connections here. Not ones I am proud of, but someone has got to step up. If I can ease the burden for my mom, I will, and by any means necessary. I know what I am about to do is taking things to a different level than anything I have done before; however hard times call for extreme measures.

The hot rod is one of those dilapidated tobacco buildings, which sits in an open field, housing the beautiful machine. She is a fully restored, black, 1967 Chevy Nova SS, and the dust settling over the car screams to me that no one is going to miss this piece of American muscle right away. *I can have her gone and to Charlie's chop shop in Virginia before anyone will notice*, I reassure myself. Besides, mom could use the money, Laney needs new shoes, and Bonnie is getting boobs now, which means an entire new wardrobe.

The thoughts of what the extra money could do for my sisters' pushes me forward. Sure, I've stolen stuff as we've needed it—I've been boosting rims and parts from a few tire shops and garages around here for the last year—but this will be my biggest haul. My buddy, Jason, will meet me and drive the car over to Charlie's. Once there, he gets paid and we split the money.

Jason is the one who gave me the location of the car, saying everything has been scouted. It is an easy in and out. Step by step, he has given me instructions on what to do. As a minor, if I get caught, the penalties are less harsh and those records get sealed. Jason is nineteen, therefore the risks and punishments are much higher for him. So this one is all on me.

Removing the cover, I swing around to the back, adding the stolen license plate to the car. There's no need to give the cops more of a red flag since the car currently has no tags. Climbing in the driver's seat, I run my hand over the steering wheel. She is one fine piece of American machinery, and I'm practically giddy when I see the key ring is dangling from the ignition. The turn of the key, the stroke of the engine as it turns over, coming to life under me—it is a moment of power and control. The rumble of the motor sends vibrations through the old building.

I'm just getting ready to put the car in gear when I look up and come face to face with four bikers all aiming their guns at me through the windshield of the beauty encompassing me. Shit just got real.

Raising my hands in defeat, I stare down the biker who is walking over to me. Today may be the end of my road, but I won't show them any fear.

"Cut my car off, boy," one of the bikers commands.

He is huge. Tall and built he has long, brown hair braided in the back with a goatee and tattoos coming down both his arms. Out of the corner of my eye, I glance at the others who are just as mean in appearance. They have since lowered their weapons but are watching me like a hawk circling its prey.

"Get out of the car, punk ass," another one with short, salt and pepper hair orders. His goatee is an even mix of gray and black, matching his hair.

Doing as I'm told without hesitation, I can't stop my mind from worrying over my mom and sisters. What will they do with me gone? My family is going to lose the only man left to protect them. Mom has always told me to stay clean, don't fall to the temptation of a quick dollar. Too bad I didn't listen.

"What's your name, boy?" the long haired, burly biker that apparently owns the car asks, stepping up to me.

"Franklin Thomas Oleander," I answer, steeling my voice to one that shows no weakness, no fear. He may kill me today, but he won't break me.

He tucks his gun back into the waistband of his jeans against his back, obviously feeling I am not a threat. Truth be told, I'm not a threat, not to him and his crew. They could each crush me with their bare hands. I am still filling out, and since Mom can't afford much, I make sure my sisters eat before I do, which means I am skinny and rough around the edges.

"You got a death wish, Oleander?" The other three bikers remain back, letting the one man handle me on his own.

"No," I answer firmly.

"Apparently, you wanna die. Why else would you be dumb enough to touch my car?"

"Umm..." I have no answer. Seeing as it is his car I was attempting to steal, I am faced with two options: man up and take what is coming to me or cower down and beg for my life. Well, no one ever calls me smart.

"You gonna kill me, kill me. You wanna beat my ass, beat my ass. Whatever you're gonna do, just do it."

Laughing in my face, he responds, "You've got balls, kid. Not many grown ass men would step up and take what's coming to them. Get back in the car, start it and follow me. If you detour, I will find you, and this will get a whole lot worse. Let's go."

I do as I am told, adrenaline building inside of me. I'm not dead yet, so maybe this will be okay after all. He could have called the cops when he found me, but these men don't strike me as the law-abiding type. Nor do I think they would call for help when they can dish out their own kind of punishment.

Following the bikes, we pull into the Hellions' motorcycle club compound. Everyone in Haywood's Landing knows who the Hellions are. Why didn't I pay better attention in the barn? I should have known with the leather cuts, guns and motorcycles who I was dealing with. I park the car beside where the guys have stopped their Harleys then get out and wait by the driver's side door.

The long haired biker is definitely the one in charge. He is barking orders and pointing inside the building in front of me before he makes his way over to me.

Before I can speak or move, he yanks me around by my shirt. His arm comes around me into a head lock as he drags me violently behind him. We make our way inside the compound, no one says a word to us or to help me. I grab at his thick forearm, trying to relieve the pressure around my neck.

"Bull, get your ass out here. Your punk ass nephew needs some words," the biker yells, squeezing tighter with his arm.

Bull, who the hell is Bull?

He releases his grip on me, shoving me forward. Two arms grab me then and pull me steady. Looking up, I am face to face with my uncle, Kenny.

"Franky, what the fuck? Why are you here and why is Roundman dumping your ass in front of me?"

"Umm…" is all I manage to stammer.

"Your boy wanted to go on a little joyride," the burly biker, who is apparently Roundman, says with a snicker. "A joyride in *my* fuckin' car."

"Fuck. Franky, what're you thinking? Have you lost your damn mind? Your momma is gonna kill you and me both."

"Laney needs shoes." It slips out of my mouth before I have a chance to stop myself.

I don't want to be rich and wouldn't have agreed to steal the car for a simple joyride. My mom is two months behind on the electric bill; it's going to be turned off any day. We have never had cable television, and currently, we don't have a phone because it was disconnected three months ago. If it weren't for food stamps and the left-over scraps from her job, we wouldn't have food most days.

My sisters get good grades and are innocent to the damage our dad's past brought down on my mom. Hell, Bonnie was only eight and Laney four when he was killed; neither of them really remember him. He wasn't around much when he was alive anyway. They do vividly remember two days later when the goons showed up and took everything out of our house to repay my father's debt, though.

That's right. They took everything, down to the very mattresses we slept on. My mother's jewelry gone, including the macaroni necklace I made her in kinder-garten. It took time, hard work, and long hours for my mom to raise the money just to get us to North Carolina where her sister lives.

Her sister, Aunt Marsha, got her a job and set us up in the small two bedroom trailer we live in. I sleep in the living room so my mom can have a bed to rest her tired feet in at the end of a long day. Pride has always kept her from telling anyone how bad our finances are.

"What do you mean Laney needs shoes?" Uncle Kenny asks, his face distorted in anger and concern.

"The electric is about to be turned off. Laney needs shoes. Bonnie needs clothes. And Mom is working herself sick. I'm the man of the house; I gotta help. I was given an opportunity, so I took it."

The swift movement of the back of his hand coming across my face doesn't register with me until I am on the floor, spitting out blood.

"Fucker, you call me. You don't go steal shit."

As soon as I am standing, the next blow comes—a punch to the gut. My breathing is coming in hard pants as the room spins around me. Trying to catch my breath and remain standing is almost too much. Before I fall to the ground again, two arms are holding me up by my shoulders.

"Enough, Bull," Roundman commands from behind me.

Turning me to face him, he smiles at me as I fight to breathe regularly and my face is rapidly swelling. "Boy, I get you've had it bad growing up, but it's time to learn about family. You want to learn about brotherhood, son?"

I can only nod in agreement. What else is there to say?

"You're young, but you're strong. You've faced what you've done with pride. Still, you've got a debt to pay for touchin' my car, and you'll start repaying it next weekend. We'll take care of your momma and your sisters; get them what they need. The Hellions are gonna make a man outta you, boy, and teach you what your daddy obviously didn't."

I nod once again in agreement. As I breathe deeply, I

realize the man in front of me is cutting me a break, which is something no one has ever done for me before.

Roundman meets my eyes as he continues, "Life may hand you a shit deal in the cards, but you have to show that motherfucker no one controls you. Rise above it, boy. Make something for yourself, your mom, and your sisters." With that, he turns and walks away.

Afterward, Uncle Kenny takes me home and agrees not to tell my mom about the shit-storm I've escaped today.

One bad choice has changed my life. The path before me that has once been unclear and filled with more struggles than I care to think of, suddenly opens to a world of possibilities and the chance to do something with my life.

Roundman and the Hellions turned everything around for me.

FOREVER RIDE

CHAPTER ONE

UNSETTLED

There are times in life where things change so much nothing seems the same anymore. Yesterday becomes some far off dream of what once was. The things that have brought me to this place feel like a faint, far off memory.

The logical side of me still screams strongly that walking away from my family, from everything I know, and from the Hellions motorcycle club is what any sane person would do. I am a grown ass adult. The lifestyle decisions of my parents should no longer dictate the choices I make with my own life. The bubble that I grew up in has popped, reality surrounds me now.

Life with Nick is safe. No crazy-ass road trips. No crazy fucker putting cameras in my house. No wild parties. No runs where the men in my life are gone for days without a word of their safety or location. Life with Nick is calm. We've come a long way from that first meeting one night at a bar. Doll and I met him before the Delatorre situation hit the fan. Nick and I went out a couple of times before I left. While I was away, I wasn't sure what I would do when I returned home. Nick was supportive through it all. Coming home to find Tank in a coma, Nick has been the normalcy I've needed. He's the opposite of everything I've ever known with the Hellions and I need that now more than ever before.

The chaos surrounding the Hellions slowly disappears from my world as each day passes. Sure, I know my mom misses me and my dad is upset that, outside of doing my job, I refuse to have anything to do with the club. It is hard to give up everything I've ever known, but my life is better this way.

Doll and Caroline are the ones who understand my reasoning the most. They are my best friends. After everything we've been through in the last year, neither have pushed the issue of why I left the club life. Doll is an 'ol' lady' now. Tripp recently proposed and she is planning her wedding here on the coast. Caroline is wrapped up in some mess at work so Rex is stepping in to help her. Caroline wants none of this, but she's backed into a corner. There is no way out of her current situation without help from the club.

I miss having my best friends around. Hell, until the ride we had to take because of Delatorre, Doll and I were roommates. Caroline lived with us in college, but she stayed in Charlotte when Doll and I returned to the coast after graduation. Now that we're safe and Doll is with Tripp, she lives in Catawba with her man and his charter club. She is in love and feels safe, so at the end of the day, I am happy for her. Caroline claims she has no time for love. Her focus is on her career and I support that. They have their lives there and mine is getting started here.

After returning, I made the decision to give things with Nick a serious try. We moved in together not long after my return. He is stable. Things are good. However, the one thing left of my old life I can't seem to let go of is Tank.

He is in the hospital because of the Delatorre situation, and the coma he hasn't come out of in almost eight months weighs heavily on my heart. There is so much I never got to say to him. I have actually said a lot of it now, but does he really know I am here and I am talking to him? The doctors say he can hear me. They tell me the last thing a person loses is their ability to hear, so I should keep talking to him every chance I can. Therefore, each morning, after Nick leaves for work, I spend an hour at Tank's bedside before I go off to my job. A job where I once saw Tank every day he wasn't on a transport.

The whole thing started when Doll and I were sent on a ride across the country with Tripp and Rex. It was to keep us safe since Felix Delatorre threatened Doll. While we were on the road, the Hellions back home handled Delatorre and his crew. I don't know all of the details of what happened in the warehouse that day, only that Bull, Perry, Pearl and Coach were all killed. I know that Roundman eliminated Delatorre, but the specifics have not been discussed. Tank, Bandit and Jag were all injured, but while they have since recovered, Tank has not.

They don't know why he isn't waking up, either. His body has completely healed. However, his mind has not.

The majority of our trip was relatively easy compared to what everyone back home was facing trying to eliminate Delatorre and the threat he posed. Rex and Tripp took care of keeping Doll and I safe. We only had one major incident, though it's one that will forever be ingrained in my soul.

Doll and I have been inseparable since childhood, my

survival sister in this crazy life. The instant Tripp's arm comes up to signal he will be turning off and Rex is to continue on forward then circle back around, my heart skips a beat. Watching my best friend pull off at the exit while we have to continue on crushes me. The millions of 'what ifs' are playing on a loop in my mind.

Rex and I continue on and circle back around as instructed, and when we finally pull up to a rundown gas station, my heart drops. I can see the Hellions cuts on the back of the men as they are guiding a group of Hispanic men at gunpoint behind the restrooms. What I don't see is Tripp or Doll. Rex taps my thigh, a signal for me to get off the bike, as he removes his helmet. Rex is not the serious type. He takes life as a ride; simple, carefree, face what comes when it comes. At this moment, however, he is stern and unsmiling as he looks at me.

"Sass, we're gonna head to the restroom and get Doll. Given where the guys came from, I'm sure that's where Tripp sent her. You don't leave my fuckin' side, though. If more guys show up, you get to the restroom and lock yourself in." He hands me a small handgun and nods at me.

I nod back in understanding. Yes, I know how to fire the weapon. Doll and I have spent as many hours shooting as we have shopping. It is the Hellion way of life—control the chaos, command when faced with the *extremes, and never be without your brother and your weapon.*

Well, I am without my sister right now and it is time to get her.

Finding courage and resolve I never knew I had, I follow Rex to the restroom. I can hear the faint whiz of the shots being fired and the men hitting the ground nearby. The boys may be using silencers on the guns, but it is still evident when you are close by what is going on. Connections will be called, markers used or owed; this mess will be cleaned up without a trace in a matter of hours. If Doll is safe, it is worth it.

Relief washes over me as my best friend comes to the door when I knock and call out to her. I can hear Tripp in the other restroom talking, but the sounds are too muffled to comprehend.

We walk with Doll over to the bikes while we wait for Tripp. Tears are streaming down Doll's face, and I'm at a loss on how to make this better for her. When Tripp emerges, she finds her calm within the storm with him.

Thinking back to that day gives me chills.

Before we left on the ride, I had decided the biker life wasn't for me. Stupid teenage fantasies had me read more than there was into the friendship I had formed with Tank. After one hookup the night of the barbeque, things changed for me. Tank's easy dismissal of me made it clear where I stand with him. It's more than that, but his rejection confirmed it, club life isn't for me.

I'm building something solid and long lasting with Nick. He's not my knight in shining armor, Prince Charming, or any of the stuff fairytales are made of—none of that shit is real anyway. He's reliable, kind, gentle and attentive. He's safe. He's secure. And he wants me. This is what I want—to be the center of someone's world, not second to a brotherhood, a club.

Why do I still feel there is something missing, though?

Darkness. Shadows. Blackness. Gloom. Sadness. I am engulfed in obscurity, vagueness and murkiness. Oblivion. I am not completely gone, but I'm not altogether here, either.

Lost. Tumbling. Absent. A soft voice comes through; gentle, kind, loving and sad. Her voice, her presence, breaks the numbness consuming me. My girl is here. The light in the dark. The sounds of her, the feel of her, knowing she's here pulls me through the shades of black. The citrus smell of her invades my senses.

I fight to open my eyes. I want to see her. No, I *need* to see her and the depths of those emerald green eyes that once danced in my presence. I crave that connection. I fight with everything in me to see her, but my body remains unresponsive to my command.

She is touching me. I can feel her squeeze my hand and rub my arm. It's a relaxed brush, a tickle almost.

Come on, Tank; move your hand, I think to myself.

Dammit, I can't do anything. Fuck, I need her to know I am right here with her.

"I have to go to work. Roundman and my dad will be by later to see you. I'll come back tomorrow," I hear her say with somber undertones.

She is carrying a heavy burden. A weight I want to lift away. I can feel her sorrow. Why? What is bothering her? Is it my situation?

Why can't I wake up and tell her it's going to be okay?

Her hands move off my arm and hand. I feel her push off the bed and lean over me. She brushes her hand through my hair and then touches her lips ever so softly to my forehead.

"Bye, Tank. Until tomorrow. Come back to us," she whispers so low it's barely audible.

The darkness threatens to consume me again as I hold tight to her words. Roundman and her dad, they'll be coming. The Hellions' motorcycle club, my brothers —my Prez and VP will be here.

Moments from the past come flooding back to me.

Since the day I became in debt to Roundman, he owns my afternoons and weekends with the Hellions. I've spent all my spare time working for him, for the club. Over time, my responsibilities gradually progress as I earn my place and the respect of the brothers around me.

At first, I was doing shop clean-up for the garage. Yet, as business picks up for the guys, my tasks become more important. In a year's time, they have me running parts and errands after they see I am reliable. Eventually, I find myself turning wrenches alongside Roundman and Danza.

My mom doesn't like me spending so much time with the club. She tries to intervene, but Uncle Kenny steps in and reminds her that the Hellions are more than providing for her and my sisters now. Since the day Roundman said he would take care of them, he has. Our rent is paid in full for the year and our electric, gas and water bills continue to show regular payments, leaving credits left over into the coming months. Not to mention, groceries consistently show up in our pantry and refrigerator while we are out. Uncle Kenny tells her not to question it, just learn to accept the hand being extended.

Uncle Kenny, being a patched member, promised to look out for me and not let me get in over my head. If my mom only knew what got me in this situation to begin with, though. Bull, as my uncle has been named by the Hellions, doesn't tell my mom my secret. However, he makes sure I bust my ass to repay my marker, my debt owed to Roundman. He also won't let me get off track with my own life, even for the club or the shop.

"Franky, tell Roundman what you told your momma, boy," Bull commands while a shit-eating grin spreads across his face.

I should have known he wouldn't let it go. My uncle is named Bull appropriately. Not only is he a big man —as in stocky—but he is also stubborn and won't back down for anything.

Right now, he is staring me down much like a bull would a matador in a fight. There's a challenge in his tone, one that says he is going to win. He is the one waving the red cape at me, rather than the other way around. Taunting, testing and teasing, all with a knowing smile.

Gathering my resolve and courage, I begin to share with Roundman and Danza my thoughts. "Business is good, and I'm learning more every day. I'm more productive and gain more life skills here in the shop than I do at school, too. Mom and I were talking the other day, and if I drop out of school, I could work here more or get a job with Rocky down at his garage," I state, confident in my reasoning.

Danza pipes up before Roundman can. "Have you lost your damn mind, kid?"

Maybe I have. At seventeen, I am ready to break free. The stuff in those history books won't help me face the hard knocks of life. I know basic math. I can read and write. What more do I really need? I don't see the importance behind a high school diploma. It's just a piece of paper.

"Danza, I want to work on cars. There ain't nothin' in that school gonna teach me about that," I reply, making eye contact with the biker.

"You're gonna finish school. I get that you think it's bullshit, but you finish what you start. You finish school, get your certification, then you can work here as a full time mechanic. If you drop out of school, we're done with you." Danza is clearly not joking.

"Done with me? Really, Danza? I bust my ass and have from day fuckin' one. Has the last year not shown I finish what I start?" The anger in me boils into a rage.

I move to make a step toward Danza when suddenly Roundman is in my face, standing over me. He's around six-feet-tall to my current height of five-feet-eight. He is also full of muscles from the years of hard work.

He glares down on me. "I believe it was your mistakes that brought you to our doorstep. We don't owe you shit, boy! You don't want to go to school? Fine, don't. However, there is no place left for you here if you walk away. You start something, you finish it. One day, a woman will come along, you'll fall in love, have kids, and shit's gonna get boring. You gonna walk out on your family?

"At seventeen, you think you have all the answers, but you don't know shit! Go to school, learn what they teach you, and take your time growing up. You've got the rest of your life to work your ass off and be a man. So, do what teenagers do; go to school, date some girls, come to the shop and work, go home, and stay outta trouble.

"You get through school, Franky, and I'll send you to get certified. After that, I'll make sure you have a good job. If you drop outta high school, though, then I've got not one second to waste with you." With that, Roundman turns and walks away from me.

"Dumb fuck." Danza is shaking his head at me. "We're gonna make a man outta you, son. Not a piece of shit man, either; but a good man. Stop thinking you know everything and look at what's in front of you.

"I get it; your old man, he did some shit that rained down on you and your mom. We've straightened that out for you. But, Franky, you got a chance here to be some-body and do something with your life. The Hellions will

look out for you as long as you look out for yourself. Dedicate finishing school to that thought."

With that memory, the fatigue consumes me, even though I fight to stay with my thoughts.

My high school graduation, the Hellions were all in attendance with my mother and sisters. Roundman, true to his word, paid for my mechanic's certification then set me up with a good job at the garage. The cards life had dealt me were starting to feel like a playable hand. It wasn't kings and aces yet, but it was a start.

Feeling cold, I can't hold onto the memories. Sass is gone again. Her touch is long since disappeared. My hand is now empty. Her voice is more like the fading sound of a faraway angel. The hold she has is slipping with each passing second as I succumb once again to the darkness and the sleep.

Keep riding with the Hellions MC in Forever Ride here!

ACKNOWLEDGMENTS

To My Readers- without you there would be no reason for the Hellions. Thank you for supporting me and giving my books a chance.

To My Family- thank you for always believing in me and dealing with everything that goes along with my writing. To my hubbub and kiddos, I love you more than I can put into words. Thank you for giving me the space and time to go after my dreams. To my parents, I know you never thought all those rides when I was younger would turn into this. I love you both. Mom #2, you said write a full length novel damn it. Okay, done! Love you. Bobo, can you believe it? I can't, lol. Love you.

To Carol and Savannah- The Hellions would not exist if it wasn't for a simple chat in a group all those months ago. Thank you for telling me to go for it. Thank you for being with me at every word, every page, every chapter, and every step all the way to the end and publish.

To JENNIFER- I would be a complete mess without you. Thank you will never say enough for all you do for me. This one has been a long project to bring to life, but you've stuck with me through the ups, downs, and the days I wanted to give up. Thank you.

To ASLI- more than my editor, you're my friend. Thank you for your input and dealing with my craziness. November 12th is an extra special day now and I will forever think of you.

To RENEE- President In Charge of all things…the many hats you wear for me. I can't say thank you enough for the support you've given me from the beginning. Thank you for helping with those 'tough' decisions and sorting through everything with me. Thank you for always being there to listen and share a laugh.

To MADELINE- thanks for keeping in real, raw, and dirty…and for trying…and putting up with all my silly messages.

To JARED, VIKKI, AND PANTARA LYNNE- thank you for the hours you put into a photo shoot for this series.

To THERESA- Thank you for the designs, the input, and your friendship. You make me laugh daily and get my weird sense of humor. D4LB!!!

To AMY- payback's a bitch. Wreck another car and

see what I come up with next, lol. My shenanigans partner, thanks for being you, enough said.

To MELISSA- two chicks from the Boro and we're doing this. Some days it still feels like a dream. Love you bunches, lady. Thank you for making my words pop and come to life with your formatting genius.

To CRYSTAL- You're a boss! Thank you for your honest feedback, your support, and our many silly conversations. I will try to tone down my proper English, but I make no promises. Commas are a lost cause, I'm addicted. Love you to pieces.

To LARAMIE BRISCOE- Thank you for the encouragement. Thank you for being scared shitless with me… no one wants to be afraid alone.

To RACHAEL- Holy pimping batman! I can't say thank you enough.

To WENDIE- My sweet swag queen. Love you.

To BRANDI- WHO DAT?! Louisiana Baby! Oh my proofreader friend…I owe you a beignet and then some!!!!

To SUZANNE- even if you are a Steeler's fan, I still love and appreciate all your encouragement. Thanks for the support you've given me.

To KELLY, ARIANA, MARISA, DEE, JACQUI, AND BOTH MY MARY'S- thank you for the chats and encouragement.

To all the members of the Shenanigans room- thank you for putting up with my silliness.

To ALL the bloggers who have joined in promoting the Hellions Ride. I could fill a book listing you all. I love all that you do for all authors, thank you for taking your time to post, read, and review.

Promoting For One Ride – a big thank you to my organizers for all swag, cover reveals, blitzes, blog tours, and fan page promoting.

Reading Renee Reviews always rocking the posts and being here to help me, thank you.

PRODUCTION ACKNOWLEDGMENTS

First edition cover photo credit: Vikki of Vikki's Portrature, Models Jared Caldwell and Pantera Lynn

Formatting by: Melissa of IndieVention Designs

Editing by: Asli of EL Edits, C&D Editing

2020 Edition cover credit to Deposit Photos

Hellions Insignia design credit: Jennifer Rivera, photo credit to Shutterstock

CPSIA information can be obtained
at www.ICGtesting.com
Printed in the USA
LVHW051912080321
680888LV00011B/1541

9 781519 784339